FLIGHT
PATTERNS

by
Jana Williams

PRINT VERSION: 978-1-7781871-0-0
eBOOK ISBN: 978-1-7781871-1-7

Printed in Canada

Edited by B.K. Editorial Services
Cover design by Milan Boro
Interior design by TeaBerry Creative

ADDITIONAL TITLES
BY JANA WILLIAMS

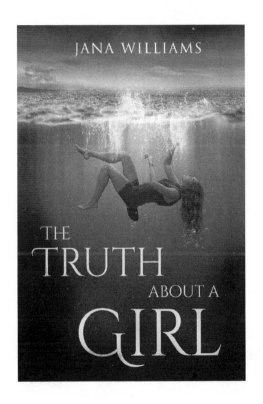

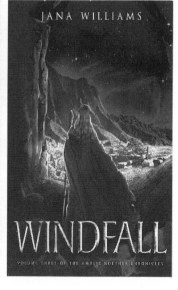

*Flight Patterns is a work of fiction based on
the real lives of women who flew
for the WASPs, ATA and WAFS.*

*Although some characters—
such as Jackie Cochran, Hap Arnold
and Mrs. Deaton—are real people,
all situations are fictional.*

*I acknowledge that I live and write
on the unceded traditional territory
of the Musqueam, Squamish
and Tsleil-Waututh First Nations.*

It's Only a Paper Moon

It's only a paper moon, hanging over a cardboard sea
But it wouldn't be make-believe,
if you believed in me.

BILLIE ROSE, E.Y. HARBURG / HAROLD ARLEN
LYRICS & MUSIC

LONDON, ENGLAND—1942

ONE

An impossibly full moon rises on an autumn night so clear you can see with a naked eye the dark circles of the craters on its surface. Commonly called a *Hunter's Moon* by the British, its clear silvery light negates the black-out curtains that hang in every doorway and window in the city of London. The full moon effectively spotlights every building in the city.

Ninety degrees from the rising moon, all along the horizon, searchlights suddenly snap on—scanning the sky overhead just as a chorus of sirens begins their high-pitched wavering wail. The hunt has begun!

Within moments the *Luftwaffe* are crossing the English Channel and approaching the coast of Kent to head for the City of London. Shortly after, hundreds of bombs scream through the air and fall on the moonlit city.

Amidst this, a very old man bicycles along a dirty, cluttered city street, wending his way carefully through piles of debris and rubble left from the previous bombing raids. Around him civilian Air Raid Wardens take to the streets in their metal helmets, adding the shrill screech of their whistles to the cacophony of screaming air raid sirens. The people who stream onto the streets looking for shelter are silent by comparison. The old man carries a canvas messenger pouch slung over one sloping shoulder. The Wardens recognize his mission and frantically wave him past.

Moments later the messenger props his bicycle against an exterior wall of a building. Overhead the swinging pub sign is rocked by the breeze.

THE GOLDILOCKS—Where the beer is never too hot,
And never too cold—Always just right

He takes one last look over his shoulder at a conflagration at the far end of the alley, and then pushes inside the pub doorway. Deep blackness greets him on the other side of the exterior door. Dank, clinging blackout curtains envelope his face.

Inside, an energetic band plays loudly on a slightly raised stage. The pub is packed with uniformed men and women drinking, laughing, smoking and singing along with the band. They dance as if unaware of the air raid underway in the beleaguered city beyond the pub door.

The old man surges through the doorway and into the chaos. It takes a moment for his eyes to adjust to the dusky, smoky light in the bar. He sorts through the bulge of envelopes in his pouch, finds the one he wants and looks up, searching the various groups clustered throughout the public house.

Near the piano bar a group of male and female Air Transport Auxiliary pilots—the ATA—are gathered. They're not military, but they're uniformed like everyone else. Among them are many old flyers who have come out of retirement to help the war effort. The ATA deliver new war planes to every airfield in England. A brand-new plane, just off the assembly line, is first flown by an ATA pilot. And there's a 50-50 chance in England that pilot will be a woman.

The old geezer spots the ATA insignia on their jacket sleeves and threads his way through the crowd. His mere presence cuts through the din like a scythe. Each group he passes recognizes the old gentleman's uniform, and thus his errand. Most stop mid song, mid joke, or mid heartbeat. All eyes follow his progress through the noisy bar. Once he's passed, the festivities rev up again.

Multiple times each night, the old guy delivers death with his telegrams. During the war, telegrams have become synonymous with grief. He ambles towards the ATA pilots at the piano. Holding his telegram aloft, he shouts, "Lef-tenant Stewart?" His British accent weights the first syllable.

A poised, dark-haired pilot raises her eyes from her mug of beer. Lila Stewart is extremely attractive and remarkable in every way. She quirks one eyebrow at the old man.

"Are you Lila Stewart then, luv?" he says.

"I suppose I am."

All the pilots surrounding Lila watch the drama play out before them. One woman reaches over and puts her hand on Lila's forearm to comfort her as the old man reaches across the piano to hand Lila the telegram.

Lila's face remains impassive as she slices open the envelope with a well-manicured fingernail. She reads the message, her face inscrutable. After a long, tension-laced moment Lila looks up at the pilots surrounding her and gives them an ambiguous smile.

"Dash it all. I'm being called back to America." She sighs dramatically.

"I've been offered a billet in Cochran's flight training program—in Texas, of all places."

An instant later, the whole building shudders from the detonation of a nearby bomb. The interior lights flicker crazily, and everyone instinctively ducks their heads. After a long moment, when nothing else happens, the band picks up its instruments and begins to play a fast-paced swing tune.

The woman next to Lila lifts her voice to shout, "You'd better start packing now if you want to get there on time. The Atlantic is going to be a bitch to cross."

Lila smiles ruefully, then puts her arm around the woman's shoulders and joins her voice to the drinking song in progress.

• • •

NEW YORK—WINTER 1942

The auditorium is filled to the rafters with military men in all their various uniforms, and their dates. Tourists too are massed inside with assorted locals from the nearby boroughs. Some patrons in the crowded space are standing in the aisles. Large numbers of soldiers and sailors whistle and heckle the stage from the sidelines.

On the stage a tiny young woman sits at a faux kitchen table, set with all the trappings of a half-eaten family dinner. Clearly a large family—a father and mother and four sons—all apparently frozen in time, mid *knosh*. On closer examination, the truth is revealed. The entire cast consists of life-sized wooden dummies. All except the petite young woman whose manic patter brings the tableau to life.

Jinx Babisch, vaudeville star, ventriloquist and *bon vivant* babbles alternately to her siblings and the audience. She offers up some real mashed potatoes to the wooden brother sitting nearest her on the stage.

"Here, eat something, you big lummox."

She carefully loads a huge spoonful of potatoes and tries to shove it into the wooden dummy's mouth.

"Ma, Pa. Bernie won't eat his spuds."

A spotlight illuminates the father's face at the head of the table, awaiting his reply. The spotlight helps hide the minor movement in Jinx's throat as she throws her voice upstage.

In a deeper voice, without a single tremor of her lips, Jinx replies, "That's because Bernie only eats *latkes*, Jinx. Potato *latkes*."

The audience titters at the comment.

At her end of the table, Jinx leaps up, startled. The spotlight finds her.

"Ow! Bernie pinched me, Papa." She turns a fearsome look at Bernie, then grabs a handful of mashed potatoes and starts patting it into a pancake shape.

"I'll give him *latkes*, Papa. You just watch." Jinx takes the flattened potato pancake, grabs Bernie the dummy and hauls him over her knee, spanking him on his bottom with the food. "Here's your *latkes*, Bernie. Eat this!"

The spotlight finds the ass-end of the dummy and Jinx's determined hand flailing at him. The shift of focus again allows Jinx to vocalize Bernie's answer while she paddles her incensed older brother.

"Ow! OW. Papa, make her stop." The wooden dummy's legs flail in time to the beating. The audience roars its approval.

After several more vigorous blows by Jinx and pitiful cries from her Bernie, Jinx relents and sits the wooden mannequin upright on her lap. She contritely tidies his hair and smooths his shirt back into place.

"Okay, okay, I'm sorry. Are you alright, Bernie?" Then she giggles. "How *were* your *latkes*?"

The spotlight hits his face and Bernie howls, "TOO HOT."

The audience instantly leaps to its feet, applauding wildly. They whistle and stamp their feet, drawing out the moment. Jinx Babisch rises, wooden brother tucked under her arm, and approaches the front of the stage and bows dramatically. The clamor in the theatre becomes even more intense.

As Jinx finally leaves the stage, a Western Union messenger steps forward from the shadows and extends an envelope towards her. He touches her shoulder to get her attention and extends the envelope one more time.

Jinx immediately sobers, signs the acknowledgment form and tears open the envelope. The remnants of it flutter to the stage floor like confetti.

The audience is still stamping and cheering.

Jinx tuns to look out at them over the top of the page. She reads the telegram again. "Congratulations, Miss Babisch, you have been selected by Miss Jackie Cochran to receive training at Avenger Field. Please report to Sweetwater, Texas by April first of the New Year. Be sure to telegraph your response."

She whispers to herself, with a distinctly British accent, à la Churchill, *"And I say, we have nothing to fear but fear itself. We will fight them in France, we shall fight them on the seas and oceans, and we shall fight them in the sky far over our heads."*

Jinx looks up briefly at the stagehands and folds the telegram neatly. She strides towards the rear of the theatre with a new purpose in life. A stagehand calls out after her, "For Pete's sake, Babisch, at least do a curtain call. They're gonna ransack the place."

. . .

MONTREAL, CANADA—FEBRUARY 1943

The dawn is a golden sliver of light searing the rooftops of downtown Montreal and disappearing into a flat, grey mass of cloud. Miriam Zimmerman and her aging parents shuffle-step towards the open double doors of the synagogue before them. Fat, lazy snowflakes are drifting down to cover the sidewalks. What is usually a fifteen-minute walk to temple has become twice as long because of the slippery footing.

The Rabbi waits at the open doorway, nodding to each of them as they enter. He reaches out and grasps both of Miriam's cold hands in his own and rubs them briskly.

"I'm so sorry we're late, Rabbi," Miriam whispers.

"It is nothing. I wouldn't have started without you. None of us want you to leave without a safe travel blessing from us all."

The Rabbi waves them into the synagogue and quietly closes the door behind them. He composes himself a moment, then walks solemnly to the head of the small space. He lifts a taper and lights three candles before looking out over the people gathered for early morning prayer.

Miriam finds a seat for herself and her parents near the closed doors at the back. The family always sits at the back of the temple for services so that Miriam's mother, Sadie, doesn't have to walk very far—and so Miriam can whisper translations of the Rabbi's French and English comments into Yiddish for her parents.

"*Bienvenue. Shalom*," the Rabbi intones from the *bimah*.

The congregants repeat back immediately, "*Aleichem shalom*."

"This morning we say *au revoir* to a special young lady, Miss Miriam Zimmerman, who is leaving us to travel to America to help with the war effort."

Miriam's face grows rosy at the Rabbi's comments and the attention of the assembled congregation that now turns towards her. Sadie has caught the tone of the Rabbi's comment and reaches over and pats Miriam fondly on the arm.

"Miriam has been selected to enter pilot training in America. Imagine it, in mere months Miriam will be flying airplanes," the Rabbi continues.

The congregation chuckles, nodding and smiling as they acknowledge the Zimmermans. Miriam can only bob her head mutely. The attention really is too much.

The Rabbi continues with a smile. "Who could imagine that your *mamele* would have such moxie, right Sadie?"

Sadie takes Miriam's hand and clasps it in her own gnarled grasp. "I can't imagine my little girl *wouldn't*," she whispers to Miriam in Yiddish.

Miriam feels a tear trickle down her cheek, but she can't stop it. Instead, she leans over and kisses her mother's wrinkled cheek.

• • •

LEROY, IOWA—SPRING 1943

The sky is indigo blue, cornstalks catch splintered shards

of light from a sun that constantly appears and disappears with the breeze. From Dodie Jackson's front porch, great swells of verdant green cornfields roll westward as far as the eye can see. Swallows flit across the sky; their small cries punctuate the precious quiet of dawn. The final star winks out of existence as the sun asserts itself on the day.

Dodie gazes out over the Iowa cornfields that inundate her home as if it were perched on a lakefront. She wipes a tear off her cheek as she gazes out at the farm and then startles at the sound of her father's voice behind her.

"We better get going. You don't want to miss your train."

Her father stands in the kitchen doorway, her suitcase in a one large, callused hand. His dusty fedora is gripped in the other hand. His face wears an expression of weariness and sad inevitability.

Dodie nods and pulls a rumpled telegram from her pocket.

"Just let me try one more time, okay, Daddy?"

Dodie crosses the kitchen and squeezes past her father into the darkened hallway. Before her, a light is visible beneath the threshold of a closed door. Dodie stops in front of the doorway, kneels down and slides a rumpled telegram beneath the door.

"Mama, I have to go now." Only silence greets her. "See? Here's the telegram from Miss Cochran."

Silence.

Near tears, Dodie whispers, "I have to go, Mama. I can't stay any longer. Won't you come and tell me goodbye?"

The telegram is shoved back out into the hallway from beneath the door and the beam of light disappears with a sharp snap of a light switch.

Silence wreathes Dodie in her misery. After a long moment, she retrieves the telegram from the threshold of the door. She stands and tucks it back into her dress pocket, then turns and walks away from the door.

• • •

OCEAN SANDS, OREGON—SPRING 1943

A single engine bi-wing plane is skimming along 200 feet above the ground following a lush stand of trees along the shoreline of the Pacific Ocean. Suddenly a break in the trees reveals the long thread of a railroad track and the pilot banks the plane to follow the track inland from the sea.

The pilot's face is partially obscured by goggles and a helmet. A long white scarf trails in the breeze behind the open cockpit. The pilot steadies the altitude stick with her knees so both hands can rein in and securely bundle the scarf for safekeeping.

Patty Yin Lee pulls the stick back hard on the airplane and it soars straight up, gaining altitude, angling towards the noon day sun. At the apex of the arc Patty thrusts the stick forward and the plane drops upside down, belly up to the sun, as it completes an inside roll.

Brilliant flecks of dust catch and glitter in the sunshine, like a fine trail of diamonds behind the plane as it turns and evens out its trajectory following the railway track inland.

The sound of the pilot's radio crackles to life. "Zebra, Delta one niner...Patty, have you found the railroad track?"

"Roger that, tower."

"Copy that. We've got a farmer with a double-wide barn

that says you can land in his alfalfa field and paint some directional signage for Portland on his roof."

Patty rolls her eyes and sighs heavily. She does not respond immediately.

"Tower to Zebra, Delta. Do you copy?"

"Oh, I copy you, tower. I already have one huge damn barn in my sights, that must be the one —and ten gallons of white paint in the aft hold of the plane."

The airplane continues along the railway track, heading for the nearby farm. Patty earns her flight time painting rooftop signposts to guide other flyers to the nearest town. As a result of hours of practice, Patty Yin Lee can land her biplane on a dime and paint legible signposts like lightning. She knows the entire Oregon coast like the back of her own hand.

. . .

SAN DIEGO, CA—SPRING 1943
A thousand miles south of Patty, a spiffy 1940 red coupe sits curbside, just outside a cozy whitewashed bungalow. The tiny house is surrounded by banana trees, bird-of-paradise and citrus trees growing in clay containers. The exterior of U.S. Navy Admiral Roger Powell's bungalow is as meticulous as any ship deck.

The screen door of the house slams open and a bevy of uniformed seamen appears carrying footlockers, suitcases, hatboxes and even a potted plant. They swarm around the shiny coupe parked at the curb and load up its trunk, double-time.

Close behind the swarm of young men, Lauren Powell—young, movie-star gorgeous, and the Admiral's only daughter—appears, laughing gaily. She turns to say something into the shadowy interior of the bungalow.

Flashing brightly in his summer whites, Admiral Powell follows closely behind his daughter, head bent solicitously to her every word. Brow furrowed, he stops at the top of the drive and bellows at the group of young seamen stowing their burdens in the trunk of the car. "You there, Seaman. Belay that order."

All the seamen immediately stop what they are doing, come to attention and turn smartly to face the Admiral.

"You with the palm tree, present yourself. Double-time it."

The young seaman with the potted palm races to position himself in front of the Admiral. The Admiral glares at the young man, then softens. "Stand at ease, sailor."

The seaman relaxes somewhat, awkwardly balancing the bulky potted plant. Lauren leans over and relieves him of his burden. She smiles, melting the young man with a glance. For a moment, he completely forgets the presence of the Admiral.

The Admiral clears his throat. The seaman snaps back to attention. The Admiral extends one hand, dangling a set of keys.

"You will drive my daughter to the train station. No detours, no unexplained stops. Your mission and your only mission is to get her there on time. Or else."

The young sailor swallows with difficulty, then gingerly takes the keys from the Admiral's outstretched hand.

"Touch one hair on her head and you'll be *lucky* to do latrine duty the rest of your life. Am I clear?"

The young man salutes smartly. "Sir, yes sir."

The Admiral snaps off a salute to the young driver. He promptly turns his attention to the other men. "Squad Commander. Assemble your men."

Another seaman takes charge of the remaining sailors and sets them in marching formation. He salutes the Admiral, and the squad marches off.

Lauren winks at the shivering Seaman designated to drive her to the train station. She turns on one foot and throws her arms around her father. The Admiral hesitates, and then bends down to kiss the top of Lauren's head.

His eyes meet those of the sailor. He glowers. "One hair, young man."

The Admiral pulls his daughter into step alongside himself as he steers her towards the back door of the coupe.

"A word of advice, honey. Jackie Cochran may have chosen you for her flying program...." He opens the back door of the car while the young sailor levers himself into the driver's seat. "Never forget she's a civilian. Not meant to command any U.S. troops, if you know what I mean."

Lauren slips away from her father and grins up at him as she slides inside the automobile. "Oh Daddy. Really."

The Admiral can't help himself; he smiles. "I know you'll be fine. You always are, sweetheart." He pats her hand as he shuts the car door. "I'll call ahead to make sure someone's there to pick you up when you arrive in Texas, honey."

. . .

WASHINGTON, D.C.—SPRING 1943

It's late at night; the hallway in which Coralee Abrahms sits is dimly lit. Even now, it echoes with muted conversations and the syncopation of heels smacking stair treads as someone exits via the stairwell ten feet away.

Coralee has just turned twenty. She has her civilian pilot's license and nearly 750 hours of flight time. She is neatly dressed and sits ramrod straight on the bench in the hall. Coralee has applied as a candidate for the Women's Air Service Pilots program, and she knows she exceeds by far Jackie Cochran's requirements.

She hopes this appointment, which Jackie requested via telegram, will confirm her acceptance into the WASP training program. The telegram is held in readiness in case Coralee might be questioned about her presence in the Pentagon at this late hour, in front of this particular door. Jackie has cautioned Coralee that she could possibly be late, but requests that she wait, if she can.

Coralee hears the unmistakable tap, tap, tap of a woman's high heels on the hardwood floors. She puts a careful smile on her face and stands up as she spots the blonde, nattily dressed woman approaching.

Jackie Cochran stops briefly in front of Coralee and offers her hand. She smiles ruefully into Coralee's eyes as they shake hands, then opens the door to usher her inside.

"Can I get you a beverage, Coralee?"

"No ma'am, but thank you."

Rather than seating herself behind the massive desk, Jackie chooses to sit in one of the guest chairs in front of it. She motions Coralee to the other chair and locks eyes with her.

"First, I want to thank you for coming in person. Make no mistake: you would be a fantastic candidate for this program. Smart, experienced, and motivated. I have no doubt that you could excel as a WASP."

Coralee's smile wilts a bit at Jackie's choice of words. *Would be a fantastic candidate. Could excel as a WASP.* Coralee has received innumerable honey-coated rejections like this all her life. She knows what's coming, but she refuses to let Jackie see her disappointment.

"And if it were solely up to me, you would have a billet in the very first training group in Houston at the start of the year." Jackie's mouth turns grim. "But let's be clear, Coralee, it is not up to me. Who I accept for training in the WASP program will be scrutinized with unremitting fervor by the Armed Forces Service Committee. They will be looking for any tiny thing they can find to throw this whole program onto the scrap pile." She slumps back in her chair, shaking her head in defeat.

"They're nothing but a bunch of jumped-up white crackers in uniform, honey. And they are determined to see this women's program fail." Jackie regains her composure and leans forward towards Coralee again. "I can't accept you in the WASP program, Coralee."

There is a long moment of silence. Coralee lifts her chin to skewer Jackie with her eyes. "Because I'm a negro." She pauses. "So why call me here at all then, Miss Cochran?"

"Because you're good. Very, very good, Coralee, and I wanted you to know that, directly from me." Jackie huffs out a breath and continues. "Now, what I *can* offer you, if you want it, is a chance to go to Sweetwater, Texas early in the new year. My House Mother, Mrs. Deaton, will need some help getting things ready for the arrival of the WASPs when they move from Houston." Jackie can't help but notice the look of offence that flits across Coralee's face.

"Don't look like that, Coralee. I'm not asking you to go down there to be a maid. I'm trying to put you directly in the path of everything those white girls are going to learn, so you can, too. I'll make sure Mrs. Deaton understands this to the T... so you will have ample opportunity to be part of this whole experiment in women flying for the Army."

Coralee's face softens a bit. "Well, that's exactly what Coffey and Robinson did in Chicago, isn't it?" She sighs heavily. "And they eventually became instructors at the Curtiss-Wright School of Aeronautics. *For negro students.*"

"So, you'll do it?"

Coralee takes a deep breath and bunches one hand into a fist and pounds her thigh. "Dammit, Miss Cochran, I am so very tired of constantly having to sneak into places through the back doors."

Jackie presses her lips together grimly. "If it's any consolation, I've been doing the same thing my whole life, Miss Abrahms. My family was dirt poor and I started off working at age ten in the town mill."

Coralee hesitates, then blurts, "Not the same thing at all. You're white."

Jackie cocks an eyebrow at Coralee. "You forgot to add the word *trash*. My family was poor white trash, Coralee. So, if we're not immediate family to the coloreds in the south, we're certainly cousins."

Coralee shrugs in response. "Maybe."

"After the mill, at fourteen, I talked my way into helping in a beauty salon. That salon training led to me starting my own cosmetics business and eventually a rich husband."

Jackie quirks an eyebrow at Coralee. "So, do you want to go discover what doors Sweetwater might open for you? Or sit here and cry?"

"Both, maybe," Coralee whispers. After a very long moment, she adds with a huff. "Oh hell, why not?"

Jackie Cochran smiles a wan smile, then stands abruptly. "I'll telegraph Mrs. Deaton to expect you then."

TEXAS, USA

TWO

AVENGER FIELD—SWEETWATER, TEXAS

Dodie Jackson stands on the outside of a large, locked wooden gate. Overhead a cartoon *Disney* character proudly ornaments a painted wooden arch that announces the entrance to Avenger Field. Dodie rattles the gate a second time to be certain, but there will be no entry until someone comes to unlock it.

She eyes the gatehouse and high fence with frustration and perhaps a bit of apprehension. "HELL—OOOO," she calls, cupping her hands around her mouth. When she gets no response, she stops to take in the 60,000 acres of nothing but sagebrush and sand that extends around her as far as the eye can see. She's hot and sweaty in the Texas sun, and more than a little gritty from hitchhiking to the base. It's all a little disheartening.

As Dodie bends down to lift her suitcase, thinking of walking away, she notices the hand-painted sign nailed to a crossbar on the gate. It reads "Cochran's Convent," with little halo lines over the o's. Only then does she hear the sound of a rasping, overheated car engine pulling up behind her. When Dodie turns, she witnesses the sorriest looking taxicab in Texas pull to a stop only a few feet from the gate.

A gruff-looking driver in faded coveralls exits the cab and stands staring at both Dodie and the gate. "Locked *agin*, ain't it?" The man lifts the lid to the trunk of the cab and pulls out a heavy leather-strapped trunk. He heaves it onto the dusty track that passes for a road. "Welp, nuthin to her, except wait." He slams the trunk down firmly and adds. "They only open 'er when the bus arrives from town."

Jinx Babisch tumbles out of the cab, shoving another huge suitcase ahead of her. She shouts at the man, "There's a bus from Sweetwater that stops here?" It's clear she furious. "Why the hell didn't you tell me that in town?"

She reaches back into the interior and pulls out a second, smaller suitcase. Her bobbed hair is plastered to her scalp with sweat and her traveling outfit is wrinkled and disheveled. She struggles, trying to balance the two awkward pieces of luggage.

"You would'na hired me then, would ya?" The taxi driver emphasizes his point by holding out his hand, palm up, towards Jinx.

From the other side of the cab, Lila Stewart sticks her head out of the passenger door, then unfolds her long legs and torso into a standing position. She plucks her medium-sized suitcase from the front seat. As she looks over the top of the grimy cab, she catches Dodie's eye. Lila spends a long moment measuring the young woman's mettle. "You still trying to decide if you want to do this?"

Dodie's eyes widen with surprise. "Is it that obvious?"

The cab pulls away in a cloud of road dust, leaving the three young women alone to assess their situation. Dodie looks down at her feet for a moment, then fidgets with the strap on her suitcase. Suddenly she notices Jinx's plight with her luggage and says, "I'm Dodie." She steps forward to help Jinx.

Lila joins them. "Nice to meet you, Dodie. I'm Lila Stewart and this is Jinx Babisch." Lila bends to help Jinx too.

Dodie hefts the larger suitcase and groans. "How the heck did you manage at the train station with all this junk?"

Lila and Jinx answer in unison, grinning, "Men."

The three women manage to accommodate the four suitcases and haul them closer to the locked gate. As they do so, the sound of gears grinding in the distance causes them to pause, turn and shade their eyes.

Hurtling down the road towards them is an ancient farm truck that may or may not stop—depending on how much of the clutch is left to grind away. The girls drop all the suitcases, poised for flight if need be.

The truck shudders to a halt mere meters away. A scraggly old man hops lightly from the cab and gallantly runs around the front of the truck to open the passenger door. He proffers his free hand to his companion, and out steps Miriam Zimmerman—as if she were the Princess *Royale*. Before she can wipe the glow from her brow, the old guy has sprinted around to the back of the truck and is hauling her suitcase off the tailgate.

The other three women exchange glances. Jinx grins and raises her eyebrows at Dodie. "Men. You gotta love 'em."

Lila laughs. "Except when you don't."

Miriam shakes the old man's hand and sends him on his way. He puts the truck in gear and reverses it back down the road, a cloud of dust billowing in its wake. Miriam looks askance at the bulging suitcase at her feet. Hitching up the strap on her shoulder bag, she bends to the task, dragging the suitcase to where the other three women stand.

"Hello. My name is Miriam." Miriam takes a step and lines herself up behind Jinx. "Is this the line to get in?" The other three women look at each other and burst out laughing. Miriam looks mystified.

Jinx recovers first. "I'm sorry (continuing to laugh). Honestly, I am. It's just…well, we're out here smack-dab in the middle of Texas in front of a locked gate, and you want to know if this is the line-up to get in."

Miriam's face remains puzzled. Jinx shakes her head and proffers her hand. "Never mind, it's nothing." She shakes Miriam's hand. "I'm Jinx Babisch, from New York." Jinx lays on her accent a bit thick, just to impress.

Miriam recovers and shakes Jinx's hand, smiling. "Miriam Zimmerman, from Montreal." She adds as an after-thought, "Canada."

Jinx grins. "*Oui*? *Enchanté* then, my dear." Jinx points to Lila next to her. "And this is Lila Stewart. Just recently arrived back in America from England." Jinx notices Miriam's eyebrows raised in surprise. "And has she got stories to tell about flying planes in merry old England while the Nazis bombed London to smithereens."

Dodie's mouth drops open in awe. Jinx chuckles and continues. "And this is…wait a minute. We don't know who you are!"

Dodie closes her mouth. "Dodie Jackson. Iowa." Dodie sounds a tiny bit belligerent about it and shakes the other women's hands with a certain firmness.

Miriam smiles winningly at Dodie as they shake. "Well, I'm certain Iowa…is just lovely, Dodie." Miriam makes pointed eye contact with Jinx. "Don't you think so, Jinx?"

Jinx looks at Miriam as if she's lost her mind. Then she catches sight of Dodie's scowling face, and the light bulb clicks on. "Aw, yeah. Beautiful, I bet. Why I was just saying to my brother Bernie the other day…" Jinx looks around her for inspiration.

"Bernie, we got to get ourselves out to I-O-way. And see the corn, and um, the corn silos, and ah maybe taste some of that the corn pone. Don'cha think?"

Dodie's scowl only deepens with every word that comes out of Jinx's mouth.

Jinx pokes her. "Aw c'mon, Dode. You gotta learn to take a little kiddin!"

Dodie takes a moment to look from Lila to Miriam and back to Jinx's grinning face.

Lila reaches out to put her hand on Dodie's arm. "The woman's right, Dodie." She nods towards the locked gate. "It's only going to be worse in there," she smiles at Dodie, "but we're going to do this together, right ladies?"

Somewhere behind them comes rapid panting matched with the thud of running feet.

"Hey. Wait up. Wait for me."

The four cadets all turn in unison. Patty Yin Lee is barreling down the dirt road towards them, waving her free hand over her head, motioning wildly for them to wait. She slides to a stop in front of Lila, little clouds of dust following in her wake. Her hair is wildly askew from the run. Her clothes are a disaster, but her smile is worth millions.

"Hey, thanks for waiting."

Lila uses one hand to motion towards the gate. "Hey, yourself. No problem. It's locked. We can't go in."

Miriam and Patty both chime. "Locked?"

Lila shakes her head. "Yes. Apparently they only open it when the bus from town arrives."

Miriam and Patty chorus. "There's a bus?"

One by one, the women all lock eyes and then shrug. Then Patty shakes her head and bursts out laughing. Fairly soon, the others follow her lead.

Finally, Patty wipes the tears from her eyes and extends her hand to them. "Sorry. My name's Patty Yin Lee." She can't help but notice the doubt that clouds all their eyes. "From Portland. Chinese-American, fifth generation, Yankee doodle dandy."

Everyone visibly relaxes—she's not Japanese—then they each shake Patty's hand. They all exchange names and stoop as one to gather their suitcases. Everyone pitches in to help Jinx with her entire collection. They're so busy moving travel trunks that they don't notice the woman who appears at the gate, and quietly unlocks it.

Out of nowhere, an Army jeep blares its horn behind the gals. The tight little group of women scatters—and none too soon. They watch transfixed as the previously locked gate swings magically open just in time for a military jeep with a uniformed driver to blast past them and through the opening. Hats blow from their heads, skirts swirl in the maelstrom of the jeep's passing. The group's hastily improvised solidarity teeters a bit.

Lauren Powell hangs off the passenger side of the jeep. She brandishes a 1000-kilowatt smile and waves grandly as she passes.

"Sooorrry. See you up there," she calls out.

The five of cadets stand mutely watching the military jeep disappear in its own dust. Before they've completely processed what has just happened, a shout from the gate snaps them back to the present moment.

Coralee is behind the now open gate, grinning. "Girls, you better hotfoot it out of the way. The bus from town is coming. And it doesn't stop for nuthin but cold beer and freight trains."

Lila turns to look down the road. A new and far more formidable cloud of dust is billowing up the road towards them. She grabs Jinx, who grabs Miriam, who grabs Dodie and Patty and they run for the safety of the gate. They plant themselves and their luggage safely behind the swing gate just as the bus hurtles past them, spewing exhaust and sand and a breeze hot as a furnace.

Once silence has returned to the scene of near disaster, Coralee grasps the gate and begins to push it closed. "Welcome to Avenger Field, gals. You'll have the time of your lives here."

Jinx grapples with her luggage and huffs, "I'm not betting hard cash on that notion."

STEARMAN BIPLANE—PT 17

THREE

Jinx, Lila, Miriam and Patty finally drag their suitcases to the covered porch of the administration building. Hot and covered in dust, they immediately slump onto their luggage to rest. The now empty bus pulls away from the building, revealing its cargo of additional cadets. The two groups stand and stare at each other in silence. No one seems to know what to say.

Finally, the quiet is broken by the appearance of two Senior Cadets who stride onto the porch, clipboards in hand.

"Alright ladies, the tea party's over. Time to get organized." One of the women strides to the far end of the porch and blows a police whistle very, very loudly. If anyone's mind had been wandering before, the whistle ensures it is focused now entirely on the Senior Cadet.

"My name is Senior Cadet Meadows. With me is Senior Cadet Jones. We will be your guides through the first two weeks of training at Avenger Field. Every graduating class provides two qualified WASPs who remain behind to shepherd the incoming new trainees. It's a way to get you up and running—and to save your instructors a lot of extra babysitting." Meadows skewers them all with a glare. "Don't make me regret my decision to stay on, ladies."

Senior Cadet Jones steps forward and blows her whistle loudly. "You ladies can say goodbye to leisurely chatting. All you will have time for in the coming two weeks is *Doing*. From six in the morning until ten o'clock at night your days will be filled with tasks and drills and chores."

Senior Cadet Meadows joins in. "Hair, makeup, fashion and men will all become ancient history to you."

"Most especially men," Senior Cadet Jones adds. "Let's be clear: you are here to learn how to fly the Army way. You are not here to meet your special someone. Fraternization is not just frowned upon, it can be cause for dismissal."

Looks of panic pass between many of the women at the word *dismissal*.

Meadows chimes in again. "Cheating on exams will have you booted from camp. Also, if demerits accumulate, they can become a cause for dismissal too."

Dodie turns to Patty Yin Lee and grimaces dramatically. She mouths the question *cheating*? Patty shrugs her response.

Jones adds, "Demerits are awarded when you fail at an assigned task, be it Calisthenics, Ground School, Flight tests, Uniform inspections, Barracks inspections or even your attitude."

Jinx locks eyes with Lila—raising her eyebrows in question.

Senior Cadet Meadows smirks. "Let's be perfectly clear:

no one here actually cares if you learn to fly, ladies, or even if you graduate and earn your wings. So *you* better care in spades and you better show it every single day."

Jones finishes, "In every way."

Both women blow their whistles at the same time, causing a deafening sound.

"We have no time for small talk, ladies." Meadows skewers them with a glare. "When I call your name, step off the porch at the far end and line up three across in marching formation. We'll march to your barracks as our first order of business."

Jones glares at the women facing her as Meadows moves to the far end of the porch. She shouts, "Adleman, Kearns, Babisch, Conroy." She stops as the women mill around trying to decide what to do. "THREE ABREAST, ladies. Did you not hear the command?" The new cadets rapidly organize themselves accordingly.

Meadows bellows out a string of names: "Lee, Powell, Stewart and Jackson."

Lila quickly steps forward and faces the Senior Cadet, which cues the other women to follow.

Meadows continues rattling off names, not batting an eye: "Crawford, Elias, Williams, Dowd and Zimmerman."

These women, too, line up behind the others. Lila turns around and quickly raises the arm of the woman behind her to measure out the distance between them. Once they've sorted themselves out, she uses two fingers to indicate that eyes should be straight ahead. Lila quickly turns back around once she sees the others are copying the correct formation.

Lila's astuteness does not go unnoticed by Senior Cadet Meadows, but she turns her attention back to the women now arrayed in a semblance of marching order in front of her.

"Right then." She steps down from the porch to join them. "This is now your marching formation for the duration of your time at Avenger Field." Marshal strides to the front of the phalanx and shouts: "On my mark, ladies. We'll march to the barracks and assign you your bunks and get your paperwork completed."

She takes a brief moment to point to Lila and shouts, "Guide to the right on cadet Stewart, maintain your distance of one arm's-length from the woman in front of you. Let's see how it goes."

Meadows turns her back on all of them, takes a single step forward and shouts, "FOR - ward, MARCH."

Lila confidently steps out the perfect distance behind the Senior Cadet. The rest of the group struggles into motion, looking rather like a drunken snake trying to organize all its parts.

Lila recognizes the others' uncertainty and begins to call out cadence. As she lands on her left foot, she shouts loudly, "ON your LEFT." And again, "ON your LEFT." Within moments the snake is looking more sober with every left step the women take.

• • •

It's late evening. Everyone has been assigned a bunk, given sheets and bedding, and designated a locker, including a limp drab green coverall for a uniform. They've all filled out innumerable forms and questionnaires. Now the women cadets are all in various stages of undress as they finish unpacking. They are all unnerved by the day. When they had set out to make the journey to Texas, every one of them had been filled with hope and enthusiasm. Now they are all amuddle, mired in disbelief at reality and more than a bit sullen and resentful. This day had not been fun at all.

Lila is carefully stowing the gear from her single bag into her locker. Her mood is quiet and considered. Next to her, Jinx has both her trunks stacked one atop the other. She drops onto her lower bunk, looking mournfully from the trunks to her open locker and back again. "All this stuff will never fit." She kicks the nearby locker. "It just won't go in."

Nearly finished unpacking, Lila turns and assesses Jinx's predicament thoughtfully. She turns back to her own locker and shrugs. "Send something back home. It's not like you'll be wearing much of it. We likely won't get time to go off into town for weeks yet."

Jinx moans in frustration. "I just can't. I can't believe this is all the closet space we get." Jinx buries her head in her hands and appears as if she might weep.

Lila pauses—clearly thinking better of it—but turns and strides over to Jinx's tower of steamer trunks. "Okay, okay. Let's see what's in here. Maybe I can help." She begins to open the latches on the top trunk, when Jinx flies off the bed, hands outstretched to stop her.

"Stop. Not that one." Jinx leans over the top of the trunk

to stop Lila from opening it. "I'll need everything in this one." She gives Lila her most winning smile. "Let's start with the other one."

Lila is taken aback a moment. "Jinx, you don't have enough room for *either* trunk in this locker."

Jinx grabs the handle on the critical trunk and pulls it off the other, onto the floor. She then drops her butt onto the trunk lid to keep Lila at bay. "The other one first, please."

Lila turns a suspicious eye on Jinx. "What's in there? I know when I'm being conned, Jinx."

The attention of the other women is pulled from their unpacking to the cubicle at the end of the barracks. When no fireworks ensue, they go back to their own tasks.

Jinx shifts herself more firmly onto the center of the trunk. *"Pssst.* Can you keep your voice down, Lila?"

Lila takes a step away from the trunk and folds her arms over her chest. "I'm waiting, Miss Babisch."

Jinx looks around the barracks to be sure no one else is listening. When it appears that everyone has gone back to their tasks, she bends down in front of the trunk and draws a key from a chain around her neck.

"Okay, okay," she whispers. "But you have to promise… on a stack of Bibles or your pilot's license or something…." Jinx inserts the key in the lock and turns it carefully. "Promise you'll never reveal what you see here today."

Jinx looks around the barracks one more time, checking that everyone is busy. Lila can't help herself; she's drawn in by Jinx's subterfuge. She edges closer to the trunk.

Jinx lifts the lid ever so slowly and steps slightly to one

side. Finally, the trunk is open enough that Lila can see inside the dim interior.

"Wow. Now that's what I call packing," says a brash whisper behind them. Patty Yin Lee has somehow appeared by Lila's side and is peering over her shoulder into the trunk. She drops her duffel bag on the floor in amazement.

"Jinxy brought her own man to training camp. Wish I'd thought of that."

Jinx slams the lid of the trunk down and wheels on Patty, tiny fists raised. She grabs Patty by the shirt front. "That's not a man, you idiot," she whispers hoarsely.

"It's my brother Bernie. And if you tell a soul, I'll...."

A look of horror paints Patty's face. "You packed your brother in a steamer trunk to bring him to a women's training camp! The only person I'm gonna tell is a shrink."

Lila intervenes, stepping forward to separate the two. "Patty...remember, loose lips sink ships."

Patty sputters, "But...."

Lila raises one finger to her lips and begins laughing softly. *"Shh."*

"But...*her brother!* What kind of woman is she?"

Jinx glowers at Patty and drops her derrière back onto the lid of the trunk.

Lila continues laughing, shaking her head at Patty. "Bernie's not really her brother, Patty. He's a dummy."

Patty takes moment to consider; then a light goes on behind her eyes. "Jinx Babisch! *The Family Babisch.* I read about you in the Portland papers when you played San Francisco! You're famous—kind of."

Jinx brightens. "Ah, Portland has newspapers? And women flyers too! I never would've imagined it."

Lila holds up one hand to silence Jinx. Then she bends down and picks up Patty's duffel bag and tosses it onto a nearby upper bunk. "It's unclaimed. And you look like you need one."

Patty nods and sits down on a lower bunk, snapping off a tiny salute to Lila.

"So, our Jinxy is a star in vaudeville. Along with her four brothers, right?"

Jinx pats the trunk she's sitting on. "Right. And Bernie's a big part of my act. I just couldn't leave him behind, Patty." She smiles one of her most beautiful smiles at Patty. "Will you tell?"

Patty grins in response. "Never. Can I stay?" She pats the bunk.

Jinx shrugs. "Why not?" After a moment she adds, "By the way, why did the other girls kick you out of their cubicle?" Patty is already unpacking her duffel and stuffing things in her locker. She shouts over her shoulder at Jinx. "Stupidity." She places a couple of rumpled shirts on a shelf and turns to smirk at Jinx. "I confessed I snore."

Jinx and Lila exchange horrified glances. Jinx whispers, "I think I need a smoke."

Lila shakes her head and adds, "Me too." She grabs her pack of cigarettes and heads for the porch. She can hear the patter of Jinx's footsteps behind her.

Lila steps out onto the wide porch and immediately goes to perch on the railing. She takes a cigarette from the pack and tosses it to Jinx. Once they've both lit up, she nods at Jinx. "You gonna survive the change of scenery, Babisch?"

Jinx exhales dramatically. "What choice do I have?"

Lila turns to stare out at the vast expanse of scrub range-land that stretches to the horizon beyond the flight line.

"My god, I'd forgotten what it is like here. In England, everything is so close, so green and so populated—at least in the south." She exhales a long stream of cigarette smoke.

"Are you sorry you came back?" Jinx whispers.

"Nooo. But being here…now don't take offence at this, okay? Being at Avenger Field is like being thrust back into elementary school after you'd finally made it to high school. Or college. I love my country, but Congress has been so wrong to do nothing while Europe suffered."

"It must have been truly horrible over there then?"

"Oh my God, no, it was just the opposite." Lila turns to looks at her. "You can't imagine the uncountable and amazing things I witnessed. The scream of the air raid sirens is only seconds old when the automatic heroism of the unarmed Barrage Balloon Girls kicks into gear. They have ten minutes to act while the *Luftwaffe* are racing over the channel hoping to annihilate them.

"Regardless of their fear, they raise those giant dirigibles into the air to help protect the city from the bombers getting too low to be effective. Every raid they put their own lives at risk. The Ack-Ack volunteer spotters, again unarmed, use only binoculars to help direct the anti-aircraft guns more effectively. The whole time the bombers are bearing down on them. The British were amazing every single day I was there."

Jinx is quiet a long moment, then sighs. "I guess we're pretty tame by comparison, huh?"

Lila stubs out her cigarette and leaves it in the nearby ashtray. "Naïve. Well-intended. There is so much vitality and life here, it's astounding. I'd forgotten how *alive* you all are."

She continues, "But I fear for the women training here. They're pinning their hopes on flying for their country. But it's a country that doesn't relish the idea of women changing, and the men sure don't like the idea of needing a woman's help. That's going to the toughest load to haul. For all of us, I think."

Jinx shakes her head sadly. "What choice do we have but to try?"

Lila smiles sympathetically. "Exactly. Let's go get some shut-eye, so we can start trying bright and early tomorrow morning."

. . .

The next morning the formal introduction to life the "Army Way" begins with two searing whistle blasts that jolt every sleeping woman awake. At the entrance to the barracks the two Senior Cadets, Meadows and Jones, stand grinning and fully dressed in perfect uniforms. As chaos erupts around them, two more lengthy blasts from the whistles silence the floundering cadets from the shock of the noise.

"First rule of thumb, ladies: Don't speak, just DO." Meadows looks at Jones.

Jones continues, "You don't need to consult with your neighbor about how to pull on your coveralls and get ready to march. See you in fifteen minutes out front of the barracks to march to breakfast. Latecomers will be given demerits."

"Fifteen minutes, ladies," Meadows repeats.

The two Senior Cadets step outside the barracks to await their charges, each very pointedly looking at her watch to gauge the time that is rapidly elapsing.

A grim silence has descended as the girls race to wash their faces, comb their hair, get dressed and out of the barracks on time. Lila had the foresight to lay out her clothes the night before, hang a towel off her locker door and place a thermos of water there too. She is perfectly ready in less than ten minutes and has time to make her bed and line up her spare shoes beneath it in a neat row.

Lila gives her portion of the cubicle one more quick look, catches Jinx's eye a moment and salutes her. "Better hurry, they're somewhat forgiving the first day—but it won't last, Jinx. If you aren't careful, you'll be back in vaudeville before you know it."

Jinx sits up in her bed and notes the water, the towel and Lila's neatly made bed. "Shit. I wondered what you were up to last night. How'd you know?"

"Later. Get moving, girl. Or start packing. It's all up to you." Lila strides from the room and out to greet the sunny day, letting the screen door slam shut behind her.

Jinx and forty-seven other women leap into action. Silent action.

• • •

Twenty-two minutes later Senior Cadets Meadows and Jones are leading a sloppy squad of new trainees towards a long, low building with a deep porch that embraces every side of it. The building is far closer to the flight line than their barracks, and the roar of airplane engines scissors through the morning air. It seems just the sound of airplane engines puts a snap in every woman's step.

The cadets have been issued their training coveralls, which consist of large masses of unstructured material apparently created to clothe giants. Most of the girls have rolled up the legs into cuffs, rolled back the sleeves and cinched in the waists, aiming to create a better fit. Mostly they look like poorly constructed rag dolls.

All except Lauren. She manages to look smart and perky in her voluminous flight suit. Her makeup is fresh and pristine, and her hair is utterly perfect. She's right up at the front, just behind Lila and Senior Cadet Meadows. As they clomp past a porch railing crowded with mechanics and flight crew who've just finished their breakfasts, a long emphatic whistle fills the air.

Meadows turns her head to identify the source of the sound and the wolf whistle immediately turns into a rendition of the folk song *Dixie*. The mechanics grin back at the squad leader, standing to attention to salute the troops as she keeps them marching past.

Lauren beams at the two mechanics in appreciation. Several of the mechanics return the grin and remain standing, smiles on their faces as the women disappear inside the building known as the mess hall.

FOUR

Apparently not caring that some women haven't completed their breakfasts, Meadows and Jones check their watches, then stand and give an enthusiastic blast on their whistles. In seconds, they have the women up and placing their dishes into bins positioned at either side of the room.

While she's busy scraping her leftovers into a bin, Jinx can't help but notice the woman who was at the gate yesterday to let them into Avenger Field. She calls out to her, "We survived the night."

Surprised at being singled out by a cadet, Coralee frowns. "Well, let's see if you're still here by the end of the week."

One of the cooks adds airily. "Or the end of the month." He and Coralee both laugh and then she disappears out the back door of the mess hall.

Jones is raising her whistle to her lips one more time when Patty Yin Lee grabs Jinx by the elbow and steers her towards the front door.

"What'dya think she does here? She's obviously not a cadet."

"Who?"

"Ladies, what is rule number one of life in the Army?" Jones shouts.

The assembling cadets shout out immediately, in unison, "Don't talk...DO."

As Patty and Jinx fall into formation, Jones looks pointedly at Jinx. "Gee, some people have already forgotten that. I was afraid you all might have."

Meadows calls them to order. "Ladies, A-TEN-tion." She takes her spot at the front of the platoon and calls out, "For-ward MARCH."

The women are a little more certain of themselves this time out. They march past the now deserted porch railing. Within moments the Texas sun is already demonstrating why every building has a wide, deep porch around it.

Ground School is only minutes away from the mess hall, a few steps farther along is the administration building and after that the Machine Room, the Parachute Riggers shack and last of all, just before the airfield itself, the Flight Shack.

Meadows calls out the names of the buildings as they pass each one. She then shouts an entirely new order: "Right Flank, MARCH."

The platoon falls apart, the women shaking their heads in confusion. Jones and Meadows simply stand and grin at the chaos. Waiting. Eventually every woman in the platoon turns to face the two of them. No one says a word.

After several minutes, Jones laughs out loud. "Very good, ladies. We pulled that trick just to see if you would all instantly forget our First Commandment."

Meadows adds, "Nicely done."

Jones walks over to stand at the far end of the troop. "Okay, Stewart. Front and center."

Lila steps from the ranks and approaches Jones, stopping an arm's length away from her.

"It seems to me that you've done a bit of marching in formation before," Jones says. "So you and I are going to show the others how it's done."

Meadows moves over to call the commands. "Everyone else merely watch." She nods for Jones and Lila to square up. They align themselves shoulder-to-shoulder. When they're set, Meadows calls out, "A-TEN-tion, MARCH."

Lila and Jones step forward, walking in unison, never altering the distance between their shoulders. After three steps, Meadows calls out again, "Right Flank, MARCH."

Lila, who is right next to Jones, immediately turns on her heel to the right and continues marching at a ninety-degree angle from their original trajectory. Jones turns at the exact same moment too—but now she's marching directly behind Lila.

"Company, HALT."

Lila and Jones each stop exactly as Meadows says the word *halt*.

"Alright ladies, did you see how that was done?" Meadows smiles. "Any platoon leader gives the platoon its marching orders in two distinct segments. First, she tells you what she wants you to do—Right Flank. Then she gives the order to do it: MARCH."

Jones joins Meadows, smiling. "Easy, right?" She skewers Lila with a look. "I know you get it, Stewart. So you're now a platoon leader. Take eight volunteers and show us how it's done."

Lila comes to attention and salutes Jones, "Ma'am. Yes, ma'am." She walks towards the assembled women and stops, then nods. "Who feels they've grasped the basic premise of this move? Hands please."

Lauren's hand shoots up into the air. Slowly Jinx raises her hand. Patty is next. Then Tex, easily the tallest, skinniest cadet. Several others step forward too. When Lila has eight women, she steps away from the larger group and motions to her. "Form up, ladies: two columns, four deep."

The women line up in front of Lila, two women side-by-side and four rows. They measure with outstretched arms the distance between each other. The arm's length gives them the room to turn as needed, and to not step on anyone else's shoes.

Lila looks them over carefully, then nods. "Well done." She walks over to Jinx and Patty, who stand next to each other. "Okay, when the platoon begins to move, everyone gauges their distance by Patty." She waits as all the women nod, acknowledging her remark. "Then, when you've executed the command, you will be guiding on Jinx, with Tex right next to her now. Okay?" All the women nod in agreement.

Lila steps back to the head of the column, about five feet ahead of Jinx and Patty, right in the middle. "A-TEN-tion." Lila brings herself to attention as well. "FOR-ward, MARCH." She steps out, feeling and hearing the women fall into line behind her. After leading them about ten steps along, Lila calls out again. "Right Flank, MARCH."

Lila makes a perfect ninety-degree turn on her heel and is gratified to see out of the corner of one eye that Jinx and Patty have executed their turn perfectly too. Lauren and Miriam are a split second late but following nicely. With minute corrections the other women lock step with their platoon. When they've settled, Lila shouts out a command: "Company, HALT." And they do.

After a brief moment, Meadows motions them to rejoin the troop. When they do, she smiles. "Not bad. Not bad at all."

Jones is smiling too. "I bet all you hotshot fly-girls are wondering what the Sam Hill this has to do with flying. You came here to fly, *dammit*, not to march around in the hot sun. Didn't you?"

Discreet coughs and guilty smiles are the only response.

Meadows's face is dead sober when she speaks. "Marching in formation is about following orders to the T, ladies. One little mistake and maybe you step on someone's toes or bump into their shoulder."

Jones adds, "But imagine being airborne at 5000 feet, flying in formation at one hundred miles per hour, with four other aircraft on your wing. And one pilot misjudges his distance. Or executes a LEFT flank instead of a RIGHT flank. What then, ladies?"

Meadows finishes the thought. "One little mistake, a single moment of inattention and a pilot may die. Or worse yet—we may lose an airplane—or even two or three. What then, ladies?"

"So, we will drill you until your feet are swollen with fatigue. Until your sunburnt skin is peeling off your nose and the tops of your ears. We will drill you until you are perfect on the ground because a mistake down here is nothing. Up there, it's an entirely different matter."

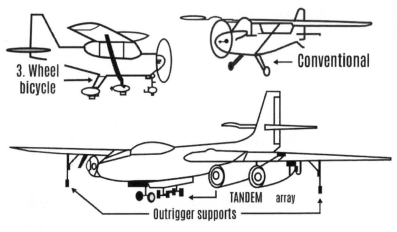

3. Wheel bicycle

← Conventional

TANDEM array

Outrigger supports

3 TYPES OF LANDING GEAR

• • •

The Ground School building is much like all the others: white siding, aluminum roof, long wide porch on three sides, and windows. Windows that are always open, even though the Texas breeze is always damn hot by midday. Warm air that moves is always preferrable to air that doesn't.

Jones and Meadows lead the cadets into the classroom just as the instructor at the front pulls down a large schematic for a biplane. Wallace Shaver turns and nods agreeably. "Good morning, ladies. Jones, Meadows, do you think we should keep this lot—or send them packing before they even sit down?" He is smiling as he says it.

Jones and Meadows both take a moment to pretend to inspect the anxious cadets. "Go ahead, everyone find a seat," Meadows shouts. She turns to the instructor. "I'd say the jury is still out, Mr. Shaver." She nods to Jones, indicating the door.

As the Senior Cadets depart, Jones calls back over her shoulder, "Be sure to let us know what you think, Shaver."

The women quickly find seats, pairing up at the two-person tables. Patty and Jinx grab seats together. Lila and Miriam seat themselves at the table behind them. Lauren gravitates to a table front and center, right in front of the instructor's desk. The seat alongside her remains empty for some time. Finally, Dodie moves from the back to sit beside the beauty queen.

While the women are settling themselves, Shaver continues to prep for the class. Two more large schematics of single-winged aircraft are rolled down to cover the blackboard behind him. As he turns back to face the cadets, he's struck by Lauren's kilowatt smile. He smiles in return, and then quite consciously lets his smile travel the room, meeting the eyes of each woman briefly.

"Good morning, again. My name is Wallace Shaver and I'll be your instructor for Ground School here at Avenger Field. You may call me Shaver, or Mr. Shaver, but never Wallace or Wally." His ready smile softens his message.

"I imagine we have quite a range of flying experience right here in this room. Jackie Cochran is very determined to prove this Women's Air Service Pilot program can be effective and so she's handpicked each one of you. At last count, I was told that there were more than 20,000 applications mailed to her—with more coming in every day. So, you all are in exalted company, gals."

Shaver sighs, blinded by Lauren's radiating smile still right in front of him. As he continues talking, he reaches down with both hands and tugs his desk back five feet and over several feet. Lauren is no longer front and center. He dusts off his hands and then places them on his hips. "Where was I? Oh, right, exalted company."

Shaver starts to pace along the front of the room. "Okay, so let's be clear with each other. Just because you made the first cut to get here doesn't mean you'll graduate. That's because you will be examined twice with every flight test you take. First, Avenger Field instructors will check you out. And then, when deemed ready, you'll be assigned to a visiting Army Air Corps flight instructor, who will be the sole judge as to whether you meet their criteria.

"We will do our utmost to ensure you receive all the training necessary to pass every test you will encounter. Part of the education is the acquisition of accurate nomenclature. Every radio call you make, every report you write must convey accurate information to those receiving it. When you encounter a problem or discover an anomaly with your aircraft, you will need to know its proper name—its Army name—to adequately report it.

"So, let's begin with the basics to ensure we're all speaking the same language. I don't want to hear any slang or shortcuts on the radio or read it in any of your reports. If you have a problem with the urination tube in your cockpit, say so. We can't give you good advice if we're left guessing about the issue. Am I clear, ladies?"

Lila prompts the others by answering first. "Sir, yes sir." The others follow suit as Shaver nods appreciatively.

"You know the old saying, 'You can lead a horse to water, but you can't make it drink!' The instructors here at Avenger Field will make every effort to prepare you for these tests. But it is absolutely up to you to succeed.

"Now quickly, let's do a hands only survey of the actual flying time in the room."

Shaver raises his hand to demonstrate what he means. "Who here has the minimum required thirty-five hours of flying time and has soloed on any aircraft? By the way, thirty-five hours flying is the standard criteria for Army *male pilots* in training."

All the cadets raise their hands.

"Good. Now, who here has 100 hours of flying time?" Shaver keeps his hand aloft, indicating he does. A few of the women drop their hands. All are looking eagerly around the room, curious to see who has the most flying time.

"Great. More than great, really!" Shaver beams at his students. "Okay, now who has 250 hours of flying time under her belt?" Most of the women drop their hands now. Shaver notes their expressions of frustration. "Hey, you all are way ahead of the game, so do not worry. And you will notice, my hand is no longer in the air."

The women titter appreciatively.

"I teach now, more than I get to fly," he explains. "But I still love flying."

Shaver surveys the room. Lila's hand is still aloft, as are Lauren's and Dodie's. Patty Yin Lee still has her hand up proudly too. Right next to her, Jinx is grinning to beat the band, hand in the air.

"Okay, five left. You gals tell me how many hours you have and how the hell you acquired them." He points to Patty.

Patty laughs and jumps to her feet. "I'm Patty Yin Lee, fifth generation Chinese-American, *just so we're all clear about that fact.* I probably have five or six hundred hours in total. I got my flying time on the Oregon and Washington coasts creating directional signs for pilots that were visible from the air. I flew six months of each year up and down the coasts finding appropriate barns and houses and silos on which I painted mostly arrows and milage markers pointing the direction to the nearest city with an airport." Patty sits down abruptly, suddenly shy.

Jinx reaches over and hugs Patty with one arm. She, too, stands up and turns to face the class, never thinking to rein in her performer self. "I'm Jinx Babisch and my vaudeville career kept me busy traveling the country performing. I discovered early on that it was simpler to fly myself to our next booking, than to twiddle my thumbs waiting for our road crew to get everything together and put it on a train. I was the youngest person in New York to ever receive a license and I've logged way over 500 hours too."

Muted applause greets Jinx as she finishes. She takes it as her due and bows before she sits back down. Miriam and Lauren dispatch their own stories promptly and sit down too.

Shaver looks over his eyeglasses at Lila. "Have we saved the best for last, Miss?" Lila stands and speaks only to Shaver. "My name is Lila Stewart. I have most recently flown with the Air Transport Auxiliary, or ATA, in England. Although it is a relatively small country, when war was declared qualified flyers from all over Europe descended on England to help them battle the *Luftwaffe*—the German Air Corps.

"The ATA crews flew aircraft just off the assembly lines to air stations near the front lines. I have flown over 1000 hours for sure, often quite short hops and often in quite rough weather. England is not known for its sunshine."

Shaver is silent a long moment. "So, are you saying you were a ferry pilot in England while it was actively being bombed?"

Lila nods. "For the last two years, Sir."

Shaver continues, admiration clear in his tone. "I imagine you've dealt with a lot more than just rough weather then?" Lila nods again.

"Cadets, if you need proof that women can serve their country in a time of war, look no farther than your classmate, Miss Stewart."

All eyes turn to Lila, who seats herself quietly, eyes straight ahead on Shaver.

It is at that moment that Coralee crosses the threshold and stops, waiting for Shaver to notice her. He continues talking. "Ladies, if you're going to fly, the first thing you need to know is what aircraft you're going to be flying."

Shaver finally notices Coralee. She's clad in a tidy light blue shirt and navy-blue trousers; not the baggy flight suit issued to the cadets.

"Ah, excuse me a moment please." Shaver strolls from the front of the class back to where Coralee waits. He smiles as he approaches her. "This is as good a moment as any to introduce Coralee Abrahms to you all. Coralee learned to fly in Chicago and would easily have qualified for admittance here at Avenger Field." Shaver watches surprise flicker across the cadets' faces.

When he moves closer, Coralee demurely offers him a telegram. She ducks her head, but whispers quietly, "Thank you, Mr. Shaver."

Shaver turns back towards the class, gesturing with one hand towards Coralee. "Miss Abrahms now works directly for Jackie Cochran and is an Assistant Administrator here at Avenger. It's likely this is a telegram from the lady, herself—asking me what's taking me so long to get the lot of you up and flying. She would prefer that it had happened yesterday."

Coralee smiles at Shaver and adds, "Oh, I'm sure Miss Cochran knows even you need more time than a single day to turn these gals into flyers, Mr. Shaver."

Shaver laughs. "Just so. Thank you, Miss Abrahms." He heads towards the front of the classroom as Coralee slips from the room unnoticed. Shaver takes up his lecture, talking as he walks.

"In front of you is a schematic for your first trainer, a PT-17, commonly known as the Stearman biplane. Once you've soloed on that aircraft you'll move on to the BT-13

Vultee. A single-wing aircraft that is quite a bit of fun to fly. And finally, once you've soloed on the Vultee, you will move up a giant step to the T6 Texan."

Shaver's smile has gotten bigger and bigger as he has progressed through the list of aircraft in which the women will train. "After you solo on the T6 Texan, the sky will be the limit for you ladies. I've heard the journey of a thousand miles starts with the first step. Let's get started, shall we?"

Shaver rubs his hands together, "Alright, in looking at the schematic of our three trainers, what do you see? What are some of the differences you notice in the aircraft? Anybody?"

"One has more wings than the others."

All the women groan in unison at the obviousness of the comment.

After a moment, Patty blurts, "Two of them have fixed landing gear; the other is retractable."

Shaver beams. "Now we're getting somewhere. What else? How can you tell it's a fixed wheel aircraft?"

Miriam raises a hand and murmurs, "The fixed wheel craft have fairings or 'pants' to help make the wheels more aerodynamic in flight."

Shaver nods his head. "Terrific. Anyone else?"

Leightyn, a pencil-thin young girl, stands up and calls out briskly, "The T6 Texan does not have the radio antenna that's obvious on the Vultee."

"Wow, good eye, Leightyn. Anyone else?" When no one raises a hand, he continues. "You'll train on all three aircraft, ladies. The biplane or Stearman is lightweight, slow-moving, and very, very stable. The PT-17 biplane is perfect for beginners." He notes some smirks in his audience. "Don't you dismiss this aircraft, gals. Any plane can kill you if you're casual about your approach to it. Am I clear?"

All the cadets nod solemnly.

Shaver lightens his tone. "The second aircraft you'll master—or else go home—is the BT-13. The Vultee is heavier and faster and will be your introduction to the use of a two-way radio and interacting with the flight tower. It too has a fixed 'tricycle' landing gear array, like the Stearman. But the Vultee has movable flaps for landing and a variable propeller. More about that later.

"And finally, once you've passed your flight tests on these two craft, you'll learn to fly the T6-Texan. This plane has a 550-horsepower engine, retractable landing gear and a 42-foot wingspan with room for a 30-inch machine gun on the starboard nose and the capability of a gun in the rear."

Shaver pauses a moment at the looks of uncertainty on some of the women's faces. "As a rule, training aircraft are not equipped with guns, but be aware that some of the aircraft you encounter in the field may have that capability."

He lets that sink in a moment and then concludes, "Once you've passed your flight tests on the T6 you will definitely be on your way. So be of good cheer, ladies!"

Shaver smiles encouragingly at them all. He understands that this is the point where some of the women will begin to rethink their commitment to flying the Army way. It's his job to remind them—to be sure they know—these are machines of war, not the aircraft they've watched doing tricks at a weekend Air Circus.

• • •

They have survived the day. If questioned, all the cadets would confess *they are too pooped to pop.* Jinx elbows Patty as they march in formation back to the barracks through the heat, the dust and the blazing sun. "I'll race you to the shower when we get there," she whispers.

Meadows calls a halt to the platoon just in front of the barracks and grins. "And now the fun begins. For those of you planning to hit the showers, I've got news for you. We're going to the toilets first. All of us!"

Jones opens the porch door into the barracks and waves her arm expansively. "After you, ladies."

Meadows takes the lead, and the cadets follow through the barracks proper and past the lounge which they eye with yearning glances. They stop abruptly at the communal washroom. Meadows grins at them and appears gleeful when she speaks. "Pair up. Find a partner and let's get to work."

By now Jones has commandeered several cadets to pull out buckets, mops and sponges and is lining them up at the entry to the bathroom. She points dramatically towards the toilets and with a tiny push encourages Jinx and Dodie to volunteer.

Jinx looks aggrieved as she approaches the first of ten toilets on her side of the washroom. "This is disgusting."

"I know, I didn't sign up to clean toilets," moans Tex, standing nearby.

Senior Cadet Meadows pokes her head into the wash-room. "Gee, neither did your mother. I guess since she's not here, someone has to do it. And believe me, ladies, it will not be me."

"As if," Jinx mutters.

"Join us in the lounge as soon as you think your toilet is *inspection ready*," Meadows intones. "And believe me, if I find any grunge, you'll be seeing a lot more porcelain in your future."

Thirty minutes later all the cadets are drooping around the furniture in the lounge, way beyond tired. Jones has her back to them and is pinning a large poster of names on the wall.

"Duty sheet." Meadows turns to point to the poster. "Also please note the Inspection Dates listed in the far column."

The bulk of the cadets whisper their response: "Inspections?"

"That's right. Every week you will clean the barracks from top to bottom. Every week it will be inspected by your platoon leader."

Jones joins Meadows in front of the group. "Snap inspections will occur intermittently by Mrs. Deaton, who is a harridan for cleanliness."

She and Meadows lock eyes. Meadows groans, "Trust me, you don't want to incur her wrath."

Jones continues, "So, you've all just had your first prac-tice run. Now let's go assess how you fared as housekeepers. Meadows will accompany the cadets in the north end of the barracks. The south end is with me."

Jones blasts her whistle. "Ladies, atten-TION."

All the cadets leap to their feet, surprise flickering across many faces.

"Aw come on. You didn't really think you were done, did you?" Jones grins at them. "Okay. Southies come with me." She pivots and leaves the lounge, followed immediately by a gaggle of confused cadets.

Jinx elbows Patty. "How clean does a toilet need to be?"

Dodie interjects, "I think we're about to find out, Jinx."

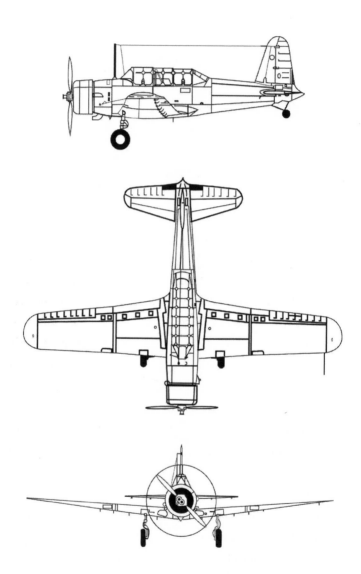

BT-13 VULTEE TRAINER

FIVE

It's evening, the sun has set and the night is alive with the sound of crickets. The WASP barracks is abuzz with a gaggle of young women in various stages of undress. Preparations for impending lights out are in full swing. Some women are still unpacking, some putting rollers in their hair or applying face cream; some are sitting on their bunks writing letters home. All are tired and a little on edge. It's been a full day. None of them could have anticipated Texas—its vastness, its dust, or its heat. Not to mention just how far away from home and anything familiar it truly is. A bass note of homesickness runs through the barracks like a fugue.

Lauren Powell is in her element. Military brats—officers' kids—get used to disruption. They become masters at pulling up stakes, moving on and blending in once they arrive. Not that Lauren could ever blend in—not with her good looks. But she does know what afflicts the women around her, and she knows what to do about it. They need someone to get 'em moving and keep them talking until they can expel the stress of the day.

Lauren slips out of her cubicle and wanders down the hall. She stops at the entrance of a nearby quartet of bunks. A woman is resolutely peering into a handheld mirror, tweezing her eyebrows.

Lauren leans over her shoulder and peers into the mirror too. "Try a little more roundness in the arch. Don't you think?"

The woman stops a moment and looks up quizzically, not quite sure what Lauren means.

"Here, let me." Lauren takes the tweezers from the other trainee's hand and bends over her, lifting her chin with one hand. "I mean, Joan Crawford's eyebrows look great on her...." Lauren plucks a stray hair. Then another. The young woman winces. "But honestly, what really separates us from the apes?" Lauren ignores the woman's flinching.

"Oow!"

Lauren tilts her head and looks at her work critically. "Just a couple more." She continues, "I tell you what the difference between us and monkeys is—makeup and accessories." Lauren spits on her forefinger and uses it to smooth the other woman's eyebrows into place. "Now, that's perfect. Have a look."

The trainee holds the mirror up to her face, inspects Lauren's work critically, and then beams.

"Wow, thanks. My name's Josie, by the way.

Lauren grins back. Her smile is truly golden. She knows this trainee can't help but feel special having been singled out for attention, no matter how painful it was.

"Don't mention it, Josie. Glad to help." And Lauren means it. She knows homesickness from dozens of military shuffles during her father's long career.

Across from Josie, a forlorn cadet is seated on a lower bunk. She has clearly been crying and is only resting between stormfronts. The girl holds a small photo in her hand.

Lauren sits down on the edge of the bunk near her. "Tougher than you thought, isn't it? What's your name?"

The sad girl nods, a tear slipping down her cheek. "Nadine."

Lauren nods knowingly. "Well, Nadine, I imagine from home this sounded like some great big adventure. And it was terrific, wasn't it, while your friends were still around and throwing you parties and saying goodbye." She reaches over and takes the photo from the Nadine's hands. "Is this your friends back home?" Nadine nods.

Lauren slips an arm around her. "They do look like fun." This makes Nadine start to cry again. Lauren pats her back gently. "And it's right that you should miss them, Nadine." She lowers her voice. "But I'm going to tell you a secret—and you're just going to have to believe me on this."

Nadine looks up for a moment, her eyes so devoid of hope that Lauren nearly starts to cry herself.

"You're going to have fun here, too, believe me. A lot of fun."

Nadine looks skeptical.

Lauren locks eyes with her. "I said you were going to have to trust me. Didn't I?" Lauren stands up and looks down at Nadine with a stern demeanor. "Just stick out the night." She lets out a big sigh. "Then, get yourself through tomorrow." She nods her head sagely. "And I promise you, something's going to happen. I don't know what.

But guaranteed, you're going to be laughing your head off by the end of the week."

Lauren is set to move on. Nadine's face clears just a bit; a tiny glimmer of hope flickers in her eyes. "Promise?"

Lauren smiles her most genuine smile. "Absolutely." She exits the cubicle and slips back into the main hallway where she nearly collides with Lila.

"Wow, that was very sweet. You did that kid a lot of good."

"Yeah, I almost believed it myself," Lauren smirks. "I've been through this a million times. Military brat—Daddy's in the navy.

Lila is a little taken aback at Lauren's quick shift from soft-hearted counselor to blatant cynic. She frowns. "So I hear. Powell, isn't it? Lauren Powell." Lila grins at her. "Daddy's not just in the navy. He IS the navy, from what I hear. Admiral Powell, Navy Air Corps?"

Very pleased, Lauren gives Lila her full megawatt smile. "Yeah. How'd you know?"

Lila pulls out a clipboard with a list of trainee names on it and consults it. "Well, I saw a Powell on the duty roster here. And I suddenly remembered a military jeep that nearly ran me down yesterday—with you in it."

All Lauren's attention is suddenly riveted on the duty roster in Lila's hands. "How'd you get that?"

"Oh, Meadows and Jones gave it to me. They made me Squad Leader."

Lauren's face suddenly loses all its warmth. "Squad Leader. Really?"

Lila is still consulting her list and doesn't notice the change in tone. "Uh-hm. They told me to pick an assistant. From what I saw just now, you'd be great." She finally looks up at Lauren's face.

Lauren quickly switches gears and puts on a *how nice for you* look. "I'm not good at that, you know—that emotional stuff. I grew up with brothers."

Lila realizes something is amiss. Something's changed, but she can't quite put her finger on it. She hesitates for the first time in her interaction with Lauren.

Ever the realist, Lauren accepts momentary defeat and agrees with grudging enthusiasm. "Assistant. Great. Thanks for choosing me."

Still puzzled, Lila's face briefly registers bewilderment. "Okay, then. Our first task is to get everyone into the lounge. Jackie wants to say a few words."

"Cochran's here?"

"Soon, yeah. I gather she pops in as often as possible to check on how the program's going." Lila stops dead at the look of determination that appears on Lauren's face. "Is something wrong?"

"Nothing that can't be fixed."

Lauren brushes past Lila and marches down the hallway towards the barracks lounge in search of Jackie Cochran.

Mystified, Lila turns and announces to the women in the nearest cubicle, "Barracks meeting at twenty-one hundred hours."

Blank expressions greet her announcement. She sighs and translates, "Nine o'clock. Military uses a twenty-four-hour clock." Lila raises her eyebrows. "Look Sharp. Meet you in the lounge. Spread the word. Let everyone know."

Lila moves on to the next cubicle while the cadets in the first cubicle are still digesting the order.

"Full barracks meeting at twenty-one-hundred hours," she shouts. "That's nine o'clock, everyone. Mandatory meeting." She moves from cubicle to cubicle repeating her message.

• • •

Patty, Dodie and Jinx stride towards the recruit lounge. From the doorway, they can see it is already packed with the other trainees. Little knots of gossip circulate through the room. Lila and Miriam are already seated; Lila in a huge armchair, Miriam perched on its more than adequate arm.

"So, you learned to fly at Dorval too?" Miriam whispers.

"No, I already knew how to fly before shipping out from Gander. But I know a lot of the gals in the ATA learned the ropes at Dorval."

On the far side of the lounge, Lauren sits on one of the three ratty sofas with Nadine and Tex, all deep in conversation. Lauren's face is like thunder.

As Jinx's group enters, all the trainees' heads immediately swivel to check them out. As soon as it's clear it's nobody important, everyone goes back to their chatter. The mood is electric—a far, far cry from the exhaustion of only moments before. Everyone wants to meet Jackie Cochran, the best woman flyer in the world.

Only Lauren still scowls, which deepens as she watches Dodie stride in alongside Jinx and Patty.

Patty elbows Dodie with gusto. "Wow, what'd you do, steal her boyfriend or something?"

Dodie looks around the room to see if she might be misinterpreting Lauren's stare. She whispers back to Patty, "I dunno. Maybe it's you, Patty."

Jinx hauls Dodie around to face her and blurts, "You stole Lauren's boyfriend!"

Dodie whispers back intensely. "No. I didn't steal anything. I don't know what's eating her. It can't be me."

Jinx turns Dodie back around and slips an arm around her waist. "She likely just can't stand it that you got to grow up luxuriating in Iowa's corn fields your whole life. "Let's just ignore her." They walk past Lauren until they're right in front of Lila and Miriam in the big chair. Jinx pulls Dodie to a stop and whines, "I'm so tired, why couldn't you guys have grabbed a sofa?"

Pouting a bit, Jinx lowers herself to the floor in front of Lila's feet. Patty and Dodie follow. Lila leans over and whispers in Jinx's ear, "Early bird gets the cushy seat, Miss Babisch."

Jinx purses her lips and blows a raspberry in response.

Across the room Lauren skewers the Brat Pack with her eyes. Dodie notices and squirms away from her glare as far as the sofa and gauntlet of women's legs will allow. She whispers to Patty, "Wow. What is her problem?"

Before Patty can respond, three silhouettes appear in the doorway, blocking some of the ambient light to the lounge. All eyes in the room turn expectantly.

Crowded into the wide opening are Meadows and Jones, turned out to the nines with creases on their trousers that could slice bread. Jones shouts, "TEN-hut, ladies."

Jackie Cochran steps from the hallway into the space between Meadows and Jones.

Instantly, all the cadets are on their feet at attention—their eyes on Jackie. Clad in pajamas, hair rollers, over-sized flight suits, bathrobes—they are a motley collection. But admiration shines on every face as they stand ramrod straight awaiting their hero's first words.

Jackie is immediately identifiable in her fashionable women's suit and perfect makeup. She could give *Lauren* lessons on how a woman can use her smile to every advantage. She has an innate energy that precedes her into the packed lounge.

As Jackie takes a step forward into the room, her smile becomes even more radiant as she makes eye contact with each woman. Then slowly, one by one, the trainees begin to applaud. Within minutes the sound is deafening. Then they begin to call in unison, "Jackie, Jackie, Jackie." Many are now crying.

Finally, Jackie raises her hands and motions for silence. All the trainees quiet immediately—not wanting to miss a single word from the woman who has brought them together. Then Jackie softly begins her own round of applause for the young trainees.

She wipes a tear from her cheek with the tips of her fingers.

"Thank you. Thank you all for that moment. It will become one of the memories I treasure for the rest of my life."

She motions for them to sit and waits patiently while they arrange themselves again in front of her. "Thank you for coming. For answering your country's call to duty. You are about to enter what will be, I promise you, one of the greatest adventures of your life."

She continues, "Many of you are already expert fly-ers." Jackie searches for Patty Yin Lee and nods her head in her direction. "Some of you, like Lila Stewart, already have ferry pilot experience. Lila served for two years with England's ATA. She has proven she can fly anything with wings while dodging bullets and bombs at the same time. Right, Lila?" Jackie nods in Lila's direction. Lila's ghost of a smile is tightly self-conscious.

Jackie uses a sweeping motion of her hand to indicate all the trainees in the room. "So many of you have already proven your grit and determination by the simple act of teaching yourselves how to fly. No easy thing for any of you. Not in a man's world."

Lauren plasters a demure smile on her face, as Jackie sweeps her eyes in her direction. "Others of you who have had every advantage, haven't risen to the challenge as far as you might have. Yet."

Jackie's eyes continue moving. "But regardless of your background, you are here now. And this is where you will prove your mettle. This is where you will take what skills you bring and hone them. Then you will prove you cannot only fly—you can fly the *Army way*." Jackie takes a breath and nods. "Avenger Field will test you as you've never been tested before."

Jackie lets a smile grow on her face as she gazes out at all the young women at her feet. "I'm certain you will make me proud. But more importantly, you will be proud of yourselves too. Your training at Avenger Field will give you the confidence to go out and succeed at anything else you choose to do in life, ladies."

Jackie begins to clap her hands softly, applauding the young women once again. Her eyes shine with more tears. "And now I'd like to introduce two people who are going to become some of the most important people in your life for the duration of your training. Please welcome Mrs. Leoti Deaton."

Mrs. Deaton steps forward and smiles at the assembled cadets. Jackie continues "Also, her most capable assistant, Miss Coralee Abrahms." Jackie encourages Coralee to step forward too. "These are the women who will coach you all through the coming months of training. If there is anything you need, any situation you question—talk to them. They always have my ear, day or night."

The cadets stand up and a wave of applause builds and rises up to engulf the three women at the front of the room. For a lovely moment, everything is in balance and perfect. Lila, Miriam, Patty, Jinx and Dodie slip their arms around each other's waist. Coralee and Mrs. Deaton grin in response. Even Lauren stands slowly and adds her applause.

All the cadets hug each other tightly, their shared dreams encompass every woman in the room. Never before have they been embraced by such a huge circle of like-minded women, and it is exhilarating.

Of course this mood can't last. Three hours later, the barracks echo with the soft sniffles of women who have left all they know, everyone they care about, to risk their futures on a roll of the dice. Jackie Cochran may tell them she has faith in them and faith in her vision for their future. But they must be the ones to prove it. And at this moment, at the midnight hour, it feels hard and unreachable.

At the midnight hour, the weight of the risk they've taken hits many of the young women hard—hard enough to bring them to tears. Many can't sleep because it's too quiet, too foreign and too different from what they've known. The beds are lumpy, the barracks austere and the landscape beyond the barracks is terrifying.

Many of the women can't forget that before lights-out Jones and Meadows specifically reminded them to check their shoes in the morning before putting them on. Rattlesnakes and scorpions from the desert beyond the door love the residual heat that remains in human shoes when they are discarded for the night.

What that means for those who routinely get up to pee in the middle of the night is too scary to contemplate. Little wonder many of the cadets fall asleep sobbing into their pillows. Some will never surmount the sense of utter dislocation—and leave before training is complete. But none of them is quite ready to quit yet.

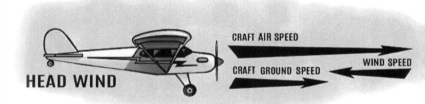

WIND SPEED FACTORS

SIX

The following morning Jones and Meadows blast them all awake again! This time though, they call Lila, Dodie and Lauren to attention and march them to the front still in their pajamas.

"This is the day, ladies, when we leave you. We're off to our own duty stations now and will hand the reins—or whistles," Marshall smirks, "over to you."

Jones continues, "Stewart, you will be the Company Commander. Top dog. Head Honcho."

Marshall interjects, "And Dodie and Lauren will be your assistants." Nearly everyone, except maybe Lauren, expected Lila to be picked as head girl. But Dodie is as perplexed as everyone else when the whistle lands in her hands. From that simple changeover, new chaos erupts that follows them through the remainder of the day.

The sun is barely above the horizon, and it's already hot. Trainees tumble from their beds, stumble to washrooms and begin to dress before their eyes are fully open. Jinx takes one look at the mayhem and rolls over in bed and pulls the covers over her eyes.

Too soon they all line up outside and begin the march to the mess hall. They look a little more awake, but their marching is haphazard and their ill-fitting 'zoot' suits do not add to the picture of military precision. Patty keeps turning around and marching backwards to talk to Jinx, who's in line directly behind her.

Lauren happens to notice and immediately blares her whistle right in Patty's ear. "Com-pany, HALT," she shouts. The cadets do so, immediately, all of them. Only Lila, the new Company Commander, has the license to pull herself from ranks to observe what's causing them to stop.

Lauren shouts, "Cadet Yin Lee, front and center. MARCH."

Patty looks around mystified, but she takes a rigid step towards her assistant commander.

Lauren eyes her appraisingly. "Replace Cadet Smith as platoon guide. All cadets will now use YOU to keep formation. Make it perfect, Lee. Give us some cadence, please."

Patty flits her eyes at Jinx as if to say, *Do I have to?*

Jinx scowls deeply at Patty and jerks her head towards the head of the platoon. She hisses, "Move your ass, Patty." Patty quickly moves up to the front rank of the platoon as Lauren has ordered.

Once the two cadets are settled in their new positions, Lauren blows her whistle again and shouts, "Company, A-ten-TION."

All the women snap to attention. Lila steps back into

place at the head of her company and calls out, "Company, FOR-ward, MARCH."

The mess hall is now only moments away, but Lauren has thoroughly made her point as to who holds the whistle.

• • •

The cadets have just finished breakfast and are lined up in formation outside the mess hall when Instructor Shaver approaches Lila from the far side of the porch.

"Miss Stewart, word has it you've been made Company Commander. Although it puts the responsibility of the platoon's daily performance squarely on your shoulders, I'm certain you will be up to the task. May I be the first to congratulate you?"

Taken aback, Lila nods, affirming his comment. She offers a very polite, "Thank you, sir."

Shaver turns back to the class. "And congratulations to Miss Powell and Miss Jackson as your squad leaders." He beams at each of the women in turn. "I thought before we launched into the classroom setting today, we could take a quick side trip to the flight line." Shaver nods his head towards the airfield. "Make sure everyone's awake for the dry, detail-driven lecture that lies ahead of us." His smirk ensures Lila understands he's being humorous.

"I'm sure a field trip would definitely get the platoon's attention," Lila responds. She turns and calls the cadets to order, explaining, "Instructor Shaver is authorizing a quick sortie to the airfield before we head into the class-room today."

"Company, FOR-ward, MARCH." Lila steps off, following Shaver's lead and marches her troop towards the airstrip. The detour has added a definite spring to everyone's step.

At the far end of the runway, an inbound T6 training plane is making a low approach to the airfield. Shaver notices and raises one hand to indicate Lila should halt her platoon before they get too close.

Lila shouts, "Company, HALT. Everyone, fall out along the flight line."

All eyes along the flight line are now fixed on the small plane as it races towards them. The pilot has too much altitude to be attempting a landing. Everyone can see that. As the pilot passes them by, the wings of her aircraft wobble from side to side. The girls can see the face of the young pilot clearly. Behind her, in the tandem cockpit, the second seat is empty. On her face is a look of terror. She continues wobbling her wings as she passes the Flight Shack and the assembled cadets.

Shaver is silent for a moment and then asks briskly as he turns towards the cadets, "What did you see as she passed, cadets?"

Plane and pilot roar down the runway away from them and begin a slow arc back around to recircle the field.

"Cadets? Anyone?"

Patty is the first to speak up. "Wing wobble means something's wrong. I would guess it's landing gear problems. 'Cause they weren't lowered yet for her landing."

Shaver nods, "Very good, Miss Lee."

Nadine adds, "She looked scared when she flew past."

Shaver nods to that too. "Just so. But that's the point of training. Rigorous training. You master your fear and perform the required flight patterns in spite of it."

"They'll work out something to help her from the Flight Shack." Shaver turns away from the airfield. "Miss Stewart, let's keep moving over to the Stearmans on the other side of the Flight Shack."

Lila puts the company into motion. They follow their instructor onto the portion of the field where aircraft are sequestered that aren't expected to be flown for the day. Shaver approaches the nearest double-winged aircraft and motions for the cadets to gather around it.

Lila blows her whistle and shouts again, "Fall out, everyone." The neat rows of cadets disperse and groups promptly coalesce around the nearest Stearman.

Shaver runs his hands over the wings and visibly relaxes as he does so. "Alright, let's start at the nose of the plane and work our way towards the tail. I'm assuming many of you learned to fly in one of these. They're simply constructed, with a metal frame for the fuselage or body, covered over with heavy-duty canvas cloth. This makes them extremely light weight and easy to repair. The wing struts are metal but the wing's structure and tail assembly are both wood, covered with canvas." He runs his hands along the struts to emphasize his words.

The cadets crowd around Shaver, shadowing his every move. "You'll notice the landing gear is fixed and stationary, with the 'pants' Miss Zimmerman mentioned. Very simple aircraft."

Standing next to Patty, Dodie whispers, "Yeah, I used to wing-walk on these to earn flying time."

Patty turns and replies too loudly for Dodie's comfort. "You were one of those crazy wing-walkers?"

The whole company turns towards Dodie, including their instructor. She seems to melt into herself, becoming smaller at the sudden attention.

Shaver smiles and reaches out his hand for Dodie to shake. "Welcome to the club. I started as a wing-walker too."

Dodie rallies and reaches out to accept his handshake. But the moment of comradery is broken by the roar of the T6 as the student flyer passes overhead again, the wings still waggling.

Shaver looks up and as the pilot passes overhead, he muses more to himself than to the cadets, "Hmm, if her landing gear is indeed stuck, the hydraulics could be faulty."

Dodie whispers back, "What will she do?"

Shaver is startled from his reverie. He frowns a moment then instantly changes his demeanor. "We should get ourselves back to the classroom, Miss Stewart. Time's awastin'."

The faulty plane approaches the runway again. Again, the wings waggle. Again, the air around them reverberates with the roar of the engine passing overhead.

Dodie's jaw tightens. "We can't just leave her, Mr. Shaver!"

Lila puts out a hand on Dodie's arm to caution her.

Shaver frowns again, "There's very little we can do. The Flight Shack will handle it."

Dodie persists. "Sir, I believe that aircraft has a manual crank for the landing gear."

Shaver turns to give Dodie his full attention. "Two. The one in the cockpit is a pump lever. Why she hasn't used it is beyond me."

Emboldened, Dodie blurts, "Maybe hers is broken, or defective." She pauses. "But the one in the rear cockpit seat should work. It's a manual crank."

Shaver scrutinizes Dodie now, assessing. "How good a wing-walker are you?"

Dodie meets his gaze unflinching. "Just about the best."

Shaver stands eye-to-eye with her a moment longer and then huffs. "Let's get over to the Flight Shack, cadet." He reaches for Dodie's forearm and tugs her away from her platoon and begins to trot towards the shack.

Lila turns and assesses her cadets, then blows her whistle sharply. "Form up, FORM UP."

All the women leap into position, shoulder-to-shoulder. Lila quickly steps to the head of the column and shouts, "FOR-ward, MARCH." She sets a rapid pace for the column, quickly walking them towards the Flight Shack at the edge of the airfield.

Dodie and Shaver have disappeared but reappear before Lila has time to line up her troops alongside the Flight Shack. They watch Shaver and Dodie race for the parked Stearman biplanes.

Two mechanics have sprinted to the flight line and pulled the guywires that anchor the leading plane to the ground. Moments later, Shaver is circling the aircraft doing a pre-flight external check on the airplane. He motions Dodie into the forward cockpit. He climbs into the rear cockpit the moment the flight check is done.

"What the hell is going on?" Patty's overly loud whisper carries way past Jinx; heads among the troop turn her way. Everyone is asking themselves the same question.

Jinx shrugs, "I'm as in the dark as you are!"

By now, the Steaman's huge motor has been primed and is roaring, annihilating any further chance of talk. The mechanics quickly remove the wheel blocks, and Shaver smoothly moves the plane forward and onto the airfield. He maneuvers it easily onto the runway and taxis into the wind, gaining some space to begin his take-off.

As the aircraft rolls along the tarmac past the cadets lining the airfield, Dodie's face is white as a sheet and a mask of intense concentration. As the aircraft nears her, Lila brings herself to attention and snaps up a salute and holds it. One-by-one the other cadets follow her example as the plane gathers speed for its leap into the air.

In the rear cockpit, Shaver skillfully guides the aircraft along the tarmac, checking the red and white windsock as he passes it. Only then does he turn the plane into the wind. The craft's full-throttled roar announces its intention and like magic it is airborne and climbing rapidly to meet up with the larger T6.

As he pulls back on the throttle, Shaver speaks into the voice tube that connects him to the front cockpit. The biplane has no radio, and no connection to the ground now that she is aloft.

"So, you understand your mission. Get yourself into that rear cockpit and immediately put on the headset to connect yourself to the pilot. Her name is Isabelle. Reassure her she's trained for this. You're just onboard as an extra pair of hands."

Shaver stares intently at the back of Dodie's head, willing her to speak. After a long silent moment, he adds. "I know you can do this, Dodie. We can't afford to lose that aircraft."

In the front seat Dodie sits and shivers with fear. Her eyes are unfocused, and all the blood has drained from her face. Somehow she forces herself to reach out and lift the speaking tube, which connects her to Shaver. "Aye, aye, sir." Her harsh whisper is forced and strained.

Shaver spots the other aircraft just ahead and to his left. He reaches again for the speaking tube. "Alright, Dodie, we'll come up under her and when I tap your shoulder, you need to be ready to make your move."

Dodie simply nods her head several times to be sure Shaver can see it.

Shaver throttles back the power and lets the aircraft slide up gently beneath the bigger and louder T6. He lets his aircraft slip a bit to the right, until the wing is just below the T6 rear cockpit. He leans forward and taps Dodie on the shoulder sharply.

As if sleepwalking, Dodie registers the tap of Shaver's fingertips as something muted or foreign—not quite there. Regardless, she unstraps her safety harness and brings her feet up onto her seat. She wears no parachute; it would simply get in her way. Even though her legs are shaking, she deftly uses the wing struts to pull herself upright until she's standing in the seat.

Never taking her eyes off the horizon, utterly relying on Shaver's expertise, Dodie again uses the struts to pull herself onto the wing. Along the horizon, wreathed over the faraway desert mountains, clouds have gathered in brilliant defiance of the afternoon heat.

Dodie can't seem to move her eyes from the horizon. Fixated there, she recalls a flash of Iowa summer. A moment when her mother swung her around and around grasping her hands while Dodie leaned out watching the summer clouds fly past overhead.

"DODIE."

Even without the speaking tube Dodie hears Shaver's voice over the wail of aircraft engines. She drops her eyes to the top of the upper wing of the craft and uses the struts to shuffle to the very edge of the wing. Shaver holds the Stearman steady, feeling the weight of Dodie's progress across the wing of his plane.

Dodie looks up and in surprise finds she's nearly touching the rim of the rear cockpit of the T6. All she has to do is stretch out her hand. She is solely focused on the rim of the cockpit, and to her utter amazement she lifts up her hand and grasps its edge. She uses that solidity to pull herself forward and up to a crouch. She then lifts a leg and hauls herself inside the T6 aircraft, abandoning the Stearman.

Expert pilot that he is, Shaver immediately corrects for the loss of Dodie's weight. He allows his aircraft to drift apart, until he can see Dodie's face in the secondary cockpit. He lifts a free hand and offers her a salute, and then banks his aircraft to the right and drops deftly down and away.

Back on the ground, every cadet has her eyes trained on the blue sky overhead. They can hear the thrum of the aircraft engines. The best eyes can see the two small specks in the sky, flying in tandem, and then the biplane is falling gently away.

Over the base P.A. system, the Flight Shack transmits confirmation. "Jackson's in." Relief is evident in the voice. "They'll do a fly-by to verify landing gear is operational. Three cheers for instructor Shaver. Extraordinary job, cadet Jackson."

A raucous cheer erupts from the trainees gathered around the Flight Shack. Grinning, Lila lets them have a moment, then motions for quiet from the troops. Their smiling faces press eagerly forward, straining for the sight of the aircraft at the end of the runway.

Shaver brings his Stearman in smoothly and taxis past the Flight Shack to allow the mechanics to return the aircraft to its berth. Isabelle and Dodie dip low and do a fly-by in the T6. Every eye is on the underbelly of that plane. As soon as it's obvious the landing gear has dropped into place, another cheer shatters the tension of the day.

The pilot roars past the assembled cadets, the smile on her face blazing with confidence.

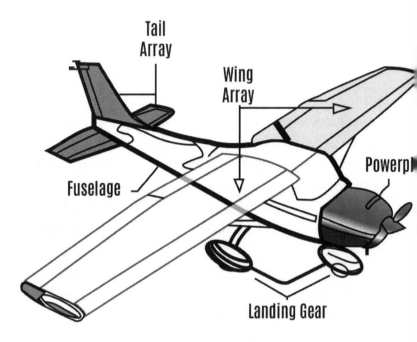

AIRCRAFT COMPONENTS

SEVEN

Lila is holding Dodie's hair back while she bends over a latrine and vehemently throws-up for the fourth time. Lila waits a moment and then hands her a hunk of toilet paper to wipe her mouth. "Better?"

Dodie turns and seats herself on the floor, inches from the porcelain. "Maybe." She pauses. "I don't think there's any way I can do lunch though."

"Honestly, I don't think you should do anything. Go back to barracks, have a nap, go for a walk. Take the time you need to settle yourself."

"But what about the others?"

"What about them?" Lila pauses to drop down onto the floor beside Dodie. "I'm sure they'll think you earned far more than an afternoon off for what you did today."

"Yeah, but here I am puking my guts out immediately afterwards. I'm such a chickenshit, Lila. I thought I was going to die the whole time I was up there."

Lila's smile is tentative. "When I flew in England, most days were so routine. Get up, get to the flight line, get my plane. Deliver it somewhere and pick up another to take somewhere else. England was so small I sometimes could do nine or ten deliveries in a day." She sees she has Dodie's attention.

"But there was one day when I was on a longer flight, headed for the south coast, right on the English Channel, and I was almost at my destination. Suddenly the closest tower announced over the radio a wave of incoming *Luftwaffe* fighter planes. It would take them ten minutes to cross the channel and hit the south coast of England. That meant I had only ten minutes to find a place to land my bird. Safely.

"Dodie, I tell you I was scared shitless. *No lie.* England has been actively farmed for hundreds of years. All those pretty little farm fields neatly bounded by large trees, hedgerows and solid *stone* fences. No matter where I looked there was nowhere I could put down safely. Before I knew it, the first Messerschmidt was coming in fast, with all its guns blazing. I ducked, I dived, I did everything I could to evade that pilot and risk losing my aircraft and my life." Lila hesitates a long moment to collect herself.

"What happened?" Dodie is slightly breathless.

"An RAF pilot had spotted the enemy plane and dove on it, strafing it as he went. He passed me on the starboard side close enough that I could see his face. And he saw mine. Then he was gone. I never saw him again or had a chance to thank him. But he got his man, before his man got me.

"In a weird way it all balanced out. I had unwittingly acted as a decoy for the RAF pilot, while he gained the advantage of height. He repaid the favor by eliminating an obvious threat to me delivering my aircraft safely to its destination.

"Moments later I was on the ground, being heralded as a hero for completing the delivery. Honestly, I couldn't wait to get away from it to a quiet place to throw up and really think about what I gotten myself into with the ATA."

Lila stands up and reaches down a hand to help Dodie get to her feet too. "I think every one of us will have our moment like that. A moment when we each recognize we've agreed to put our lives on the line for something we believe in…and we deserve a moment in return to check in with ourselves to see if that is still what we honestly want."

Dodie nods her head slowly, agreeing. "So, is that why you came back to America to fly instead?"

Lila smiles, shaking her head no. "Oh no. I flew through far worse than that, for over a year before I got Jackie's telegram. But I'm flying now with my eyes wide open, Dodie. And I think you will be too from now on."

They both exit the washroom and wander into the empty barracks. Lila cocks her head at Dodie and repeats her previous advice. "Take the rest of the morning off, Dodes. We'll catch up with you at the barracks before dinner."

Dodie smiles a grim little smile in response. "I know you're probably right. Thanks, Lila." Dodie walks with Lila as far as the porch and stops to wave her goodbye. "Maybe I'll go for a stroll in the rose garden."

Lila turns and gestures around them at the miles and miles of arid, dusty desert stretching to every possible horizon. "Good luck with that, Dodie."

. . .

Eventually, Dodie does find herself walking. Head down, putting one foot in front of the other to no real purpose but to provide movement—something for her body to do while her mind replays the morning's events. She walks robotically, turning right at the arched Avenger Field entrance and following the fence. She loses herself in thought. So she is more than a little surprised to find herself circling the barracks and various other field houses, following the definite smell of *roses*.

What Dodie discovers when she looks up is a stand of cottonwood trees—likely planted as a windbreak—that hides a small white clapboard house. No, a *tiny* clapboard house with the prerequisite deep porch, but this one is embellished with two rocking chairs and a pair of climbing roses on either side of the door. She stops in consternation. It's as if she's entered an alternate universe to Avenger Field. Although she can still hear the whine of aircraft engines and see the glimmers of the planes in the clear blue sky, her mind is stymied by the sight of the cottage set within the shade of the trees.

Dodie can see that the front door is open, the entryway solely protected by an old wooden screen door. She steps closer and can hear someone in the interior singing along with a radio. It's a nice voice, a low contralto that matches Joan Stafford's on the radio. "You got to give a little, take a little, let your poor heart break a little."

Curious, Dodie steps onto the porch and peers through the screen. She thinks she has been completely unobtrusive.

"You may as well come in as stand there and stare."

Dodie immediately steps back and offers a quavery, "I'm sorry. I didn't mean any offence."

"Get your sorry ass in here and explain why you're peeking through my screen door instead of busting your keister in Physical Training."

This comment brings Dodie up short. Now she opens the screen door in puzzlement, not mere curiosity.

Coralee Abrahms is in the small kitchen, clad in shorts and a sleeveless top, punching dough on a bread board. She places her floury fists on her hips and scowls as Dodie steps inside. Coralee doesn't give her a moment to breathe. "Why the hell aren't you in PT right now?"

Dodie ducks her head and blurts, "Lila gave me the day off to umm…" she hesitates. "To, umm, collect myself, she said. After the wing-walking thing."

There's a moment of silence, and Coralee nods her head. "Ahhh, so that was you that did that fool thing? *Dodie*, isn't it?"

"Yes, Miss Abrahms. Dodie Jackson. From Iowa."

Coralee picks up a tea towel and wipes the flour off her hands. "I was hoping for a little break from pounding this dough. Let's go sit on the porch for bit, Dodie." She crosses the room and leads Dodie outside to the two rocking chairs. Coralee picks one and waves a hand at Dodie to take the other. They both sit for a moment and rock in silence.

Without lifting her head, Dodie whispers, "So, you live here, not in town?"

Coralee stares out over the bone-dry desert that stretches to the horizon. "I do. Jackie wanted you gals to always have a woman on hand…and Mrs. Deaton goes home to Sweetwater every night to her husband. And to be honest, Sweetwater would not welcome me. So here I am."

Dodie continues to rock in her chair but looks sideways at Coralee. "This is nice."

Coralee meets her eyes. "How *are* you doing, Miss Jackson? Miss Stewart was right to give you some time off to settle a bit after the morning's events." Coralee hesitates. "Will you stay on at Avenger, do you think?"

Dodie straightens immediately and fixes her gaze on Coralee. "Of course. Why wouldn't I? Did I do something wrong?"

Coralee huffs a little laugh. "You did everything right, Miss Jackson. But two women in your company have handed in their resignation…and they were only on the ground watching."

When Dodie doesn't respond immediately, Coralee continues. "No one would blame you if you packed your bags and left, you know."

Dodie tries on a tentative smile and responds, "They'd have to drag me kicking and screaming out the front gate, Miss Abrahms."

"You're sure?"

"Absolutely."

"I will let Mrs. Deaton know then. She was worried we'd lose you." Coralee stands and cocks her head. "I was going to make some tea. Would you like a cup?"

"That would be perfect, Miss Abrahms, and very much appreciated." Dodie settles into the rocker and sets it in motion.

. . .

The bulk of the platoon is spread out in small groupings trying to find what shade they can to eat their brown-bag lunches. If it's this hot outside, the mess hall is ghastly. All of them are suffering from the Texas heat. Their flight suits are half unzipped; the sleeves are rolled up to their elbows. Nothing helps. They all pick at their sandwiches with little enthusiasm.

Of course, Lauren is the exception. She survived the mornings PT workout somehow more glamorous than when she started. She alone still looks fresh and cool and composed. "You know, we looked pathetic this morning, marching to PT." She takes a nibble of her sandwich. "My god, what an embarrassment. We need to practice more."

Miriam pulls a huge dill pickle from her brown bag and sucks the brine off the outside. "We'll get better with time." She puts the pickle back in her mouth and sucks diligently. "It's my experience that you can master any situation, no matter how BIG—with enough practice."

Jinx has been lounging in the shade, refusing to eat. She opens one eye and peers at Miriam: her pickle, the sucking. She begins moaning in rhythm to Miriam's sucking. "Ooh, baby. That's it, you tell 'em. I'll practice, practice all you want."

The group turns as one and stares at Jinx as if she's lost her mind. Unwittingly, Miriam seems driven to more rapid mastication of her pickle. Jinx notices and ups the tempo of her commentary, throwing in some panting.

"Hah, hah. Oh yeah, that's it. Practice, practice, practice."

The rest of the group makes the connection and suddenly erupts in a chorus of delighted—and horrified—laughter.

Moments later, Miriam gets it too and squeals in horror. "Eeewww, Jinx. Stop it." She throws the pickle at Jinx, who is now killing herself laughing. "You're disgusting, Jinx Babisch."

Jinx is laughing so hard that she's holding her sides. She manages to squeak out a rejoinder. "Practice, practice, practice, kiddies, if you want to be the best."

The group finally settles back into some semblance of normalcy. Lauren stretches out a leg and pushes at Jinx playfully with her toe. She is smiling and shaking her head in dismay. "It's not exactly what I had in mind. But you do get my meaning."

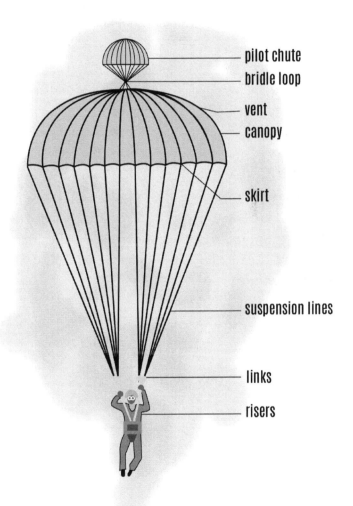

pilot chute
bridle loop
vent
canopy

skirt

suspension lines

links
risers

PARACHUTE COMPONENTS

EIGHT

Outside the Ground School classroom Instructor Shaver is deep in conversation with four other men. The WASP trainees are standing clumped together in a huddled mass in the shade of the shack. Shaver breaks from the coterie of instructors and addresses the cadets.

"Alright, gals, I know you thought you'd had PT today, but we're going to work outside some more to get you ready for your first trip up in an Army Training aircraft. No one flies an Army aircraft without knowing how to use an Army parachute." Shaver motions for the other instructors to step forward and spread out in front of the massed trainees. "Lila, Patty and Jinx, let's get the company spread out only two deep—so everyone can see."

Each of the men holds a parachute packed and ready to use in front of them. They lengthen the space between them to help all the cadets get a good view.

"Now, I want your absolute complete attention for the next few minutes, as the information I'm going to give you could save your life.

"Arrayed in front of you are my fellow instructors, Mr. Anderson, Mr. Bittern, Mr. Wadge and Mr. Riley. Each holds an Army issue parachute in his hands. Each 'chute serves the same purpose—to save your life.

"Now before you go thinking the U.S. Army invented parachutes, I want to set the record straight. Parachutes were being used in circus performances in China as early as 1350 A.D. to entertain the emperor. Those performers were jumping off roofs, the tops of temples, you name it—for the sheer fun of it, all those centuries ago.

"And let's be clear, it's not just men that love to jump. As early as 1911 women were making good use of parachutes, again for entertainment. Georgia 'Tiny' Broadwick is credited with over 600 parachute jumps and earned the nickname 'the first lady of parachuting'. So, if Tiny can do it, so can you—if the situation calls for it."

At the questioning looks on the faces of the nearest trainees, Shaver explains,

while motioning the next instructor forward. "Anderson, can you please step forward and move your 'chute around so the cadets can see every angle as we discuss it. And Mr. Bittern, could you step up beside Anderson so the gals can compare the two 'chutes for a moment."

Frank Bittern has a craggy, dour face. He does as ordered and moves to stand beside Anderson, but glowers at the cadets while presenting his parachute for examination.

Shaver continues. "As you can see, all the parachute packages consist of a tightly bundled pack attached to an adjustable harness that allows it to cling to the flyer." Shaver catches sight of Bittern's glower. "Don't let Frank's face put you off the parachute he's holding. Packed inside is over 30 yards of nylon, meticulously sewn to maximize its strength.

"Now, can I get a volunteer please?"

Not a single woman raises her hand. Shaver waits patiently. Finally, Lauren raises her hand and plasters a megawatt smile on her face.

"Perfect, Miss Powell, thank you." As Lauren approaches, he lifts the parachute from instructor Anderson's hands. "Alright, Miss Powell. First step is put the parachute on like a heavy winter coat. Hold both arms out to your side."

Lauren holds her arms straight out from her sides, and Shaver and Anderson each take a grip on the harness and help her slip it on over her shoulders. As they release the weight fully onto her, she groans. "This is heavy."

Shaver laughs, "What'd I tell you. Each 'chute weighs roughly 35 pounds. It's heavy because this parachute, when fully opened, is 28 feet across. That's as wide as our Ground School classroom.

"Okay, so you'll all note that the harness has multiple places where you can adjust it to suit your body. You'll want it snug, but not tight. The 'chutes you'll be using actually have you sitting on the parachute itself, so adjust the tension accordingly."

Lauren grasps the surplus webbing flowing down her shoulders and gives it a firm tug on each side. She also tightens the belt around her waist, so now some of the weight is held up by her hips.

"Good, good. I see you've done this before." Shaver's tone

is approving. "Have you ever actually jumped, Miss Powell?"

A flash of fear ricochets across her face, but she immediately smiles again. "No sir, Mr. Shaver. Will we be practicing a real jump?"

Shaver huffs out a laugh. "No, no, not for ages yet. But we will be practicing the fundamentals of how to jump, in stages, so that you're all completely comfortable with the idea before you ever actually jump out of an aircraft for practice. The best advice I can give all of you is stay with your aircraft in any emergency, if at all possible. You must use your parachute only as a last resort to save your life.

"So, we have the adjustable parachute harness, the parachute pack which is the most any of you may ever see of your 'chute. But folded inside, to very exacting standards, are the cords which attach the harness to the 'chute.

"Also, the 'chute itself is folded in a very specific way that enables it to be extracted from your pack with utter efficiency. Tucked into the 'chutepack at the very top is a tiny baby 'chute called a drogue. When you pull that 'D' ring right there on your left chest harness it releases the drogue or DRAG 'chute first. This tiny 'chute is what actually deploys the main 'chute out of your pack."

Shaver motions to Bitter. "Frank, will you bring that unpacked 'chute over here so the gals can have a gander at just how much is stuffed into their new seat cushions?"

Bittern shuffles over to the group dragging a fully extended military parachute which he hauls by the drogue 'chute at the top.

"Okay, so you all can see the tiny 'chute Frank has in his hands is firmly attached. It's not going to come loose from your main 'chute for any reason. Now below that is the main 'chute, which when fully inflated would easily cover up all of us. Frank, show them the vent at the top."

Frank lifts up the top of the 'chute and shows the women the expandable vent.

"Now when you pull the 'D' ring, the little drogue 'chute fills and drags the main 'chute out of the pack. If it's folded correctly, it will pull out neatly, filling as it goes, until it's fully inflated and then the baffle over that hole in the top covers itself over. By then your harness has jerked you into an upright, sitting position—as if you were sitting in a swing in the play yard at school—and you ride the 'chute all the way down to the ground.

"But when you hit is when you realize just how fast you've been falling. So, to help minimize the accident rate upon landing, we're going to push you to build muscle and conditioning in Physical Training. Not only will you be conditioning your muscles but your mind too. We'll have you practice jumping from higher and higher levels of the jump tower, while also learning to roll when you land and even how to climb your own suspension cords to safety if you end up swinging from a tree. We want you gals ready for anything that comes your way."

Shaver is not unaware of the nervous glances that flit back and forth between the women in the platoon as he finishes his presentation. He beams a reassuring grin at each one of them.

. . .

All the cadets are in a frenzy to get out of their horrible, heavy, sweaty flight suits and into something less cumbersome. They have a full hour and a half until they have to march to the mess hall for dinner, and they want to make the most of it.

Some are lounging on their bunks, reading, or writing letters home. Others have stripped down to their skivvies and are applying wet cloths to their sunburned faces. Whatever they're doing is a mostly vain attempt to bring back some of the normalcy of civilian life to the chaos the military is imposing on them.

Jinx and Miriam have just finished a quick sponge bath and have put on shorts and sneakers. They both have their hair tied up in ponytails, trying to keep cool.

Patty appears out of nowhere and sticks her head inside the cubicle that their bunk beds and lockers form. "You guys ready?"

"Where you been?" Jinx's tone is snappish with the heat.

Patty grins maniacally, "Oh just procuring a little something to brighten our day."

The three are just about to depart and join the others streaming out of their cubicles when Patty stops dead in her tracks. She eyes a sleeping form tucked into the top bunk. The only thing visible from under the blankets are hair rollers and a kerchief.

Patty lowers her voice immediately. "Whoops, sorry. I didn't know someone was sleeping." Suddenly very officious, Jinx hauls Patty from the cubicle, clearly hustling her along.

"Hey, who is that? That used to be Helen's bunk, right? But she abandoned ship after dear Dodie's heroics." Patty stops dead in her tracks and becomes an immovable object, no matter how hard Jinx tries to tug and pull her along the hallway.

Jinx exhales a big sigh and turns Patty around back towards the cubicle. She plasters a patently fake smile on her face and whispers jovially, "I'm sure you remember BER-neece, Patty." Patty's face scrunches up in puzzlement.

"Remember? You met *HER* the other night. When I was unpacking?"

Dodie joins them in the hallway, staring into the cubicle with them. "How can that woman be sleeping when it's 95,000 degrees outside?" Patty furrows her brow in concentration. "And how can anyone sleep with rollers in their hair? I've never been able to figure that out."

Jinx shrugs. "I dunno. I think maybe she was up all night. Let's just let her get some shut-eye."

Patty takes a step towards the upper bunk. "Ah, Jinx, I don't think she's actually breathing."

Dodie leans towards the woman and gasps. "She isn't breathing. Holy cats, we better call a doctor." She quickly turns to exit the cubicle, but Jinx grabs her arm hastily and hauls her back inside.

"Oh Jesus, you two. Okay, this secret has to *die* with us, you hear?" Jinx whispers harshly. "That's *Bernie,* you idiots."

"Your brother?" Dodie gasps. "And he's dead?"

Patty chuckles. "Relax, Dodie. He's WOOD."

Both the gals turn quizzical expressions on Jinx.

Jinx sighs dramatically. "We've always been close. He's my favorite brother and I felt awful leaving him stuffed in a steamer trunk. When Helen decamped, I thought what the heck, we've got the room now. He can move in with us."

. . .

WASHINGTON, D.C.

Jackie is seated at her desk, looking out a tiny window, talking on the phone. She is dressed in open-toed heels, a crisp women's business suit and a stylish hat. Her nails are perfect and her makeup flawless. In contrast, the office of the head of the WASP program is military spartan: drab gray-green military issue and a bit worn around the edges. "C'mon, Hap. These girls put their lives on the line every single day. The least we can do is recognize their contribution with a real uniform."

On the wall behind Jackie's desk are numerous plaques and citations. The most impressive is the citation confirming her rank as a Flight Commander for Britain's Air Transport Auxiliary. Even though it was an honorary citation, Jackie loves it and feels it adds weight to her bid to become the Army head of the WASPs, once she finally gets them military status.

Atop a nearby filing cabinet sit several impressive trophies won in flying competitions: Bendix trophies, Harmon trophies and a model B-17 bomber commemorating her flight as the first woman to ferry an aircraft across the Atlantic Ocean.

"Honestly, they deserve a standardized, military-issue uniform that says *plainly* for all to see WHO my girls are and WHAT they do. Surely you can understand that."

Jackie turns and breaks a pencil point by pressing too hard on her notepad. "For God's sake, right now my girls are being mistaken for bus drivers, airport attendants you, name it."

She sighs into the phone in exasperation. "They go off on a cross-country ferrying job and then spend *hours* once they deliver a plane convincing the base duty officers of their right to temporary quarters and a meal."

Jackie doodles on the notepad. "No, Hap, I understand. Alright, I'll wait for the committee meeting. Thanks, Hap."

Jackie hangs up the phone and pauses, staring thoughtfully down at her suit jacket. It is beautifully tailored, with lovely brass buttons down the front and on the sleeves. She fingers the buttons a moment, thinking, then reaches over and picks up the phone again, dialing rapidly.

"Antoine, Jackie here. Listen, I have an important meeting with General Hap Arnold next week and I need your help."

Jackie is excitedly tapping her stub of a pencil now. She's scribbling ideas on the notepad. "How long would it take you to sew me a new suit?" She sketches a pair of wings, widespread, as if in flight. She blocks in the letters WASP across the top. "You know, like the blue one, but with a couple of tiny changes…."

NINE

Lila sits in the forward seat of one of the biplanes. Instructor Shaver is seated behind her, clipboard in hand. He's scribbling notes as Lila meticulously guides the plane through a left roll, right roll, chandrelle and finally a series of loops. All the while Shaver is jotting notes on his clipboard, as casual as you please.

As they come out of the final loop, Shaver taps Lila on the shoulder. When she turns, he gives her a thumbs-up and motions for her to take the plane in for landing. Lila smiles in acknowledgment and banks for the turn to line them up with the runway.

Just outside the Flight Shack, Lila's platoon is huddled, watching her bank the craft and head for the runway. Lauren is amongst them, and she seems to be scrutinizing Lila's performance with a keener interest than most.

Nadine has one hand shading her eyes as she watches the far end of the runway. "She's good." She turns to Lauren for agreement. "Good enough to teach the course herself, don't you think?"

Lauren turns away, unimpressed. "Oh, I don't know… *anyone* can learn to fly with enough practice. Even you, I bet." Nadine sucks in her breath, wounded.

"It's the principles, the mechanics, that are tough." Lauren softens her tone a little. "Don't you think?"

Nadine replies after a moment's hesitation. "I dunno. I think it's all hard."

Lila coasts the airplane to a halt in front of the little group. She leaves the engine running because Shaver remains in the back seat awaiting the next cadet. She clambers out of the cockpit and slides down to the ground. Sprinting over to the cadets anxiously eyeing her, she says, "Okay. Who's next?"

No one in the group moves. Lila scans their faces, seeing worry and insecurity. She tilts her head and then simply chooses the next candidate herself. "Okay, Lauren, why don't you take it for a spin?"

Once she's sure Lauren's on the move, Lila steps up to another recruit and taps her shoulder. "You're next. Then you…and then you, Tex."

Lauren straightens her spine and steels herself as she marches towards the waiting airplane. Behind her all the other gals melt again into a huddle and watch the aircraft as it begins to taxi past them onto the runway. In the front seat, Lauren casts a glance their way that is both filled with pride and awash in anxiety.

As the aircraft stutter steps past the assembled flight team—stopping, starting, stopping, starting—Lauren's attention is pulled immediately back to her duties in the cockpit.

Lila bows her head, putting both hands over her face and shaking her head in disbelief. In the rear seat, Instructor Shaver's head is snapping back and forth, back and forth, like a spring dolly made for the dashboard of an automobile.

Nadine, misreading Lila's gesture as concern for Lauren, leans over and shouts above the rising engine noise, "She'll be fine, I know she will. Right?"

Lila removes her hands from her face, trying to disguise her dismay from the other trainees. She whispers under her breath, "We will be here the rest of our lives at this rate."

Noticing Nadine's look of concern, Tex interjects, also raising her voice. "Of course Lauren will be fine! We're all going to be fine. We'll fly this turkey till it's roasted. And then serve it up for dinner."

Nadine looks from Tex to Lila and back again. Lila laughs. "That may be a Texas bit of slang that has no ready translation, Nadine. We'll all be fine. Don't worry."

The windsock atop the Flight Shack, which shows pilots which direction the wind is blowing, snaps and twists in the afternoon breeze. It flies first in one direction then does an about-face and swivels from the opposite direction. Near the end of the runway, Lauren's aircraft proceeds towards takeoff. It bobbles a bit, gathers sufficient speed and is gone into the blue and rising off the horizon line.

As it clears, another craft already airborne centers itself and sets itself up for landing. It lands with a solid thump onto the far end of the runway and coasts to the Flight Shack. Patty Yin Lee jumps from the cockpit and exchanges a salute with Dodie, who is next up to fly. Patty is totally pumped after her flight.

Dodie is a bit more understated. She shrugs into her 'chute and climbs into the cockpit Patty has just vacated. She makes a point to salute Mr. Anderson and then gets down to business. She points the nose of the aircraft down the runway and lets the throttle out. Moments later the plane has seemed to simply leap into the air.

Overhead another aircraft lines itself up on the runway for landing. It drops down and nails the landing with exquisite force, then drifts towards the Flight Shack. Lauren exits the cockpit and descends, using the wing edge as a slide to drop to the ground. Nadine runs out to take her place in the cockpit.

Lauren trots exultantly towards her flight group, dust swirling around her as she approaches them. Grinning, she reaches out for the canteen one of the trainees offers her and raises it to her lips as everyone pats her shoulder in congratulations. Lauren turns expectantly to Lila, her eyes asking, *How'd I do?*

Lila hesitates, then reluctantly slaps Lauren's shoulder. A roiling gust of wind wreathes them in a shower of dust and sand. On the flight line, it's clear Shaver is calling it a day. In fact, every aircraft up in the air slowly begins the line-up to start the descent homewards. The windsock overhead is like a tilt-a-whirl—swirling first in one direction, then another and back again.

Relieved of his aircraft, Shaver finds his group of trainees and hustles them towards the Flight Shack to get out of the wind that's now growing ever fiercer.

"I think something big's blowing in. We'll have to call it quits for the day on the flight line."

• • •

Outside the barracks, a dusty twilight world has descended upon Avenger Field. The wind is rattling gates and doors and windows, as well as the shutters designed to protect the windows from breaking. The sound is reminiscent of a brass band that's forgotten its melody.

Lauren, Lila, Jinx, Miriam, Patty and Dodie, along with about twenty other trainees, are killing time in the barracks lounge. They've spread around, casually draping themselves over every available piece of furniture.

The moan of the wind rises and falls, rises and falls. Jinx is seated deep in a dilapidated armchair. She suddenly leaps to her feet and wails along with the wind. "I am *sooooo* bored. I can't believe we are confined to barracks for our own safety." She turns and does an impromptu backbend over the old chair she just vacated. Upside down she shouts at Patty, "Go look and see if you can see anything, P.Y."

Patty dutifully rouses herself and plods to the window and raises the blinds. "There's nothing to see, Jinx. There is a curtain of sand between us and every other thing out there. I can't even see those big cottonwoods just behind the barracks anymore."

Tex looks over Patty's shoulder at the swirling dust. Her local twang adds weight to her comment. "Well, that's the thang with twisters down here. There's so much dirt in the air you don't see 'um. You don't see 'um and then BANG.

They drop down and just nail you. Best thing is to keep busy and not worry till something happens."

Jinx, still bent over the back of the chair, flips herself upright and ends up in the chair seat where she started. She jumps up and skips across the room to Patty, leaping nimbly onto Patty's back.

"Hey!" Patty shouts in surprise.

Jinx whacks Patty with her hand and yells, "Giddy-up horsie. Get me outta here before the twister lands." Trainees titter in nervous appreciation.

Patty trots obligingly and then turns to the others. "C'mon, all of you get yourselves some horses. We're gonna have a rodeo."

Jinx whips her horse over towards Tex and they bump her into moving. "C'mon, gals, get a move on it."

Nadine leaps off the other sofa and onto Tex's back. "Yeehaw. Ride 'em cowboy."

Tex and Nadine join Jinx and Patty in the middle of the room. A tall, lumbering lass approaches Lauren and offers her back. Lauren climbs onto the arm of the sofa and leaps aboard. Meanwhile Dodie obligingly lifts Miriam onto her back. Soon horses and riders are lining up in the center of the room.

Lila levers herself out of the decrepit club chair she's been occupying and strides over to the milling mass of women. "Alright, I'm the starter then."

Patty surges out of the crowd under Jinx's heavy spurring.

Lila shouts, "And the judge too, Miss Babisch. You wouldn't want to be disqualified, would you?"

Lila lines up all the horses and riders and explains the rules. "The racecourse consists of a trip down the hall, through the bathroom and circle back out into the hall and back to the lounge—two times. Got it, ladies?" Lila holds up two fingers, just to be clear.

The notion of getting to best Patty and Jinx at anything has snared Lauren's interest. She shouts, "Where's the finish line?"

Everyone looks but it's Dodie who shouts, "Right where Lila's standing."

All the women shout, "Got it."

Lila crosses to the big open threshold of the lounge, lifts her arm and yells, "Ready, set.... GO."

Horses and riders leap from the start and head for the first turn like an undulating jellyfish. First Dodie and Miriam are in the lead. Then they are sucked back. Lauren and her lanky filly round the turn and take the lead. They, too, get sucked back.

Lila maintains her position in the doorway. Her raucous laughter draws other trainees from the rest of the barracks. A crowd begins to gather in the doorway.

In last place, Jinx slides off her steed and she and Patty shove one of the ratty sofas directly in the leader's path. Jinx leaps back astride and is off again, slipping as she and Patty round the second turn.

Surrounded by a pack of horses and riders, Dodie and Miriam fail to see the booby trap in time. They careen into the sofa, falling, laughing, rolling over onto the floor. Others topple over them.

This is very popular with the gang in the grandstand. Everyone cheers as Jinx and her worthy steed, Patty, sprint into the lead. The sofa is a mass of teeming trainees—arms and legs sticking up in all directions.

Laughter echoes up and down the barracks hallways. The trainees are so absorbed that no one notices Mrs. Deaton letting herself in through the front door. She hesitates a moment, her face wearing an expression of incredible sadness. In one hand is an envelope, the lifted flap clearly indicating it has been read.

After a long moment, Mrs. Deaton draws herself very upright and proceeds down the hallway towards the unruly crowd of young women cheering on the horse race in the lounge. She weaves her way through the mayhem; each trainee she passes takes one look at Mrs. D's face and freezes. It's wartime. Mrs. D's look can only mean one thing.

Mrs. Deaton finds Lila, indicates the telegram in her hand and looks around the craziness still proceeding in the lounge. Lila leans towards Mrs. D and the woman whispers a name in her ear. Lila's face immediately clouds with concern.

Jinx has used the sash from her old bathrobe to lasso another rider and haul her to the ground. Like the natural showman she is, Jinx turns to the grandstand for approval. All that greets her maneuver is Mrs. Deaton's careworn face. Jinx motions for Patty to stop and she slides to the ground.

At the same moment, many of the other riders become aware of the change in atmosphere and stop their horseplay as well.

Total silence blankets the lounge. All eyes turn to Mrs. Deaton and Lila. The crowd begins to file from the room quietly. As Dodie files past her, Lila reaches out and grasps her hand and pulls her gently aside. Dodie struggles briefly, trying to escape.

Lila gently folds Dodie in her arms. "It's your mom, Dodie," she whispers. "I'm so sorry. She's died."

The room is too quiet now. Even the wind seems to have taken a moment to rethink its course. There is nothing to hear but the sound of Dodie's sharp intake of breath.

"*Noooo.* Please, please not my mom."

. . .

It's 3:30 a.m. and the wind has picked up again while Lila and Dodie were talking. They are the only two women awake in the barracks. They huddle together beneath the implied warmth of a single table lamp in the lounge. Everyone else has gone to bed.

Lila simply sits and lets Dodie talk. It's clear from Lila's face that she's been crying. Dodie's face is unmarked by tears. Lila looks at her friend and thinks, *she must be in shock. She's still trying to assimilate the information of her mother's death.*

"My mom used to grab me by the hands, when I was little, and twirl me around and around and around. I swear that's why I love to fly, being up there right in the clouds that used to twirl over my head. It's weird. I hadn't thought about that in years, and then just the other day, when I was up in the plane with Shaver, I felt like a kid again. Like my mom was swinging me by the arms and the world was twirling overhead faster and faster and faster. And yet, I was safe, perfectly safe, with my mom."

Tears roll down Lila's cheeks. Dodie doesn't notice.

"And you know what else is weird? I've begun to think that maybe I started flying because my mom became so afraid of living. She wouldn't ever leave the house; it was too risky. Didn't want me to go to school 'cause it was too risky."

Dodie presses her lips together, steeling herself not to cry. "I became determined to risk anything—everything—just to prove that I wasn't like her. Not at all."

Dodie whispers, "But ya know what? I think she spent all those years in furious battle with her own fears to make *me* feel safe in the world...until she just couldn't do it anymore.

"And the only thing I could see, Lila, was that she quit." Dodie hangs her head in shame. "I never even noticed how hard she tried."

Now Lila is obviously sobbing. Dodie notices but continues anyway. "I'm really sorry I never got a chance to say that to her, Lila."

Dodie puts her arm around Lila's shoulders to comfort her. But she gazes off into the distance and shakes her head sadly. "I get it now. The real challenge in my life will be to learn how to be that brave."

Lila looks up at Dodie's still-dry face and whispers, "Mrs. Deaton said she can make sure you get a flight home, Dodie. I think your dad will want you there."

Dodie sighs heavily. "I know I should go, but there is this part of me that is a little afraid I won't come back."

Lila nods slowly. "If you're certain you want to come back, then promise me, Dodie—right now. Do right by your dad but come back to Avenger Field and complete your training. Okay?"

Dodie's smile is wan, but certain. "You can count on it."

Suddenly, the lights in the lounge go off, which brings an instant halt to further conversation. Lila wipes her face with the palms of her hands and looks out the window behind the sofa. "All the lights in the base have gone off too."

Lila can't see Dodie's frown, but she can hear it in her voice. "Must be the storm. I guess the wind finally toppled something important."

Both women listen intently to the sound of the wind. Suddenly, they can hear the thump of footsteps on the porch outside. Lila spots the beam of a flashlight playing across the porch.

"Someone's here. Wonder what's up?"

The front door to the barracks crashes open, and the flashlight beam bursts inside. The beam rakes across the lounge itself, and a voice booms out.

"Good, someone's up. Help me get everyone awake and outside, pronto."

"Is that you, Miss Abrahms?"

A powerful flashlight approaches and plays across Lila's and Dodie's faces. "Yes. Come on, we have to hurry. All hands at Avenger Field are ordered to the flight line because of the storm. Help me get these girls up and MOVING. NOW."

Coralee Abrahms hands Lila a flashlight and shouts, "There are more flashlights in the emergency locker by the front door. MOVE."

She starts blowing her whistle loudly and repeatedly until she hears movement. Sleepy trainees stumble from their beds, grumbling as they try to make sense of what's going on.

Lila and Dodie grab more flashlights from the safety locker and race from the lounge. They run the length of the barracks urging trainees out of their beds and into flight suits.

Coralee shouts, "No time to get dressed. Let's go NOW."

The three women manage to get all the trainees from their bunks and out of the barracks in record time.

Outside the wind is tearing away anything that is not nailed down. Tumbleweeds fly past, pieces of corrugated tin from roofs, hair rollers and sashes from the trainees' nighttime apparel go flying.

Thoroughly spooked, the cadets follow Coralee and Lila through the inky blackness. Converging on their destination are battalions of other admin personnel, mechanics and all the flight instructors. Each group is pinpointed by the bobbing flashlights at their helms.

The trainees race to the Flight Shack where instructors Shaver, Bittern, Anderson, and others await to direct them. The young women huddle in a tight group trying desperately to hear Shaver's instructions over the ROAR of the wind.

Shaver cups his hands. "Pair up, everyone." He grabs two trainees, forces them to clasp hands and pushes them towards an aircraft. "The aircraft tie-downs can't hold the craft against the wind—it's creating too much lift." He grabs two more women, pairing them up like a harried Noah. "To counter that lift, we need to get as much weight as possible onto the wings of these aircraft. I don't care how you do it—but get yourselves up onto those wings."

The trainees catch on and start peeling off in pairs, racing down the flight line.

"We cannot afford to lose these aircraft, ladies. We save them tonight or there will be no Avenger Field tomorrow morning."

Lila and Dodie grab hands and race down the runway towards one of the airplanes. As they run, they can see the wings of the aircraft around them being buffeted by the gale blowing in across the open desert. The windsock atop the Flight Shack is being torn from its moorings. Rain begins to splatter their faces. Lila bends, lacing her fingers together, and boosts Dodie onto the wing. When Dodie's in place, she hauls Lila up after her. The sound of the storm is deafening.

Just behind them, Jinx and Coralee have paired up and run towards the opposite side of the same aircraft. Coralee offers to hoist Jinx aloft. Jinx doesn't hesitate a moment. She steps in the hand Coralee holds out and vaults onto the wing. She reaches down and grasps Coralee's hand in hers and hauls her aboard. Their eyes meet just as Coralee slides up and over the wing. Their heads are mere inches apart as they spread their bodies out along the wing.

"Spread out, make yourself as flat as possible to maximize the effect of our weight, Jinx."

Jinx does as she is told, but her head comes up again when Coralee shouts her name. Their eyes lock again, just as a lull in the wind allows the aircraft to settle.

"Brace yourself. This isn't over yet."

Before she can stop herself, Jinx blurts, "I'm not sure I want it to be." Neither of them wants to be the first to break their eye contact. Their plane is hit by another gust of wind, but they're still smiling.

On the opposite side of the aircraft, Lila prods Dodie and nods for her to look up. Lila points to the entire flight line in front of them. Aircraft lie helter-skelter, covered with living deadweights draped on them like half-clothed sandbags.

Now a torrent of rain begins to fall. A huge gust of wind slams into the aircraft on which Dodie and Lila are precariously perched. If feels as if the plane cannot help but become airborne. Lila screams and holds on for dear life. "THIS IS CRAZY!"

Dodie can just make out the sound over the roar of the storm. She turns and is suddenly grinning into Lila's rain-soaked face. Dodie screams too, "AND I LOVE IT!"

Laughing now, they both continue to scream for the sheer joy of being alive.

Knots
.5 Km/h
.5 mph
.5 m/s

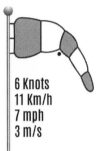

6 Knots
11 Km/h
7 mph
3 m/s

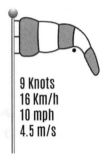

9 Knots
16 Km/h
10 mph
4.5 m/s

2 Knots
22 Km/h
4 mph
m/s

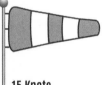

15 Knots
28 Km/h
17 mph
1.5 m/s

WIND SPEED INDICATOR
(WINDSOCK)

TEN

By the weekend Avenger Field is back to normal. Sunday morning, Lila and Lauren are making the rounds, shaking trainees awake, reminding others of the day's agenda. Many are already up and half dressed, working on makeup, ironing a civilian dress or blouse and skirt for the morning's chapel attendance.

Lila approaches the last cubicle in the barracks; its lights have been dimmed and the lower bunk against the wall has a very large, black-fringed shawl tucked under the mattress of the upper bunk to create a kind of gloomy canopy for the lower bunk. Both bunks contained hunched bundles— apparently sleeping trainees who are in no hurry to rise.

Lila leans down and shakes the shoulder of the trainee on the bottom bunk. "Jinx. You better get up. You'll miss breakfast."

Lauren shouts from the cubicle across the way. "Chapel bus leaves at 09:00 hours, soldier."

Jinx's voice is muffled from beneath the covers. "I can't go."

Lila stops immediately, concern in her voice. "Are you sick? Should I send for Coralee, or Mrs. Deaton"?

At the mention of Coralee's name, Jinx rolls over halfway and pulls the covers off her face. "Chapel is against my religion, Lila. The name's Babisch. I'm Jewish."

She rolls back over, pulls the blankets back up over her head, then whips them off, grumbling, "How can it be so hot already?"

Lauren stops mid stride as she overhears the conversation. A clear look of disbelief washes over her face. "You're posturing, Babisch. Zimmerman is going."

Jinx is silent, musing. "Of course, she is...she's Canadian. She'd rot in *hell* before she'd be impolite enough to say *no* to someone." Jinx sits up and fixes her eyes on Lauren and Lila. "She'll be exorcised as a Jew, you know, if she goes to chapel with you. But would she ever say? *No way.* Not her—but I'm telling you."

A look of fury comes over her face. "Don't you guys know *anything*? You make us eat all this *unclean* food, you won't let us study our Yiddish or Torah—and now you're insisting we desecrate our Sabbath."

Both Lila and Lauren take a step back, instantly apologetic.

"Holy cats! We didn't know, Jinx."

Lauren looks from Lila to Jinx and then her attention turns to the upper bunk. The trainee there has not moved a muscle throughout the ir conversation. "What about Bernice?"

Jinx looks up and pushes against the mattress over her

head to deflect the attention away from her. A grumpy voice from the upper bunk booms, "Sorry, gals, Orthodox Jew here."

Lauren colors slightly and turns aside. "Gads, I should have asked sooner. I'll let Mrs. Deaton know she'll be short three trainees this morning."

Lila watches Lauren leave, then reaches over and raps quite firmly with her knuckles on Bernice's exposed shoulder. A definite THUNK, THUNK, THUNK echoes in the cubicle. "Sounds more like wood up there than orthodoxy, Jinx." Lila sighs. "I guess you can take the girl out of vaudeville...."

Jinx swings her legs over the side of the bunk and reaches for a cigarette. She takes a deep drag and exhales. "Ahhhh, but taking the vaudeville out of the girl—now that would be a trick worthy of the great Houdini himself. Don't you think?"

Jinx smiles sweetly at Lila. "Should I relay the news to Miriam of our newly won freedom of religion. Or will you tell her?"

Lila turns on her heel, shaking her head. "I'll tell her. You and Bernice can grab some more shut-eye."

•   •   •

Jinx is lying on one of the ratty sofas in the lounge, her head in Bernice's lap. She's puffing on a cigarette, one leg dangling across the other.

Miriam is seated across from her, knitting. She glares at Jinx. "Okay, Miss Smarty-pants. Now that we've been given our very own Yiddish study hour, speak up. Let's hear some good old-fashioned Jew talk from you, Jinx. Maybe you could recite the *Amidah* for us, eh?"

Jinx grimaces through the cigarette smoke that clouds the air between them. "*Oy vey*. Potato *knish*. Happy Hanukkah." She flaps the dummy's hand in Miriam's direction and Bernice chortles, "I don't see what you're so pissed off about, missy."

Needles clacking furiously, Miriam mutters, "You know I don't like to lie, Jinx."

Jinx interrupts. "Neither do I."

Clack, clack, clack. Miriam looks over at her. "Hah!"

Jinx bolts upright and turns to face Miriam. "I don't, honestly. But at least I know how to—when it's necessary." Jinx leans forward earnestly. "In fact, if you're going to be in this girls' Army, Miriam, I think it's time you learned how to lie with impunity."

Bernice butts in, "Who's Impunity? Is she that new girl?"

Miriam can't help herself; she laughs out loud and throws her knitting needles and wool at Jinx and Bernice on the sofa. She sighs and sits back in her chair. "I suppose I had better teach you some Yiddish just so I don't have to lie when they get back."

"And I'll teach you the fine art of prevarication." Jinx smiles grandly.

Bernice interjects. "And I'll put up $10 that says Miriam will put Jinx's training into practice before Jinx ever uses hers!"

Miriam studies Jinx and Bernice a long moment and then reaches out her hand for Jinx to shake on the bet. "We probably should *help* Bernice back to her bunk before the others get back, don't you think?"

Jinx leaps from the sofa and grabs the dummy around the waist. Bernice immediately shrieks. "Unhand me, you cur, before I call the military police!"

"What's going on here?"

Jinx immediately drops Bernice in surprise and Miriam puts a hand over her mouth in shock. The jig is clearly up as they both turn and find Coralee Abrahms standing in the doorway of the lounge with a look of bewilderment on her face.

A lengthy silence ensues in which Jinx stares down at Bernice but fails to pick her up again.

"Is that a new trainee? Is she okay?" Coralee's voice is filled with hesitation.

Jinx looks up and plasters a smile on her face, formulating a response, but Miriam beats her to it.

"Bernice is just a little faint. Jinx and I were just helping her back to her bunk."

Bernice laughs out loud...and so does Jinx. "YOU owe me ten bucks, Miriam."

"What is going on here? Mrs. Deaton asked me to come by and check on you two. She didn't mention a new recruit."

Jinx looks slightly abashed. "Come and sit down, Miss Abrahms. As you can see, Miriam and I are fine. And it's time you officially met Bernice, I think."

Coralee hesitates but decides to hear the explanation. "This better be good, Babisch."

Miriam laughs. "Oh it is, Miss Abrahms. It is!"

. . .

An hour later Jinx and Coralee Abrahms are carrying a long duffle bag between them, slugging through the heat and the stand of cottonwood trees to Coralee's house. As they break through the low limbs of the trees and the substantial stands of tall grass the sight of the little clapboard house stops Jinx in her tracks. "No one would ever guess this little place was here without someone to guide them."

Coralee smiles and shrugs. "I suspect it was meant to be that way." She shifts the duffle bag handle to her other hand. "I'm told the original owner of this ranch wanted to stay on, but his wife wanted some privacy from the goings-on at the base." Coralee takes a step towards the house, and Jinx follows, holding the other end of the long duffle.

"On the original ranch, they planted the cottonwoods intentionally close together so they would provide shade for the house, but now it's become excellent camouflage to hide the existence of the house to any casual passersby at the airstrip."

Coralee proceeds onto the front porch and sets down one end of the duffle bag. "I've got some iced tea in the icebox—you want a glass?"

Jinx smiles. "That would be great. While you get that, I'll pull poor Bernice out of her carry bag."

Coralee disappears into the house and returns moments later with a pitcher of iced tea and two glasses. She sets them on the small table between the two rocking chairs.

Jinx props Bernice up and fixes the wig on her head so

it sits straight. She pats her cheek and then plops down into the nearby rocker. She takes a glass of tea and lightly clicks it against Coralee's glass. "A toast to rocking chairs on porches."

For the first time, Coralee's smile seems completely genuine. It's so lovely that Jinx feels as if she has a momentary rift in her heart.

Coralee counters, "To iced tea and the man who invented the icebox."

Jinx grins back at her. "Or the woman."

"The woman what?"

"Or the woman who invented the icebox."

"Oh, did a woman invent the icebox?"

"I dunno. Did a man?"

Coralee shakes her head in confusion. "I don't know. I was asking if you *knew* for sure that a woman invented the icebox."

"No. But then I don't know for sure that a man did either."

Coralee peers at Jinx over the rim of her glass. "You are one strange bird, Miss Babisch."

"So I've been told. I just don't like to assume men do everything strange and wonderful in life. I like to think there are some strange and wonderful women out there too." Coralee's laugh is so unexpected and merry that Jinx can't help but smile in response.

"Okay. I didn't want to ask while we were scheming to find our Bernice a new home, but now that she's here, can you show me how you do what you do?"

Jinx quirks one eyebrow across her glass at Coralee. "So you want a free show in payment for helping me?"

Coralee is aghast at the phrasing. "No. No, that's not it at all," she sputters.

Jinx laughs. "I was teasing you, Coralee. Didn't you have brothers at home growing up?"

Coralee stops a moment, blushing. "Yes, you may call me Coralee in private, JINX." She emphasizes the use of Jinx's first name. "And no, I didn't have brothers. Do you really have four?"

"Oh God," Jinx sighs dramatically. "Yes. But never on stage. They literally grew up in vaudeville and had enough of it. The family act was kind of winding down by the time I came along, but I still wanted to be on stage. So it was always just me and my wooden siblings in the spotlights."

Jinx bends over and lifts Bernice onto her lap. She uses one hand to fuss a bit with the back of the dummy's clothing. Suddenly Bernice's eyelashes are flapping, she's raising and lowering her eyebrows and turning her head from side-to-side.

"Okay, that is just a bit weird," Coralee stammers.

"Yeah, it is at first. But remember, even in the front row you'd be about forty feet away from Bernice. We have to make her movements and expressions big so the audience can see them."

"Should I move farther away then?"

"No, stay here. The rockers are nice. When the curtain goes up, house lights go down and Bernice and I are on stage in a spotlight of our own. We usually start with a conversation, or we sing."

"Bernice sings?"

"Sure." Jinx fusses a bit getting Bernice sitting just right on one knee. "Good evening, m'lady. Tonight, my friend Bernice and I will serenade you with an old show tune we love." Jinx launches into a jaunty popular song in a high, clear voice.

"*If you knew Susie, like I know Susie.*"

Bernice picks up the next line, a definite alto. "*OH! Oh, oh what a gal.*"

Jinx picks it up again. "*There's none so classy as this fair lassie.*"

"*Oh, oh, oh what a gal.*"

Coralee interjects, "How can you do that? How can you make her sing and move like that?"

Jinx laughs, delighted. She moves her rocker closer to Coralee, so they're sitting face-to-face. She reaches out and takes Coralee's hand in her own. "May I?" A slight scowl of indecision crosses Coralee's face.

"I'm not going to hurt you," Jinx says. She places Coralee's hand on her throat, meets Coralee's gaze, and says, "This is me talking. Feel the movement?" Coralee nods.

"Bernice, say something."

Coralee half smiles, her hand still on Jinx's throat, and watches her mouth. Jinx's lips never move except to smile.

In a much lower voice, Bernice whispers, "You have truly beautiful eyes, Coralee Abrahms." And then Jinx leans over and kisses Coralee's lips so softly, neither breathes while their lips touch.

ELEVEN

In Washington, D.C. a late spring has sprung and the weather outside is glorious. Cherry trees blossom and lively clouds scud across a blue sky. But in the large, stuffy Pentagon conference room there's no sign of spring at all.

Jackie is seated on one side of a huge oval table. She sits impatiently tapping a finely sharpened pencil on the top of the table. As always, she's dressed in a smashing two-piece women's business suit, this one in periwinkle blue with a filmy blue scarf tied around her neck.

Across from Jackie, and shooting daggers at her every chance she gets, is Olveta Culp Hobby. Olveta is head of the Women's Army Corps. She dearly wants to incorporate Jackie's WASPs into her command. Olveta looks rumpled and uncomfortable in her poorly tailored Army-issue uniform. They are the only women at the table, among nearly a dozen men of various ranks.

At the head of the table, and clearly chairing the meeting, is General Henry "HAP" Arnold. He consults a piece of paper in front of him, smiles briefly in Jackie's direction, and then continues.

"The final item on our agenda is the question of a uniform for Jackie's WASP personnel. As you all know, she now has nearly 400 women performing various flight functions across the U.S. and another 300 in various stages of training at Sweetwater."

General Arnold consults his notes again and looks around the table. "With more than 750 recruits expected to graduate this year alone, and 1000 more slated for fiscal 1944, we are fast running out of time to finalize this issue."

Olveta Culp Hobby raises her hand for permission to speak.

"The chair recognizes Mrs. Hobby."

Olveta stands and takes a moment to direct a smile to every man seated around the table. "I would just like to reiterate that the Women's Army Corps has uniforms, already sized to women's proportions, which would solve the problem without further debate. And once we agree to militarize the WASPs...." She sits down and shrugs as if the rest is self-evident. If WASPs wear the Army Corps green uniforms, they will by default be under her domain.

Jackie meets General Arnold's gaze; he nods permission to speak. She, too, stands and smiles at all the men around the table. She winks at one of the generals, who quickly ducks his head, pretending to read notes. A tiny smile betrays his pleasure at being singled out.

"Make no mistake, gentlemen, I have nothing against the uniform of the U.S. Army. It has a proud tradition that mirrors that of its service to our country. But we're building a modern new addition to the American military here. With a dedicated Air Corps, we will need uniforms that stand out, uniforms that mark our men and women as something other than either the Army or the Navy. We need uniforms that mark them as Air Corps."

Jackie graciously extends a hand across the table to Mrs. Hobby.

"Mrs. Hobby, if you could indulge me. Would you stand and step away from the table and give all the gentlemen here a chance to admire the Women's Army Corps uniform?"

Blushing profusely, the matronly but attractive Mrs. Hobby rises coquettishly and moves away from the table.

"That's it. Just stroll up and down there for a moment."

Looking like the cat who has eaten the canary, Jackie draws the generals' attention back to herself. "Now, gentlemen, if you please. I've taken the liberty of throwing together an idea of what I have in mind." Jackie leans over and presses a buzzer in the middle of the conference table. "A little something to illustrate what I think could be a terrific option."

At the far end of the room, a door swings open and all eyes turn to witness a young, willowy, very attractive woman stride into the room. She is wearing a smartly tailored BLUE uniform, patent leather pumps and a snappy beret. She strides closer to the table, turns 360 degrees, and then positions herself in direct contrast to the doughty Mrs. Hobby.

Jackie smiles and concludes. "Air Corps Pilots should wear blue, don't you think? Blue as the sky in which we'll chart our destiny and that of the country that we love."

The model takes one more turn around the table. None of the men can take their eyes off her. Grinning like a fox, Jackie adds one final comment. "This uniform is smart, crisp and dare I say, memorable. Wouldn't you agree?"

Jackie notices the nodding of heads. "We can act on this right now and give our women cadets a uniform to be proud of, gentlemen." Jackie smiles at General Hap Arnold. "Could we put it to a vote, General Arnold?"

Olveta Culp Hobby does not look pleased.

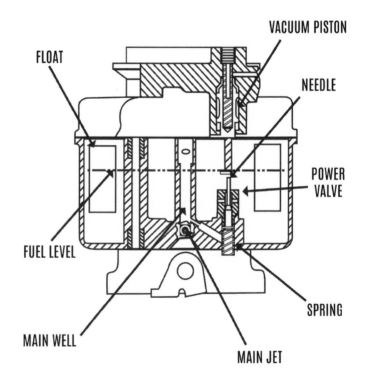

SIMPLE CARBURETOR

. . .

At the machine shop, the trainees are all lined up at long work benches, clad in their coveralls, with bandanas around their hair. In the sweltering Texas heat, they look like hell.

Spread before them on the table are the innumerable parts of several aircraft engines. Each woman is picking through the pieces, trying to create an entire component according to the diagram she's been handed. No one is having any great success at it. Well, no one except Patty Yin Lee.

Patty is off at one end of a table by herself, tongue sticking out of the corner of her mouth in concentration. Admittedly, she is covered in guck: grease, dust and perspiration, but her carburetor is far closer to completion than anyone else's in the shop.

Instructor Shaver stops to look over her shoulder. "That's looking good, Lee."

Patty ignores him.

"Problems with the rebuild?"

Patty continues to work doggedly. Belatedly she notices that Shaver has said something to her, and she looks up. "There's no problem. The final piece is just not here." She shrugs as if it's the clearest thing in the world.

Shaver looks down at the debris on the workbench, which stretches nearly the entire length of the room. "Not here?"

Patty looks at him sideways as she continues to fiddle. "Oh, you've put a ton of junk on the table alright." Patty reaches over to her neighbor Miriam's pile of stuff and snitches an item. "And I could probably steal Miriam's float valve and she'd be none the wiser."

Patty's and Miriam's eyes meet. Miriam flashes Patty a sardonic grin. "But it seems kind of unfair. Especially, since I know what's missing."

Patty lays her part on the table. "It's as done as I can make it, Mr. Shaver."

Shaver picks up the part and inspects it—then winks at Patty. "Guess you've earned your morning cigarette break, Lee. And a PASS on the course work too."

· · ·

Five minutes later all the cadets are gathered outside, lolling in what shade they can glean from the side of the building. Some are smoking, some snacking; everyone's kibitzing. Miriam, Patty, Jinx and Lauren are lounging together, sharing a smoke and yakking as they sop sweat off their foreheads.

Miriam uses a foot to poke at Jinx, who's sitting next to her. "So, I got something I wanna ask all you gals. But I'm afraid you're gonna laugh at me."

Jinx immediately sits up and takes notice. "Oh yeah. What is it? We won't laugh, will we girls?"

Miriam hesitates. "You gotta promise. All of you."

Lauren and Patty immediately chime in. "We promise."

All eyes turn to Jinx, who vacillates. "What if I promise I won't laugh...*right now*. But reserve the right to laugh a lot later?"

All the girls' eyes bore into Jinx. Patty tosses cookie crumbs at her. "Not good enough, JB."

"Oh, alright. I won't laugh, *ever*. Period."

The girls sigh as one, then lean eagerly towards Miriam.

"Okay, so my question is about the, you know—the exam the other day."

"Flight trajectories?" Patty queries, a frown on her face.

A light goes on in Jinx's eyes. She reaches over and whacks Patty on the arm. She splays open her thighs wide and adds, "The *other* exam, stupid. Has the heat gone to your head, Patty? She means the pelvic exam."

Miriam blushes furiously but nods her head in confirmation. All eyes are now rivetted on her. "Well, anyway, what I wanted to know is because of the exam…are we all still virgins?"

Utter silence ensues. It stretches on and on. Finally, Jinx takes a drag on her cigarette and exhales. "Well, *technically* speaking? No." She inhales some smoke. Now all the cadets' eyes swivel to Jinx.

Jinx shrugs at their obvious horror. "Well, I mean in the strictest sense of the definition of *virgin*…we're not." She blows out more cigarette smoke. "Intact hymen and all that." She pauses, holding her cigarette aloft. "On the other hand, in the romantic fall-in-love-and-get-married sense of intact hymen, we are all still virgins."

Relief is clearly visible on the girls' faces.

Miriam grimaces slightly. "I, uh, have a second question, then."

They all turn slowly, anticipating Miriam's next query with a kind of morbid curiosity.

"Does simply being married always mean…well, that you're *not* a virgin?"

All eyes once again turn to Jinx.

"Well, Mimi, generally speaking that is why people get married. So, they don't *have to be* virgins anymore." All the girls actively shush Jinx. This conversation is maybe veering a little off track.

"Well, it's true," Jinx insists. "You get married mostly 'cause that's the only way your mom and dad will be okay with you *doing it...you know.*" Jinx stubs out her cigarette and skewers Miriam with a meaningful look. "Is there something you'd like to share with us, Miriam?

A tear starts to slide down Miriam's cheek and she nods her head slowly. "I think maybe I'm not a virgin then, *technically.*"

This news prompts everyone's mouth to drop open in shock. A chorus of questions follows: "What? Who? Where?"

Jinx cocks an eyebrow at Miriam and grunts, "Spill it, girl. What happened?"

Another tear trickles down Miriam's cheek. "You know my parents immigrated to Canada just before Poland fell to the Germans. I knew we were leaving Warsaw and I was so torn about going. So I married my friend Henryk in secret, hoping it was a thread that would bring us back together somehow."

Miriam wipes her face with her hand. "At first, after I left, we wrote pretty often. Henryk was going to learn to fly and then escape from Poland to find me." She sniffs loudly. "It's why I took up flying lessons at Dorval. I thought we could fly together someday."

When Miriam doesn't continue, Jinx steps in. "But then,

one day the letters stopped coming. And then the rumors began about what the Germans were doing to the Jews in Poland, and you began to wonder...." Jinx can't go on because Miriam has started to cry in earnest now.

"Today was his birthday. My Henryk, he would be twenty four today."

Everyone is patting Miriam's back in sympathy. Jinx lets out a deep breath.

"Wow. You Canadians. You're quiet, but *deep.*"

• • •

After class, Miriam is leaning over the mechanics' benches, reading a mimeographed piece of paper.

Jinx approaches her cautiously. "Hey. You okay?

Miriam looks up and gives her a lopsided smile. "Yeah. Thanks." She looks back down at the paper. "Ya know, it says here Jackie's finally got a uniform approved." Jinx looks over her shoulder at the sketch that accompanies the article. "What is this, Mimi?"

Miriam looks up. "Oh, it's *The Avenger*, a kind of news-paper for the WASPs. Miss Abrahms started it and they're looking for cadet reporters. You wanna volunteer with me?"

Jinx flicks the page with her fingernail and scoffs. "Nice uniform; can't wait to see it." She pats Miriam patronizingly on the cheek. "Take my advice, Mimi, never volunteer."

• • •

Immediately after lunch, Instructor Shaver has his squad huddled in front of the Stearman biplane. With his clipboard in hand, he is giving them a pep talk prior to the flight. He has everyone's undivided attention. Similar groups are huddled in front of every other biplane aircraft down the line.

Shaver looks up from his clipboard. "Okay. We've got an Army flight inspector here today, which means some of you have a chance to solo." He looks at his notes.

"Lila. You up first, please. I'm sure you're ready. Miriam, you want to try too?"

Miriam takes a deep breath and nods.

"Great, you're second then." He continues to study his clipboard, humming to himself. "Patty, you should be a shoe-in."

Lauren interjects, "I'd like a chance to try, Mr. Shaver."

Everyone turns their full attention on Lauren. Shaver looks at her as if she's daft; then his expression softens a bit and he nods in agreement. "Why not? You get three tries. This time can help you relax if you need to try again. You'll know what to expect."

Lauren's eyes meet Lila's as if to say, *See?*'

If their instructor picks up on the look, he ignores it. "Right, then. Let's not forget, this is not a do-or-die situation. Each trainee has up to three chances to solo on a craft before she is washed out of the program. So stay calm, stay focused, gals."

Out of the corner of his eye, Shaver can see the uniformed Army officer approaching his group. "Alright now, let's look smart, girls."

Shaver turns to lead all except Lila back towards the Flight Shack. "Oh, and good luck to everyone!"

Lila remains at the front of the aircraft, awaiting the officer. When he's within range, she extends her hand and introduces herself. "Lila Stewart, sir. Pleased to meet you."

The officer looks at her hand as if it is contagious and keeps on walking towards the aircraft. "Let's ignore the niceties, shall we? Get me back on the ground alive and I may consider shaking it."

They climb into the cockpit, setting themselves up for the flight. The officer is seated in the rear seat, a grim expression on his face. Lila is at the controls in the forward cockpit. She turns the ignition and sets the engine rumbling. The whole plane shakes until the engine warms up.

A mechanic runs out and removes the chocks beneath the wheels and then salutes the cockpit smartly. A signalman steps into view where Lila can see him, stands flags in hand, waiting for the thumbs up.

Lila is calling out her preflight check on the engine and instruments. She picks up the talking tube on the old biplane and announces to the Army officer that she's ready to taxi. She then signals the man on the ground that she's ready. He motions her forward and she eases the aircraft from the flight line and points it towards the runway. As she taxis past the signalman, she drops him a crisp salute.

The remainder of Lila's training group is clustered around the door of the Flight Shack watching her guide the aircraft down the runway towards takeoff. Farther down the flight line other flight inspectors are climbing into other aircraft with other trainees. A second airplane roars to life, then inches itself onto the runway, 500 feet behind Lila. A third aircraft promptly follows behind, and then a fourth.

In the lead biplane, Lila is in complete command of her aircraft. It rises off the runway like silk, gains altitude without effort and banks slowly west. The inspector ticks off notes on his clipboard. Ten minutes from the training center, he taps Lila on the shoulder and motions for her to execute a series of rolls.

The plane peels off left, falls away towards the earth below, then straightens and peels off right, following the same procedure. As the craft rights itself, the officer is busy making more notes. His face gives nothing away.

He taps Lila again, motioning for a series of loops. The aircraft rises, gaining altitude and then loops forward like an airborne roller coaster across the sky. Lila's face is flushed with excitement by the end of the maneuver, the inspector remains impassive.

Finally, he taps Lila and indicates a dive. She banks the plane in a slow spiral, ascending, ascending through the thin line of clouds far over the Texas plains below. Then abruptly, the inspector taps her shoulder once again and the nose of the airplane drops suddenly. The inspector's hand remains aloft inches from Lila's shoulder, ready to signal for her to pull up.

The aircraft races towards the ground, gathering gravity-induced speed as it falls. The altimeter races backwards. Lila's eyes flick towards the hand near her shoulder, and then back to her controls. Finally, she feels she's reached the point of no return. She pulls up on the controls and wrestles the aircraft back into level flight. The inspector relaxes back into his seat in the rear cockpit and lets Lila pilot the aircraft back towards the runway and home.

She lines the plane up for landing, then guides it into the flight path. The plane drops onto the tarmac as smooth as milk pouring out of a pitcher. As soon as the wheels touch the pavement, Lila throttles back the engine and lets the aircraft coast to the line. Once the mechanic chocks the wheels, she leaves the engine running and extracts herself from the cockpit.

Lila glances briefly back at the officer in the rear seat. He makes a final note on his clipboard and tears off the sheet and hands it to Lila. He stretches out his other hand to shake. "Obvious *Pass*, Miss Stewart. It's clear you're neither self-destructive nor stupid." Lila shakes his hand, her lips pursed in thought.

"Send the next trainee out please."

A huge grin washes over Lila's face as she jumps off the wing. She shoves the evaluation sheet inside the breast pocket of her flight suit and sprints the distance to the group in front of the Flight Shack. Pulling the sheet from her suit, she waves it over her head in triumph as she runs.

Miriam gives Lila a quick hug and then races over to the waiting aircraft, where the inspecting officer is waving impatiently. Lila is swamped by the other trainees before she can impart any words of advice to the anxious Miriam.

Twenty-five minutes later, Miriam climbs from the cockpit. Her face is a study in shock. The officer rips off a page from his clipboard and hands it to Miriam. Her expression changes only marginally as she grips the paper and climbs down from the aircraft. She wanders towards the other trainees outside the Flight Shack like a zombie.

Lauren races past her towards the waiting aircraft and the inspector. "Well, did you pass?" Lauren's gone before Miriam has time to reply. She stops in her tracks and finally looks down at the sheet of paper in her hand. Handwritten across the top in giant letters is the word *PASS*.

Miriam's expression of shock changes instantly. A huge smile spreads across her face and she laughs out loud in surprised delight. She raises the sheet of paper over her head in triumph and dances around in circles. "I passed. I passed."

Lila races out to pull Miriam away from the flight line. Miriam grabs Lila in a bear hug and makes her dance with her back to the Flight Shack.

PRE-FLIGHT CHECK

TWELVE

The next day, Mr. Shaver is standing at the front of the classroom as the cadets enter, a big grin on his face. He claps his hands, rubbing them together as if in anticipation. As the cadets find their usual seats, he says, "Don't get too comfortable." His grin widens. "We're going to play a little game now that we have a bit of mechanics under our belts."

The cadets aren't quite sure what to make of his statement, so no one responds.

"Ahh, cat's got your tongue, does it?" He picks up a large jar stuffed with folded slips of paper and clutches it to his chest. With one hand in he swirls the paper bits around so they're thoroughly mixed up.

"Volunteer please."

Lauren's hand instantly shoots into the air. She has a big grin on her face too.

Mr. Shaver looks askance at her. "You either know where this is going or you're a very trusting soul, Lauren Powell."

She laughs. "Trusting. I haven't got a clue what you're up

to, but your expression says it will be fun, so I want to play."

Shaver nods his head approvingly. "Okay. This game is called *Fix it, to fly it.* The first volunteer gets to choose her partner rather than draw from my jar." Shaver notes the glum expressions that sweep over the cadets' faces. "See. Volunteering can pay off."

Shaver points directly at Lauren and intones in a very dramatic voice: "Lauren Powell, you and your teammate are out for a flight and are forced to land on a desert island due to mechanical difficulties. You have 30 seconds to name your partner."

Lauren doesn't even bat an eyelash. "Patty Yin Lee."

A resounding silence descends on the room. Except for Patty, who bolts upright and sputters, "Whaaa- at?"

Shaver takes over again. "You heard the woman, Patty. You two are now joined at the hip for this exercise." Patty continues to stand and sputter. "But she doesn't even like me. Why pick me?"

Shaver pins Lauren with a look and sighs deeply. "Could you please put Miss Lee at ease so that we can get on with the thrilling particulars of our quest?"

Lauren rises and turns to face Patty. "Pat-teee, I don't dislike you! But you are irritating as heck sometimes." Lauren looks at the other cadets for confirmation and various heads nod. "But I'm not stupid. If I'm going to be stranded on a desert island because my plane has crapped out on me, I want you in the other cockpit. No contest." Lauren sits back down.

Shaver smiles and waggles his head. "Proof that Miss

Powell is not just a pretty face." Then he raises the jar over his head. "Okay, someone get up here and draw a name." He holds the jar out for the first contestant.

"Patty and Lauren, pair up over by the door for the next phase of the contest."

. . .

Out on the flight line the cadet duos are lined up next to a Stearman biplane. Shaver stands between the rows of airplanes so all the gals can hear him. He is still grinning as he consults his clipboard.

"Alright now, flip a coin to decide who's going to pilot and who's going to mechanic. Make sure you call out the name so I can jot it down."

Up and down the line of aircraft coins rise in the air and are caught. Lauren looks at the coin in her hand and smiles at Patty. "You're the pilot."

Patty grimaces. "C'mon, Lauren. Work with me here." Lauren's eyes hold Patty's for a long moment. "*You* work with *me*, Patty. I can do this." She immediately calls out to Shaver. "Lee's our pilot."

A chorus of *ooohs* echo up and down the flight line. This is shortly followed by a staccato burst of names that Shaver records on his clipboard. He lifts a whistle so everyone can see.

"On my mark, everyone will start by having the pilot climb into the craft and attempt to start the engine. Keep plenty of distance, gals, as you troubleshoot the problem. I don't want anyone to go to the infirmary today. Mostly because it means you flunk this test. If no one has completed the task by the time I blow the whistle again, you all walk to the plane to the south of you and we start over. The winner, obviously, is the team that gets the airplane into the air."

Shaver blows the whistle and mayhem erupts along the flight line. All the designated pilots scramble into the cockpits. Their mechanics perch on the wing close to the cockpit. All except Lauren. She has the presence of mind to begin to walk around the aircraft to perform the standard pre-flight mechanical check.

Shaver blows his whistle loudly and the chaos halts immediately. "Very well done, Miss Powell and Miss Lee." Shaver skewers the other cadets with a venomous look. "Ladies, I cannot stress strongly enough that nothing should preclude your pre-flight check." All the other cadets hang their heads in shame.

Shaver nods to Patty and Lauren. "You now have the option to continue with the competition. Or you can rest on your laurels if you like for the remainder of the day and watch the merriment that ensues from the sidelines."

Patty and Lauren lock eyes. Patty shouts, "We'll continue, Mr. Shaver."

He claps his hands and then blows his whistle. "Once again, people."

Lauren is now on the wing, watching Patty perform her pre-flight instrument check. Lauren nods. "All good? Let's see if she'll start."

Patty turns the fuel lever on, primes the pump three quick times and sets the fuel mixture to rich. Then she turns off the fuel pump, waiting to see if the engine will catch. She flips the starter toggle on her right and holds her breath.

With a bluster and a burst of exhaust near the propeller, the Stearman's huge, exposed engine bursts into life. Both girls watch the propeller intently.

Then the engine dies. The silence in the cockpit is deafening. Patty turns to look at Lauren. "Ideas?"

"Let it sit a moment to drain out any excess fuel from the carburetor. Pull back on the mixture this time. Not so rich."

Patty nods. "My thoughts exactly."

Both women zero their focus to the sound of their engine amidst the roaring and sputtering of the flight line around them.

. . .

The sun is angling towards the horizon, and the flight line is a jumble with Stearman aircraft sitting all helter-skelter along it. The mess is mute testimony to the cadets' utter failure to achieve any *sustained* momentum from their craft.

Shaver blows his whistle a long, loud blast and all the cadets stop mid-fidget. They drop what they're doing and slowly coalesce around their instructor.

"Harder than you thought, isn't it?" At least Shaver has the grace to appear sympathetic. Behind him a troop of mechanics is approaching with T-bar tows in hand. They fan out and tackle the motley assortment of aircraft, putting them back to rights for the night.

Shaver turns and calls out to them. "Thank you, guys. Don't forget to pass along to me what you jimmied on each of them so the gals can go over it with me in class tomorrow."

Shaver nods at his trainees. "Go on. You've all earned a beer with your dinner tonight at the mess hall."

Patty perks up. "There's beer?"

"Ah...no," Shaver grins. "But you gals sure worked hard enough for one." He notices their expression and adds, "There's an important life lesson here. Always be good to your mechanics. DIS-missed."

Neither Lauren nor Lila makes the cadets form up into a squad just yet. It's important sometimes to be able to drift to the next moment with your tail between your legs.

• • •

Patty Yin Lee is standing in front of her locker, toweling off after her shower. She's barefoot and moving around the cubicle, fussing—plumping her hair, girl kinds of things. Sweat immediately begins tricking down her temple. It is still so friggin hot—any shower is only a temporary respite.

Jinx is in the lower bunk, having a nap in her skivvies, completely unaware of Patty. Patty pads over to her lower bunk and her bare foot lands in something sticky and icky. PY stops dead in her tracks. She lifts a foot gingerly and looks down to the sole of her foot. She pulls off a squishy glob of chewing gum.

"Jinx Babisch, I swear if this happens even one more time...." Patty goes ballistic, ripping off her towel and throwing it at Jinx.

Jinx awakens and sits up rather nonchalantly. Yawning,

she tosses the towel on the floor at her bedside. "Patty, when are you going to learn to pick up your stuff?"

Patty grabs her grimy flight suit and pulls it on as fast as she can. She barely buttons it closed before she spins around and grabs Jinx's flimsy mattress and hauls both it and the cadet from the bed. "That's it. You are outta here."

Jinx watches from the floor, grinning. She sits calmly, eyes gleaming, draped in linens, and watching the whirling dervish. Other trainees notice the commotion and slowly make their way down the hallway to see what's amiss.

Patty reaches into the overhead bunk, grabs the mattress and bedclothes and hauls them down onto the floor next to Jinx. She then throws herself onto Jinx's bunk and uses her legs to lift the top bunk off its moorings. It tilts crazily but Patty reaches up and eases the frame to the floor. With the bunk beds now separated, Patty grabs the post of Jinx's bed and hauls it towards the back door of the barracks, straight outside into the yard. The door slams behind her.

Now there's a whole roomful of trainees watching the melodrama unfold. Jinx is still seated on her own mattress, covered in bed clothes. A playful smirk is anchored at the corners of her mouth.

Moments later, Patty storms back into the room, wipes a stream of sweat from her brow, and bends down. She picks up Jinx and her bed clothes and heaves them over her shoulder. Without missing a beat, Jinx blurts, "Wow. You are freakishly strong, Patty."

Patty hauls her trophy out into the yard and dumps Jinx unceremoniously onto her waiting bunk. "You can come back inside when you learn used gum belongs in a wastebasket!"

The whole platoon is gathered, tittering, on the covered porch outside the back door of the barracks. Lila and Lauren push their way to the front of the group and confront the two feuding trainees. Lila raises her arms in exasperation. "Alright, what IS going on here?"

There is a long moment of absolute silence. All eyes are on Jinx, who sits in solitary splendor in the middle of the yard. The first stars are just appearing over her shoulder. She shrugs. "Patty just had a stupendous idea." Jinx fixes Patty with a mischievous look. "And you know her—she had to act on it. We thought we'd move our beds outside for the night."

Jinx straightens the covers a bit and snuggles in. "It will be *sooooo* much cooler out here, don't ya think?"

Murmurs of assent whisper among the trainees gathered on the porch. They all

turn to see what Lila's response will be. After a long moment, she shrugs. "I can't see there'd be any harm in it."

Lauren grabs Lila's arm as she turns to go back inside. She shouts, "Lila, you can't let them do this. It's…it's unladylike, it's undignified, it's UN-MILITARY."

Patty and the others have been listening to this exchange in complete silence. There's a long pause after Lauren finishes and then Patty races back up the stairs into the barracks and turns around to shout, "What're we waiting for, gals?" All the other trainees swarm past Lauren, back into the barracks to get their mattresses and bedding.

Excited voices echo from inside the sweltering barracks.

"Patty, how did you get the bunks apart? Patty, will you help me?"

"Hey, has anyone got mosquito repellant?"

Lauren is abandoned on the porch by herself as the barracks door slams on the final trainee rushing to move her things outside.

. . .

All the trainees' bunks except Lauren's are now scattered in groups around the yard. Some women are already fast asleep. Some are just lying awake, having a last smoke and looking at the stars. A couple are taking photos with their Brownie cameras. Sporadic camera flashes pop in the darkness.

Jinx is smoking, lying on her back. Patty's bunk is on one side, Miriam's on the other. Miriam snaps a photo of Jinx. Lila is caught off to one side of the photo, in the background, with her arms crossed beneath her head.

Jinx skewers Miriam with a look. "Mimi, do that again and you die." She exhales smoke loudly. Her tone changes abruptly, turning nostalgic. "Me and my brothers used to do this all the time in NYC. 'Cept there it was rooftops. In the summer, New York gets so hot, the road asphalt goes all goopy." She takes another drag on her cigarette. "Sometimes we'd scratch our names in the melted tarmac. I'd always do mine in gigantic letters."

Patty rolls over and stares at Jinx. "Now there's a surprise, JB."

Jinx eyes Patty. "If you blend in old bubblegum, it mixes

with the road tar and lasts forever…but you have to save your old chewing gum." Jinx smiles. "That's how I became Jinx. Writing *Joanne* Babisch required too much bubblegum."

Lila stirs at that comment. "Joanne?" Jinx sighs. "Yeah. That's my given name. Someday I'm going to go legit…. you know, on *Broad*way. Or maybe in the movies."

Suddenly self-conscious, Jinx changes the subject. "How 'bout you, Lila? You grew up in New York too, right?"

"Umm, not really in the city. On Long Island. My brother and I had a treehouse. We kind of threw it together ourselves as a secret hideout."

Miriam chimes in softly. "From your parents?"

Lila laughs softly. "Gads, no. We hardly saw *them*. It was our nanny. My brother Robert and I hated her. I think my father thought that meant she was doing a good job." Lila laughs louder and shakes her head in disbelief. "It sounds absurd to even say it, but I kind of miss that nanny."

Jinx takes a final drag on her cigarette and tosses it aside. "No kidding, I miss the sounds of the city. What about you, PY?"

"I miss the smell of the ocean—and cedar trees in the rain."

Miriam smiles wanly. "Montreal bagels, hot out of the oven. With sixty tons of butter and my mother's homemade jam."

Jinx sighs. "Variety. The newspaper. Reading show reviews."

Lila laughs out loud. "My damned brother Robert."

"All four of my brothers," Jinx chuckles. "I never thought I'd say that!"

They all fall quiet for a long moment. The stars wink overhead, a soft breeze blows off the desert, bringing the smell of sage and aircraft fuel. Miriam snuggles down into her sheets and whispers, "Goodnight, everyone. *Joanne*, this was an inspired idea."

Jinx smirks boldly at Patty, who is three feet away in her own bunk. "Hey, thank Patty. She's the wild child genius among us."

· · ·

The barracks is empty, the moon shines in through a side window, left open to encourage any little breeze to come inside and introduce itself. But that's not happening. Alone in one of the middle cubicles is one solitary bed with a lone occupant.

Lauren is tossing and turning, getting no sleep whatsoever. Her hair is plastered to her temples from sweat. Her baby doll pajamas stick to her like second skin—damp second skin—all because of her stubborn refusal to follow the others outside.

Finally, she can't stand it any longer. She heaves herself out of the bunk, grabs a corner of the mattress and hauls it from the bedframe. She pulls the mattress and all the bedclothes behind her like a cotton sack. At the screen door to the back porch, Lauren stops and looks out. Everyone is already sound asleep in the yard. She eases open the screen door and gently pulls her mattress out onto the porch. She's desperate not to make a sound. As she eases the door closed behind her, the catch audibly clicks into place. Lauren stops, frozen in her tracks. When no one stirs, she hauls her mattress into a nearby corner hidden from sight of the others.

Lauren allows herself to slip beneath the bedclothes. A slow smile spreads across her face as she closes her eyes and the fitful breeze toys with her hair. Without another thought in the world, she slips into the most profound sleep she's had in weeks.

· · ·

Patty's eyes pop open; she's suddenly wide awake. She yawns and stretches, then rolls over to see who else might be awake too. On the other side of Jinx, she sees Miriam's eyes are wide open. Patty motions UP with her thumb. Miriam nods and carefully sits up on the cot. The springs beneath the mattress squeak in complaint.

No one notices. The other trainees slumber while Miriam and Patty get up and make their way towards the barracks porch. Miriam quickly steps inside; Patty's right behind her. They both notice the snippet of bedsheet at the far end of the porch. Ever curious, Patty tiptoes over to investigate. There, just around the corner, is a slumbering Lauren, totally oblivious to the morning birdcalls, the breeze lightly playing with her hair or Patty's devilish grin. Patty is quite obviously struck by an inspired idea.

She turns as quietly as possible and scoots back to the screen door to the barracks where she runs into Miriam. Patty pushes Miriam back outside with a *shush* signal to her lips.

"Do you still have that Brownie camera stashed under your blankets outside?"

Miriam nods.

"Go get it, and hurry, okay. But be quiet!"

Patty instantly disappears off the porch, trotting towards the cottonwood trees across the field. At the other side of the stand of trees, she stops and listens intently. Coralee's small house is dark; there's no sound but the morning breeze. Bernie sits upright in one of the rockers, which is just what Patty had hoped to find. She sneaks up to the dummy, lifts it gently from the rocking chair, and scurries away with her catch. She drags the dummy back onto the barracks porch just as Miriam appears with the Brownie camera. Miriam stops in her tracks at the sight of the *man* in Patty's arms.

"Patty, please tell me you are not going to get us both in trouble." Miriam's face is dubious as she offers Patty the camera.

Patty is nearly breathless with excitement. "Hold it a minute, okay?"

Miriam nods in the affirmative. Just as Patty is about to walk away, Miriam grabs her shoulder and leans forward to whisper: "Patty, are all the brothers Jinx talks about *wood*?"

Patty looks blankly at Miriam. A l-o-n-g moment passes as if she is assessing the woman's competency. Then she shrugs. "Who can say, with Jinx? But according to her, the wooden ones are smarter than her flesh-and-blood brothers."

Dummy in hand, Patty proceeds around the corner where Lauren is still dreaming and looking angelic. Patty steps up to sleeping beauty oh so carefully and gently deposits Bernie by her side. Patty admires the effect for a moment;

she isn't completely happy with the composition. Bernie's past life as a tree is way too obvious. Patty deftly leans over and turns him on his side slightly, then pulls part of the sheet up over his shoulder. Definitely better. Grown completely brazen by her success so far, Patty leans down and drapes one of Lauren's arms over the now slumbering Bernie. *Ahhhh, perfection!*

Patty steps back and turns to Miriam, hand outstretched for the camera. Lauren grows momentarily restless. Patty points the little lens at her tableau and clicks the shutter. Her still life is captured for all eternity by Kodak.

"This is a photo both families will cherish for decades," she whispers.

She fiddles with the camera, advances the film and sets up to shoot one more time. "And now one for her friends!"

Whoops, this time the flash goes off right in the sleeping Lauren's eyes. She awakens with a start to find her arms around a *man*. She screams loudly and bolts upright in shock. Bernie the dummy *thunks* over onto his back. Whoa—a second piercing scream erupts as Lauren concludes she's been sleeping with a corpse.

Out on the lawn, trainees are starting to rouse themselves, especially after that second scream. With a big *whoop*, Patty tosses Miriam the box camera and shouts, "Run, Miriam."

Their fellow cadets are up and starting to check out the commotion. Miriam runs. Patty reaches down and scoops up Bernie, dragging him down the porch and into the barracks by one hand. Just as Patty disappears, Lila sprints around the corner of the barracks and enters the fray. "What the hell is going on out here?"

• • •

Several hours later, the barracks has been restored to its usual configuration. The bunks are back in place; all the trainees are now fully dressed. Lila is in deep conversation with Lauren Jinx is back on her own bunk, watching the full length of the hallway, reporting to Patty and Miriam their squad leader's every nuance and gesture.

"Lauren has her hand on the door. She's stepping out. Whoops, no, she's stopped again and is chewing Lila's ear some more."

Jinx skewers Patty with a look. "You are in such deep, deep elephant poo on this, Patty Yin Lee."

Down the hall it looks like Lila is doing her best to bite her lip and keep Lauren moving towards the doorway. Finally, she leaves, slamming the door behind her.

There is silence in the entire barracks for one long moment.

Lila turns and marches down the hallway straight towards the cubicle where the girls sit. A smattering of cadets falls into step with her and tags along. Jinx slips down beneath her covers, shakes her head in dismay at Patty, then disappears beneath the sheets.

Lila stops in the entrance of the cubicle, points a finger at Patty and motions her outside. She turns to the assembled masses. "This is a private conversation between Miss Yee and me, ladies." Lila glares at Patty. "YEE, OUTSIDE. NOW."

Patty's grin has vanished from her face. She brushes past Lila and exits to the porch.

Lila turns to follow Patty but stops. "The rest of you, get ready for your first 24-hour pass to go to Sweetwater for some R&R." The assembled trainees erupt in wild enthusiasm. "A weekend pass that I barely managed to *retain* for us, thanks to Miss Yee's shenanigans."

Lila turns and pushes through the screen door to confront Patty. Her face is grim. She stops inches from Patty's face. Her eyes bore into Patty's. Certain no one else will hear, she whispers, "You are likely in a world of shit, Patty Yin Lee. But none of that matters right now. The only thing that really matters, Yee, is, did you get the goddamn photo?"

Utterly surprised, Patty snaps to attention and salutes smartly. "Roger that, commander. Mission accomplished, and then some."

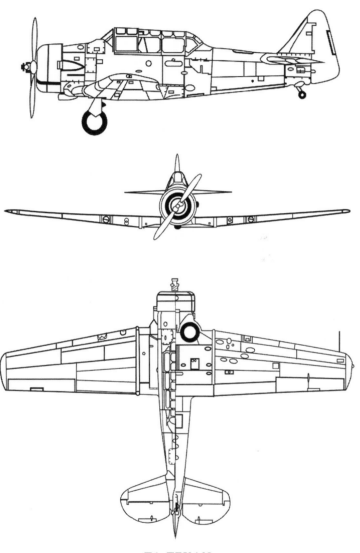

T6 –TEXAN

THIRTEEN

SWEETWATER, TEXAS

An Army bus shudders along the main street of downtown Sweetwater and grinds to a halt at the local five-and-dime. Before it's even completely halted, anxious trainees pound on the folding doors, trying to claw their way out. The doors open and a throng of eager young women pours out of the bus and directly into the department store.

It's impossible to see through the giant plate glass window at the front of the store; the glare from the intense Texas sun obscures anything beyond the hand-painted sign of the mercantile. No matter, the final trainee has barely gotten in the door when the first young woman is returning—several packages of nylon stockings held triumphantly over her head.

Having attained her first goal, she stops a moment on the street and lights a cigarette to await company for the next expedition. When a smattering of trainees have gathered, they raise their hands to shield their eyes from the sun and set their sights somewhere—anywhere—now that they're free from Avenger Field. With one glance down the main street, they're off.

There is only one ice cream parlor in Sweetwater. Two hours later it is completely overrun by the gaggle of women cadets that have descended on it. They're hanging out at the soda fountain, chatting up the 50-year-old soda jerk as if he were the last man on earth, and sipping on sodas—gloriously cold ice cream sodas that make your head ache if you drink too fast.

A group of gals in the booth closest to the doorway have sculpted their ice cream sundaes to resemble certain male body parts. The poor young busboy blushes furiously when he swoops by to deliver a milkshake to one of them. The girls erupt in spasms of laughter at his discomfort.

Outside on the sidewalk, Wallace Shaver strolls along and hears the laughter from inside the soda fountain. He stops and peers in through the plate glass window and smiles at what he sees. His cadets are roaring with glee.

He's about to continue down the main street but stops when he glimpses one solitary woman seated at the far end of the soda fountain. Without a second thought, he steps inside the door and removes his fedora. After crossing the room, he pauses before approaching.

Lila Stewart looks up from her magazine and notices Shaver's hesitancy. She smiles and says, "Yay, some adult conversation. Please join me, Mr. Shaver."

Wallace Shaver's smile is not at all ambiguous. He

immediately seats himself on the stool next to Lila, grinning. "My lucky day."

Lila laughs. "And here I thought it was mine."

. . .

WASHINGTON, D.C.—ROTARY CLUB

A group of influential congressmen and business leaders are being fêted at some luncheon or other. They're all just finishing the main course. Some waitresses are busy removing the soiled tableware while others start serving coffee and pastries.

At the head table, General Hap Arnold is just finishing what appears to have been a lengthy speech. Seated on the other side of the podium is none other than Jackie Cochran, dressed in her version of the newly approved WASP uniform. She looks a tad nervous but is definitely game.

General Arnold winds down. "In closing I'd just like to say that a fully trained and properly utilized Air Corps can minimize ground troop and infantry losses. It can be the key in neutralizing strategic enemy installations, becoming the leading wedge that can open tactical doors that at first glance appear to be sealed."

No one's listening. They've heard this kind of military blah, blah, blah thousands of times before. The General continues nonetheless. "The critical factor of course is funding, for a strong and thoroughly trained air support corps, for our troops. And the critical factor in achieving that end is judicious and persistent use of women pilots on the home front."

This last bit catches a few old duffers' attention. Heads slowly begin to turn away from coffee and pastries back to the head of the table.

"I'm here to say we can't afford to dawdle in our efforts to train women to fill the gap, and train them now."

More and more eyes are pivoting in the General's direction and now he is more than a little anxious to get out of the line of fire. He wraps up quickly.

"We have with us here today one of the foremost authorities on women in the Air Corps, Miss Jackie Cochran. Please welcome her, gentlemen."

Arnold leads the applause as he nods to Jackie and then takes his seat on the other side of the podium. Jackie is pulling herself together for one of the tougher road acts she performs for her girls: getting old men to give her money.

She takes her place behind the podium and stands a moment observing the congressmen seated around the room. She notes who is applauding, and more importantly, who isn't. She smiles one of her most radiant smiles.

"Gentlemen, thank you. Thank you very much for inviting me here today. Most of you know that John Costello,"—Jackie nods in Costello's direction, acknowledging his presence—"the representative from California, will be presenting a bill later this month to officially militarize the women's ferry pilot service known as the WASP program. I believe most of you have heard of it."

Low murmurs arise throughout the room. "Damn waste of money." "Psst, women flying—next we'll be training monkeys. Or darkies." Jackie nods, acknowledging the comments. She's heard most of them before.

She smiles out at the room of men again, giving them fair warning. "Before you turn back to that pastry, thinking this doesn't concern you at all—*Cochran and her flying witches can burn in hell before I'll vote to let them into this man's Army....*"

Jackie's comment causes quite a stir among the men. She shrugs, "Oh please! You think I don't know what you say? When your own daughters who want to fly, your wives who want to fly, even your old maiden aunts who want to fly call me at all hours of the day to report it to me? Across the country, from every state in the union they call to warn me what half of you *honestly* think about women flying." She cocks her head. The room is silent.

"But we're not here to talk about that; we're here so I can tell you about a man I had to fire last week. A man who put his own life in jeopardy, but also the lives of other flight instructors in jeopardy, not to mention his female trainees— all because he desperately wants to go to the front to fight."

All eyes in the room are now rivetted on Jackie Cochran.

"And you won't let him! We cannot let him. Not yet." Jackie pauses. "If he leaves, *if every man* leaves for the front, who will test fly new airplanes, who will ferry old ones that need fixing back to the factories, who will help test the new aeronautical advances the United States of America is creating by the scores, week after week after week?"

She pauses and leans forward, putting both hands on the podium to meet every eye in the room. "Gentlemen, if you send every available male flyer to front, who will do all the flying stateside?"

She watches her comments sink in, sees men's minds turning over what she has just said. "Women will do it, gentlemen. For the sheer love of flying, they'll do it. But honestly, is that what you want to tell your grandchildren about how you won the war? Will you confess you refused to pay for the work their own grandmothers did during the war just because they loved what they were doing so much that they'd do it for free?"

A vast silence fills the room for a long moment. Jackie scours the room with her eyes. Some men return to their coffees, chastened. Others slowly begin to applaud her remarks and then rise to their feet to clap more loudly.

• • •

Dusk is settling over Sweetwater and with it comes a comforting quiet. The sound of persistent applause seeps from the brightly lit windows of the Bluebonnet Hotel. The source is a local swing-band warming up to begin their set in the hotel lounge bar. The first notes of a popular tune, *String of Pearls*, drifts into the dining room.

The trainees are just finishing their sumptuous evening meal. They are grouped about the hotel dining room, sipping coffees, drinking *aperitifs*, and sharing desserts. They are gossiping and showing each other their day's purchases.

MAIN STREET—SWEETWATER, TEXAS

Miriam is sitting at one end of the dining table, head in hand, staring dreamily across the room to the dance floor. Jinx is busy next to her, scribbling something on a tiny piece of paper. She folds that scrap twice, then begins again on another. Patty leans over and tries to see what Jinx is up to, but Jinx covers over her work with her free hand, scowling at Patty in the process. "This is none of your beeswax, Patty."

"*Pardonne-moi, chérie.* I was wondering if you needed help."

Jinx raises her fist, which is about the size of a radish. Patty winces, feigning fright. "Oh, please spare me your displeasure, you brute."

At the far end of the table, Lauren scowls at them both and turns to Lila who is caught delicately wiping her mouth with her cloth serviette. "My god, those two should not be allowed out in polite society. Besides, they're up to something. Just look at them."

Lila in turn frowns at the two girls and mouths *behave*. They pretend to not understand her, smiling in response.

"Well, Lauren, we can only do so much in the time we've been given." Lila sets her napkin aside. "At least they don't bite and scratch in public any longer."

A shadow appears at Lila's side; she assumes it's the waiter. "Could we get our bill when you have a moment, please?"

A woman's voice responds. "You can, as long as I don't have to pay it." Dodie chuckles at her own witticism.

All the trainees at the table look up and smiles leap to their faces. Dodie grins in response. "How are all my favorite people?

Lila shouts her name and rises quickly to embrace her. All the trainees start peppering Dodie with questions. Miriam calls from down the table, "Welcome back. How are you?"

Jinx murmurs, "How's your dad? How was the funeral service?"

"It's so good to see you," Lila adds. "How is your dad doing? She immediately grabs an empty chair from a nearby table and drags it over next to Dodie.

Dodie drops gratefully into the chair and waves to a couple of gals at the far end of the table. She notices Jinx's preoccupation with writing notes but says nothing.

"The hotel manager pointed you out when I was registering." She leans over to whisper to Lila. "What's the *Jinx* up to?"

Lila merely shrugs. "Best not to ask. This is the first time I've smiled in days. Sympathetic nods all around the table.

Dodie picks up a teaspoon and fiddles with it. "Mom's service was lovely. Dad's gone to stay on Uncle Beemer's farm for a couple of weeks till he adjusts." She lets out a big sigh. "It's close enough he can still work our farm, but at least he doesn't have to be there all alone. He insisted I come back to training. Said it was no good me hanging around and the two of us being miserable."

Dodie breaks down a little at this. Lila wraps an arm around her shoulders and catches the eyes of a couple of the other trainees. "Maybe we can talk more about this later." Everyone at the table agrees heartily. "Yeah. Sure. It's just good to have you back, Dodie."

Lila stands up and turns to Lauren a moment, placing some money in front of her. "Could you organize paying the bill? The bus to take us back to the base will be here in about fifteen minutes." She lowers her voice. "I just want a couple of minutes alone with Dodie."

Then she turns to Jinx and adds sternly, "Jinx, I don't know what harebrained scheme you're up to, but you have exactly fifteen minutes to execute it."

Lila turns to Dodie and motions for her to follow.

"C'mon. Let's go talk in the lobby for a minute."

Lila and Dodie stroll from the dining room. Lauren immediately flags down the *maître d'* and inquires after the bill. Jinx tosses some money on the table and grabs her purse, stuffed with folded bits of paper. She murmurs to the group, "You guys, I'll be back in a wink." Jinx turns to head back into the dance lounge. "And PY, don't you dare let them leave without me, either."

Patty and Miriam exchange mystified expressions as Jinx hurries over to the dance lounge entryway. All they can glimpse from the dining room is Jinx approaching a soldier leaning against the bar—and apparently handing him one of the little slips of paper. Then she moves on to another soldier, and another, giving each a note.

Patty smirks, "Could she be that desperate for a date, that she's giving men her phone number?" Then she reconsiders: "What phone number?"

Miriam gathers up her things, opens her compact and applies some lipstick using the small mirror. "If I have learned one thing so far in training, it's don't ask after Jinx's little schemes." She finishes with the lipstick and snaps the compact closed. "Unless you want to be an accessory after the fact."

The smirk evaporates from Patty's face. "So you think it might involve eventual litigation too, hey?" She shakes her head in amazement. "That girl has so much gusto, doesn't she?"

"Gusto. There's a word that suits her perfectly."

. . .

Lila leads Dodie over to a couple of overstuffed chairs next to a fireplace. She seats herself in one chair and motions for Dodie to take the other. Lila takes a moment to examine Dodie's face. Dodie can't continue to meet Lila's level appraisal.

"Dodie, are you sure you're up for this?" Lila's voice is pitched low so that others won't hear. "It's awfully soon to come back to this mayhem."

Dodie nods her head slowly, silent.

"Dodie, you just buried your mother. No one will think less of you if you take another week, or even a month." Lila stops.

Dodie's hands in her lap are visibly trembling. She notices and spreads them out along the tops of her thighs to stop the shaking. She looks up to see if Lila has noticed too. If Lila has, she doesn't let on.

"When I was flying in England," Lila says, "bombs were falling and the Germans shelled us almost daily. I saw a fair number of people die—and I saw firsthand how it can affect the *survivors*." Lila leans forward and takes Dodie's hands in hers. "I will help you, but only if you promise me something."

Fear in her eyes, Dodie is silent a long, long moment. Finally, she murmurs, "What?"

"Promise me that if it gets to be too much., you'll say so. Promise you'll tell me." Dodie whispers. "Okay. I promise."

Lila lets go of her hands. "Okay, then. Are you registered to stay the night?" Lila's tone is lighter, more upbeat. "Or will you come back with us?"

Clear relief on her face, Dodie rises and squares her shoulders. "I'm registered. But I'll go get my bag."

"Great. I'll let the others know."

Dodie rises and crosses the lobby and begins to ascend the stairs, just as the other trainees start filing into the lobby from the dining room. Lila stands up and meets Lauren halfway. A bit apart from the others, they confer.

Lauren watches Dodie walking up the stairs. "Is she okay?"

Lila looks to make certain they cannot be overheard. "A bit shaky, but I guess that's to be expected. She said she wants to come back with us."

Lauren nods, then indicates the front door of the hotel lobby where the crappy Army bus has just pulled up outside.

Lila continues, "She just went to get her bag. Let's get everyone else loaded and give her a minute." Lauren and Lila arrange themselves on either side of the line-up of trainees and start doing a visual check of everyone who passes through the doors. Absentees begin to become apparent. Lauren checks her list. "Where's Tex?"

Nadine grins. "Little girls' room. Said she'd be right out."

There's a sudden roar of laughter from the lounge. The next moment Jinx spurts through the doorway and races across the dining area towards the lobby. She arrives breathless, but basically on time. She waggles her eyebrows at Lauren as she passes her. "Oooops, sorry. No demerits for me this trip, Lauren."

Lauren purses her lips tightly but manages to say nothing.

Lila smacks Jinx's backside with her purse as she passes by. "It's a long drive back to base, Babisch. I wouldn't count my chickens just yet."

Jinx is the last trainee to board the bus, except Dodie, who still has not appeared. Both Lila and Lauren cast wary glances up the stairway leading from the lobby. The hotel desk clerk notices their glances and shrugs. "First door, top of the stairs on your left. Maybe she had more packing to do than you thought."

Lila consults her wristwatch, then makes a decision. "Umm, she was kind of shaky. I'll go check on her." She heads for the stairway. "If I'm not back down in five minutes, get everyone back to the base so they don't miss curfew." Her foot on the bottom stair, Lila turns and catches Lauren's eye. "That's an order, cadet. I'll be along as soon as I can."

Lauren is clearly shocked. "What'll I tell Mrs. Deaton and Miss Abrahms?"

Lila stops just shy of the top stair. "Basically, tell her the truth. We ran into Dodie. I got tied up sorting out details. We may stay the night in Sweetwater."

Lila is about to continue up the stairs, then turns back. "Lauren, please don't say anything about Dodie's *state of mind*. I think she deserves a break on this."

Lauren frowns and appears ready to say something, but Lila gives her no option. She disappears into the upper hallway, fully intent on finding Dodie's room.

FOURTEEN

In the hallway outside Dodie's hotel room, Lila stops a moment, gathers a breath, and then knocks gently on the door. There is no response. After several seconds, she knocks again, more loudly. Again, there is no response. Lila hesitates and is about to turn away when on impulse she tries the door handle. It's unlocked. The door swings gently open.

The sound of the swing band in the lounge drifts up the stairs. Lila takes a step forward into the room and nearly stumbles over Dodie's suitcase. The door swings softly closed behind her. The room appears to be empty. Curious, Lila approaches the bathroom and opens the door. Empty. She crosses the room to the only window and looks out. It's a straight drop down three floors. She attempts to open the window, but it won't budge.

Very odd. Lila crosses to the bed, bends down and lifts the bedspread and looks beneath. Nothing. That only leaves the closet. Cautiously, not certain what she will find, Lila crosses to the closet door and opens it. Her hands rise slowly to her mouth to stifle a gasp; then she sinks to her knees, almost in supplication.

Lila extends one hand forward and whispers, "Dodie. Dodie, it's Lila."

On the floor amidst spare linens and pillows and blankets Dodie is huddled, knees drawn up to her chest with both arms wrapped tightly about them. Tears are streaming down her face. Her eyes are squeezed shut, her face screwed up as if in great pain or great fright. Sobs wrack her body.

At the sound of Lila's voice, Dodie tries to speak. "Lila? Lila, where have you been?" She begins sobbing again. "I thought you would come get me and now, now it's too late."

Lila reaches out and puts one hand on Dodie's, just resting it there. Dodie grabs Lila's and with both hers and hangs on, as if she's been thrown a lifeline.

"No, it's not, Dodie. It's never too late." Lila looks wildly around the room, looking for a way to summon someone. The sound of the bus horn blaring comes in through the open window. Distracted, she whispers *crap*. Then catching sight of Dodie again, Lila does the only thing she really can do at this moment. She climbs into the closet with her and wraps an arm around her shoulders.

Over Dodie's sobs, Lila can hear the grinding of the transmission as the bus pulls away from the hotel. "It's okay, Dodie. I'm here now." Lila hugs Dodie tightly. "What scared you all of a sudden?" Lila slowly begins to rock Dodie back and forth, softly humming a children's lullaby in time to the rocking. After a moment, Dodie's sobs begin to grow softer and eventually cease as the rocking continues.

"I started thinking about my mom. That she died."

"And that scared you?"

Dodie suddenly opens her eyes and turns to look directly at Lila. "Kind of. I mean because my mom was...well she was the crazy one in the family."

A flicker of doubt flashes across Lila's face.

"No. It's true, Lila. She hadn't come out of our bathroom in three years. It's where she died." Dodie turns away for a moment as if the truth of what she has just said has suddenly struck her. "We used to pretend it wasn't a problem, me and my dad. We never talked about it. It was just how Mom was; end of story."

Dodie turns away from Lila. Not daring to look in Lila's eyes, Dodie whispers this last part of her confession. "We chose to let her stay there because the alternative was to face that she might be sick. Really sick, and we could lose her if a doctor came. They might have taken her away from us."

Dodie's hands fly up to cover her face. She begins rocking back and forth, back and forth, sobbing again. "But the worst thing is, I didn't push Dad on it 'cause I thought if my mom could be crazy then maybe I could become crazy too. We were all so tied up in our fears, none of us knew how to help the other. And so we did nothing. And she might still be alive if only we had only done something, Lila. *Anything.*"

Lila wraps her arms around Dodie again, pulling her close. "We can't know that, Dodie. When someone we love dies suddenly it is natural to have regrets along with the pain of their passing. That will ease a bit over time. So let's get through tonight, and then tomorrow. I'll be here for you to talk with, okay?" Lila grabs one of the pillowcases from the pile and uses the edge to dab at Dodie's face.

Lila stands up and looks down sympathetically at Dodie, who is still sitting on the closet floor. "What you can do is to make the decision to live your own life, Dodie. The best life you can create for yourself—and bring the memory of your mother with you as you live it."

Lila steps out of the closet. "Take some time for yourself tonight, Dodie. Have a soak in the tub, get a good night's sleep. We have plenty of time to pick up our lives again tomorrow, don't we?"

Lila reaches down her hand and helps Dodie to her feet. "Don't kid yourself," Lila continues. "This is not an easy thing to do. But then neither was leaving your farm. Nor was rescuing Isabella when her landing gear got stuck. You can do this, too, Dodie. I know you can."

Dodie throws her arms around Lila and hugs her tightly. "It would be impossible without a friend like you, Lila. I'll see you in the morning then?"

"You betcha. I'll come get you for breakfast."

• • •

Early Sunday morning at Avenger Field Mrs. Deaton is seated behind a desk. On one side Coralee Abrahms stands at attention alongside Lauren Powell. Their faces are intentionally expressionless.

The office is filled with wall charts, records books, and assorted boxes and bookcases. A small, battered cardboard box sits off to the side of Mrs. Deaton's desk. On the other side of the desk, in front of Mrs. Deaton, stand Lila and Dodie. They both look somewhat anxious.

Mrs. Deaton taps a pencil against the top of the desk blotter, thinking. Her eyes are scanning the pages of an Army Code of Conduct military manual open before her. She looks up and appraises the two trainees standing in front of her.

"From my reading of the Army manual, there is no *reasonable* charge I can bring against you, trainee Jackson."

Dodie's eyes shift to the small woman seated at the desk in front of her. It's clear she's relieved at the announcement.

"Even though you weren't officially due back until tonight, every instinct tells me there's more to this story than either of you is saying."

Dodie and Lila risk a quick glance in each other's direction.

"I will charge you with two demerits for causing another trainee to miss curfew. I don't want to pry into the circumstances further."

Lila begins to speak in Dodie's defense and is elbowed into silence by Dodie.

"As for you, Miss Stewart, it's not just that you missed curfew, you did it intentionally and without plausible explanation."

Mrs. Deaton taps her pencil erratically on the desktop and shakes her head in dismay. "As squadron leader, it's up to you to set the example. So, four demerits and three weeks confined to base. And suspension as leader for those three weeks."

Lila opens her mouth to protest, then immediately closes it when she sees Mrs. Deaton isn't quite finished.

"Your assistant, Miss Powell, will take over as squad leader for the platoon during your suspension. Miss Jackson will continue with her duties to assist her."

Mrs. Deaton meets Lila's eyes momentarily. "Miss Stewart, you recognize that another demerit will have you thrown out of the program?"

Lila meets the stern woman's gaze. "Yes, ma'am."

"And there's nothing else you'd like to say on your own behalf?"

"No, ma'am."

Dodie clears her throat loudly, as if she might speak. Lila turns a threatening look in her direction and Dodie hesitates, then looks down at the floor.

"Fine then. You're both dismissed." Mrs. Deaton looks down at her notepad. "Next."

Lila catches Lauren's eye and smiles grimly, then shrugs. Both she and Dodie pivot in unison and march from the room. Coralee follows them to the door and bellows out a name. "Joanne Babisch. Front and center." Coralee refuses to acknowledge Jinx's presence as she strides past her, even though Jinx throws her a smile.

Mrs. Deaton reaches over and closes the Army manual. Beneath it is a small square of folded notepaper. She opens it, examines the indecipherable scrawl, then refolds the note. She slides a small box to the middle of the desktop.

Jinx Babisch crisply stops at attention in front of the desk. Mrs. Deaton looks up at Jinx and sighs heavily. "Do you know why you're here, Babisch?"

"No, ma'am, not at all."

Mrs. Deaton lifts the folded notepaper from her desk and extends it towards the trainee. "Perhaps this might shed some light on it."

Jinx steps forward to accept the note. Even as she does so, she begins to blush.

"Open it, cadet."

"I don't need to, ma'am...but I can explain."

"Oh, I'm certain you can. And you will. In good time."

Mrs. Deaton stands up and comes around to sit on the corner of her desk in front of Jinx. "Miss Babisch, I don't have any idea *what* this note says." She takes the note back from Jinx. "But I DO know how it looks. And at face value, it looks as if you are either a spy or a *harlot*."

Utterly shocked, Jinx draws herself up for a vehement response. She can feel a pointed stare from Coralee at Mrs. Deaton's choice of words. Mrs. Deaton cuts Jinx off with a wave of her hand. "I said, that's *how it looks*." She sighs again. "Miss Babisch, we are in a state of war. Has this fact escaped you completely?"

Mystified and somewhat chastised, Jinx slumps her shoulders. "No, ma'am, of course not."

"Well praise the good Lord for that small blessing. Because, Miss Babisch, one wrong look may be all that stands between you and a military bullet next time you make a mistake like this."

At the astonished reaction by the other three women in the room, Mrs. Deaton continues. "Soldiers are trained to shoot first and ask suspected spies questions afterwards." Mrs. Deaton pulls a small box from the desktop and holds it in her lap. She taps it with her fingertips.

"And then, oddly enough, just this morning a young pilot from an air base in Romulus, Michigan—enroute to Houston for training—stopped here first." Mrs. Deaton holds out the box for Jinx to take. "He dropped this off, to your attention, Babisch. You distribute a suspicious note in a foreign language and then this arrives the next day."

Jinx's eyes are huge as she accepts the box from Mrs. Deaton.

"What do you have to say for yourself?"

Jinx's eyes are wide in surprise. "Wow. Now that's service."

As Jinx lifts the lid, both Abrahms and Powell strain from their positions behind Mrs. Deaton to see what's in the box.

A huge smile spreads across Jinx's face. "Holy smokes, thanks, Mrs. Deaton."

Mrs. Deaton reaches over and attempts to take the box back from Jinx. Jinx hangs on for dear life. "Oh please, please, Mrs. D, don't take them." Jinx pulls the box to her chest and wraps her arms around it tightly.

"Give me one good reason why I shouldn't confiscate those for the sheer amount of trouble you've been, Babisch."

A cascade of emotions cross Jinx's face. Mrs. Deaton continues, "Make that three good reasons: for the notes, the box and why I shouldn't wash you out of the program right now for importing goods of foreign origin to a military facility."

Mrs. Deaton crosses her arms over her chest and settles in to await Jinx's tale. Jinx inhales the scent of the contents, and then folds the box top back over to contain the aroma. She looks at Mrs. Deaton as if the explanation is the simplest thing in the world.

"First, they are the proof that my Yiddish studies are proving useful. The notes are in Yiddish, of course. And number two—although these are of foreign origin, they are from Montreal, Canada. Canadians are our staunchest allies and partners in this war."

Jinx reaches into the box. "Here, try one. They're called bagels. And they're an important Jewish religious *sacrament*."

At Mrs. Deaton's severe look of disbelief, Jinx backtracks slightly.

"Well, okay…they're not part of the religion, exactly."

Jinx delicately puts the bagel back into the cardboard box. "But they're an important part of *home* in Montreal for one of my cube mates, Miriam." Jinx shrugs.

"She's been really lonely lately and I thought a little taste of home might cheer her up."

Mrs. Deaton still looks very, very skeptical. "And the notes?"

"Like I said, I was practicing my Yiddish. Miriam says Saul the bagel guy only speaks Yiddish." Jinx's eyes entreat Mrs. Deaton to believe her. "I can't be sure, but I'm pretty sure the notes said *Need Rabbi, and many bagels. Come quick. Avenger Field, Sweetwater.*"

After a tense moment, Mrs. Deaton laughs out loud and then rises from the edge of the desk and returns to her chair. "Well, you got the phrase *'come quick'* correct, for certain. And someone showed it to the Rabbi at Love Field who translated it for us. He's the one responsible for the box of bagels."

Jinx beams and holds the precious box more tightly.

"Just so you know, the Rabbi contacted a Houston Temple for you. Their Rabbi has kindly offered to fly up two Sundays a month to celebrate a belated Shabbat service at the barracks with you three girls while the other cadets attend Mass.

Jinx's eyes widen in question. Mrs. Deaton can't help but notice. "There are three of you in your squadron, correct?" She consults a piece of paper on her desktop. "You, Miriam and Bernice? That's the information I've been given."

Coralee and Lauren exchange quick glances.

"Ma'am. Yes, ma'am. Three trainees, although Bernice isn't that devout."

"Fine then. Tomorrow morning will be your first service. Dismissed."

Jinx brings herself to attention and executes a perfect *about face* while hugging her box of bagels. Grinning broadly, she marches from the room.

Mrs. Deaton calls out after her, "And I don't want to see you in here again, Babisch. Ever."

"Yes, ma'am." Jinx raises the box of bagels over her head and calls back, "And thank you, ma'am."

Mrs. Deaton slumps against the back of her desk chair and motions to Coralee to usher the next cadet into the room. Coralee calls out into the hallway, "Cadet Mendez, front and center. Now."

Coralee can't stop herself from admiring the way Jinx saunters along the passageway, bagels in hand.

• • •

Several hours later, the cadets are wasting the remaining hours of their weekend. Some paint their fingernails for the week ahead, knowing that the first round of mechanics class will chip and grind it all away. But it's a soothing, *normal* thing to do after dinner on a Sunday night.

Jinx pokes Patty in the arm with her toe. "I'm going for a smoke, wanna come?"

Patty has her nose buried deep in a novel. She shakes her head *no* without even looking up.

"Fine." Jinx grabs her pack of cigarettes and matches and heads out of the cube. In a few strides, she's out the back door of the barracks. Several other cadets are lounging on the porch, sitting on the railing. None of them is doing much of anything—and enjoying it immensely.

Lila notices Jinx as she steps off the porch and into the yard and calls out, "Lights out in an hour, Jinx."

Jinx waves a hand over her head and calls back, "Just out for a smoke, honest." Everyone on the porch laughs companionably. Lila sighs and looks at Dodie. "Let's hope!"

Jinx paces beyond the porch lights and stops to light her cigarette. She looks left—should she stroll towards the flight line or turn right towards the front gate and the open desert. She's just about to choose when a hand grasps her arm quite firmly. Jinx tries to shrug it off and groans. "Oh, come on. I truly am just out for a smoke. I don't need a chaperone, Lila."

"I am sooo beginning to wonder about that."

As Jinx turns, she catches sight of Coralee. Her hand drops as soon as Jinx turns around. "After that meeting with Mrs. Deaton, I'm not sure anyone thinks you should ever be left on your own—ever again, Miss Babisch."

Jinx smiles slowly. "So join me then. Want a cigarette?" She begins walking, hoping Coralee will follow. She does.

"What were you thinking, Jinx? You could have been washed out of the program just like that." Coralee snaps her fingers. She shakes her head in dismay. "There are hundreds of women who have prayed to be selected for this program… and you risked it all for what? A prank, a joke?"

Jinx stops and turns to face Coralee. She studies her for a long moment. "For friendship, Coralee. Miriam misses her parents, her country, her community so much. I wanted her to know someone sees her, really sees what she's giving up to help us. I wanted her to know she matters—to me anyway, if not to anyone else."

Coralee is silent a long moment and then shakes her head. "You honestly do take the cake, Jinx. I can't ever figure you out from one moment to the next. You pull that baloney about Bernice being Jewish…."

Jinx objects: "She is Jewish. Or at least that's how I think of her."

Coralee waves her objection away. "Putting your flying career on the line, lying to Mrs. Deaton without a second thought—all to help ease a friend's homesickness. I don't think I'll ever understand you, Jinx."

Jinx meets Coralee's eyes and a genuinely sweet smile

spreads across her face. "But you want to try, don't you, Coralee? That's why you're so upset that I risked my flight status at Avenger. I'd be gone and you wouldn't have anything to puzzle over at night."

Coralee's response is to arch her eyebrows at Jinx's assumption and then grasp her arm firmly and propel them both forward. "Maybe we should just keep walking, Miss Babisch." Two steps later, "And I will accept that offer of a cigarette, if I may."

Jinx slips her arm through Coralee's and slows their pace. She reaches up with her free hand and takes the cigarette from her mouth and offers it to Coralee. Coralee stops and focuses on the cigarette. The imprint of Jinx's lipstick is curled about the filter tip like a rose-colored wreath. She deliberately brings the cigarette to her lips and inhales.

As Coralee exhales the smoke, Jinx stretches up and puts her lips over Coralee's mouth, catching the smoke in her own mouth. Her eyes glitter with mischief as she exhales the secondhand smoke.

"I'm pretty certain that I should walk you home, Miss Abrahms."

"Are you, Miss Babisch?" Coralee reaches out and catches a handful of Jinx's curly hair between her fingers and caresses the length of it. "I love your hair. I have done so since the moment I spotted you standing at the main gate that first day."

Jinx smiles and steps extremely close to Coralee. "Funny, I never liked it because it always made me stand out." She runs her finger along Coralee's collarbone. "You might convince me that's not a bad thing, Coralee."

Coralee smiles. "I'll keep trying."

Jinx reaches up and kisses her again. "Will you? When?"

Coralee chuckles and wraps an arm around Jinx's waist to move her forward. "Just as soon as I can move you out of the middle of this damn cow pasture and into my house." She looks down at Jinx, who has fallen into step beside her, heading for the anonymity of the cottonwood trees. "Or are you having a shy moment, now that I've called your bluff?"

Jinx laughs and replies. "Would it be hugely unromantic for me to shout *Race you* and break into a run?"

Coralee laughs too—and then they both start running.

• • •

"Coralee, you think I don't know what people think and say about me? You think I live in a self-made bubble oblivious to others' opinions?"

Jinx turns over in bed and leans on her elbow so she can see Coralee's face. "I know. I'm too much, too happy, too loud, too honest. I blurt things constantly—things other people just think." Jinx flops back down on the bed and shoves her forearms underneath her head.

"I remember in fifth grade my classroom was getting ready for a parents' night. The teacher had assigned us an art project to decorate our school room for the event with our posters. The theme was the holidays, so I drew a menorah on a tabletop with a *challah* and some wine glasses. I thought it was beautiful and perfectly depicted the holy days to me."

"It does sound wonderful, Jinx."

Jinx grimaces. "She refused to hang it up with all the other art works. When I asked her why, she said she meant posters about Christmas—so everyone would be comfortable when they visited.

"I remember shouting at her, 'What about my family being comfortable? Do you think we're the only Jews in this whole damn school?'"

A long silence ensues. Finally, Coralee leans over and brushes aside a wisp of Jinx's hair. "So, what happened?"

A tear rolls down Jinx's cheek, and she frowns. "She suspended me for swearing at her and made me take home a note to my parents requesting a meeting with them after the holidays to discuss my behavior."

Jinx wipes the tears off her face with a furious scrub of her palms. "With one stroke she erased me and my whole family and the problem they presented to her vision for parents' night."

"Damn you, Jinx Babisch!"

Incensed, Jinx turns furious eyes on Coralee. Her fury evaporates when she sees Coralee's smile, which widens when Jinx leans over to kiss her again.

"Damn you all to hell," Coralee whispers again, and kisses her softly.

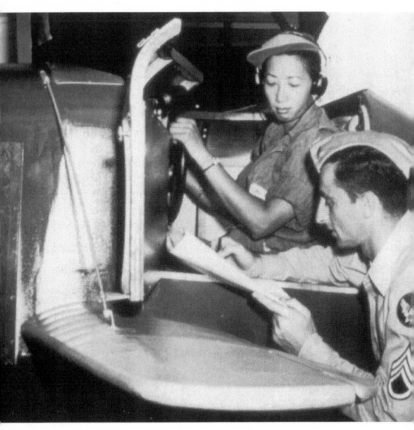

LINK INSTRUMENT TRAINER

FIFTEEN

It's cooler in Hell than it is in southern Texas in May. And it's hotter than that inside the Link Trainer, better known as the *box* at Avenger Field. The Link Trainer is designed to mimic the cockpit of a T6 aircraft. It sits in the middle of the room on a short pedestal and can be tilted and spun quite easily by the Flight Instructor in attendance. Just like with the real cockpits, there are drapes that can be drawn so that the pilot sees nothing but the gauges normally used to fly her plane.

The trainees are gathered in a tight group around Instructor Shaver. Patty's sweating her guts out inside the box. Shaver calls out flying directions to her while he sets the box whirling. Patty's job is to control the tilt of the box merely by watching the dials in front of her and making the appropriate corrections.

It's hard, sweaty work. It's also the only way to prepare for the grueling process of learning to fly an aircraft by only using your instrument panel. This is critical instruction for pilots caught out at night in a storm or trying to land a plane on the deck of a ship tossing at sea.

Exhausted, Shaver and Patty stop for a moment and Shaver opens the door to the training box so Patty can get some fresh air. "The goal, gals, is to be able to fly without looking outside your window for references. Charts and the instruments in your cockpit will tell you where you are, and how you're flying, if you trust them."

Shaver catches Patty's eye. "And to trust them you have to practice, practice, practice before you ever try this at 5000 feet in the air."

Sharon Rogers, one of the Senior Cadets, appears in the doorway to the classroom dressed in her flight suit. Instructor Shaver notices and acknowledges her with a wave. He rises from the stool next to the Link Trainer and starts walking towards the door, indicating that the group of women should follow.

"All the training aircraft have the ability to curtain off one of the cockpits. Once you're comfortable in the Link Trainer, we'll start practicing takeoff and landing with the curtains drawn so you'll rely only on your instruments."

Nadine instantly raises her hand, but Shaver has anticipated her question. He motions for them to follow and picks up his parachute near the door. He keeps walking out into the sunlight with Sharon right behind him. Lila and Lauren bring along the remainder of their platoon.

Shaver continues his march towards the Flight Shack. He stops at the flight board outside and adds his and his copilot's name to the list. He turns abruptly and continues lecturing his class. "The forward cockpit will be covered completely in black cloth. Sharon here won't be able to see out; no light will get in. Sharon, how many hours do you have in the Link Trainer to date?"

She stops to think. "Eighty...maybe more."

Shaver continues, "You will each learn to fly completely by your instruments."

Jinx interjects, "Takeoffs and landings?"

Sharon nods. "Takeoffs, landings, rolls—you name it."

Miriam whispers to Jinx, "Holy cats, that sounds crazy."

Shaver turns to face the cadets, a sympathetic grin on his face. "Just to show you it *can* be done by both young and old alike...." He turns and with a wave of his hand grandly includes his companion. "Sharon has agreed to join me today in a short demonstration of blind flying. I'll simply be along as backup."

Shaver turns towards the waiting aircraft and indicates the senior trainee should go first. "Ladies before gentlemen, madam."

Shaver's eyes make brief contact with every trainee. "You have nothing to fear but fear itself. Remember that, okay." His last look is for Lila. He holds eye contact with her a long moment, until he sees the glimmer of her smile. With a quick salute to them all, he turns on his heel and follows the senior trainee to the aircraft.

They execute a quick walk-around to assess it as flight worthy, then clamber aboard. The senior cadet seats herself in the forward cockpit and Shaver helps arrange the blackout curtains to completely cover the canopy windows from inside the craft. The whole platoon spreads outside the Flight Shack to watch the takeoff.

The aircraft's propeller leaps to life and the roar of the engine drowns out any further communication among the students on the ground. Slowly the aircraft eases away from the flight line and turns for the runway. The assembled trainees watch the progression with apprehension.

Jinx whispers loudly to Miriam, "I don't think I can watch!"

Nearby, Dodie shakes her head in disbelief. "Oh man, I'm not sure I'll ever be up for this."

Patty grins. "At the same time, imagine the freedom of being able to fly without having to constantly look at the ground for clues to where you are!"

They all watch as the aircraft makes its turn and gathers speed coming down the runway into the wind, heading for takeoff.

"Trust me, they won't let you even try it if they don't think you're ready," Patty says. There are murmurs and assents throughout the large group, but all eyes are glued to the aircraft racing down the runway. It has reached lift-off speed and begins that slow graceful movement when gravity is denied.

All the trainees who have been holding their breath let out a collective sigh. Light as a butterfly, the craft lifts from the tarmac and then suddenly SLAMS nose first into the pavement.

The screech of metal scouring the runway splinters the quiet Texas afternoon. Instinctively, all the cadets reach up to cover their ears. Their eyes are huge with horror as a fireball erupts from the aircraft and a massive explosion rattles the glass in the Flight Shack windows behind them.

Several cadets scream. They all turn away, shielding themselves from the blast. And then, pandemonium breaks loose on the flight line as mechanics run towards the wreckage.

The ambulance immediately begins its futile journey to the end of the tarmac, sirens wailing. The fire truck careens from its station near the flight line, firemen barely managing to hang onto the handrails as it accelerates towards the smoking ruin at the end of the runway.

A number of cadets have started crying. Someone is shouting, "No, no, no."

. . .

In Washington, D.C. Jackie's office is its usual drab, Army-issue spartan. Everything in it is a little worn around the edges. The sole spot of color, apart from Jackie herself, is a potted orchid sitting on the window ledge behind her desk. It's lit as if the sun outside shines solely for it.

Jackie is looking a trifle worn. Despite her smart summer suit and open-toed shoes, she's tired with a capital T. The intercom on her desk buzzes loudly and Jackie jumps slightly, then bends and presses a key to listen to the outside receptionist announce an appointment.

"Send them in and see if we've got coffee to offer, okay?"

Jackie hasn't even finished her instructions when her office door opens and two tanned, casually urbane civilian men swagger into the room.

Surprised, Jackie quickly regains her composure and offers them a seat. "Mr. Conners, Mr. Cohen, please have a seat."

The men position themselves in the two guest chairs that face Jackie's desk. Mr. Conners very carefully adjusts the crease on his trousers so as not to muss it while sitting.

Jackie leans over the intercom once again. "Shelly, can you bring our guests some coffee?"

"Miss Cochran?"

"Please, both of you, call me Jackie. Mr. Connors, you were saying …."

"Jackie it is then. General Arnold assures us we'll receive full cooperation from your department."

Jackie smiles cheerfully. "Well, that depends on what you're asking for and when you want it, gentlemen." She chuckles.

Smiling in return, Simon Cohen nods. "Of course, of course Miss…*Jackie.* We understand you have innumerable young women to train."

Shelly appears in the doorway holding a tray with three cups of coffee.

"500 this year alone; more, maybe 750 next year. Pretty close to innumerable, I'd say."

Jackie motions her secretary into the room. Shelly enters and sets the cups of coffee on the desktop and leaves. Both men nod eagerly for Jackie to continue; they completely ignore Shelly.

Jackie calls out after her departing secretary, "Thank you, Shelly."

Putting on her business face, Jackie turns back to the

two men. "So, yes, you can have access to my girls—but only for one week of filming and research." She pauses, significantly. "And only as long as it doesn't interfere with training."

Connors nods avidly. "Absolutely. You have our word."

Jackie takes a sip of coffee and eyes her guests over the rim of the cup. "Report to Avenger Field by Friday. If you check in with my liaison, Mrs. Deaton, as soon as you arrive you should have ample opportunity to shoot daily routine and then classes starting again on Monday."

It's clear from their expressions that's all the two men wanted to hear. They hastily replace their cups on the desk and rise to go. Connors stands and offers his hand across the desktop. "That's perfect, Jackie. *Movietone News* will make a newsreel you and your girls will be proud to show your friends and families."

Jackie takes another sip of coffee and considers for a moment longer; the two men fret awaiting her final dismissal.

"Yes, yes gentlemen." She frowns and adds, "Mrs. Deaton is a fierce gatekeeper for our program out there. Whatever she says goes. Are we clear?" She sets her cup down. "And remember, we can be in touch at a moment's notice through the teletype machine."

The two men rise, smiling assurances while they turn and head for the door. Jackie slumps back into her chair and takes another sip of coffee.

Across from Jackie, the teletype machine clacks into gear and the latest news from Avenger Field begins spanning the hundreds of miles and three time zones between them, printing word for word the details of the fatal accident.

Jackie rips off the lead page and begins to read it, then swears vehemently to herself. *Christ and his little kittens.* She leaps around her desk and sprints to the office door, shouting, "SHELLY, have those yahoos with *Movietone* left yet?"

Shelly stammers a reply. "Y... yes, Miss Cochran, I believe I just heard their car drive away.

"Shit and double shit."

Aghast at Jackie's language, Shelly murmurs, "Pardon, Miss Cochran?"

• • •

The trainees are all gathered in the barracks lounge, sadness, anger and bewilderment color their faces. Some girls huddle together, some hold hands, others sit mutely apart from the group. Each is attempting to process her grief in her own way.

Mrs. Deaton, Coralee and an unfamiliar Army Chaplin are standing before the assembled cadets. The Chaplin begins speaking.

"It's important to remember why you're here at Avenger Field...why Mr. Shaver and Sharon Rogers were here. What we do is risky. We train as hard as we can to mitigate the risk, but it's part of flying—it's part of learning to fly." He lets that sink in. "It's part of war."

Mrs. Deaton takes over. "We have given some thought to whether we should hold classes tomorrow, and we believe you all will be better off if we continue with our normally scheduled training. She hesitates. "We are as shocked and saddened as all of you at today's events—but classes will continue tomorrow without interruption."

Mrs. Deaton reaches over and hands Nadine a couple of sympathy cards and a pen. "Please pass these cards around for you all to sign for the families." She turns to Coralee. "Could you stay behind and collect the cards when the girls are done with them, please?"

"Yes, ma'am; happy to be of use."

One of the nearest young women raises her hand with a question. Mrs. Deaton nods to her. "Go ahead, Tex."

"Is it true the Army is *not* going to pay funeral costs or transport the bodies back to their families?"

An uncomfortable silence fills the room for a long moment. The Chaplin finally offers an explanation. "As a *civilian* instructor and flyer, neither Shaver nor Sharon Rogers qualifies for Army military benefits." He looks truly uncomfortable. "Including burial and transportation costs."

All the cadets' faces register shock. Lila finally breaks the silence. She stands up, reaches into her pants pocket, and pulls out some folded money and drops it into her ball cap and passes it on to the woman next to her. "I say, we take care of our own then. If the Army won't acknowledge their contribution, I will. Damn it."

"Me too. That's the right thing to do. This is ridiculous."

The cap is passed around to everyone in the lounge. In minutes it's filled and passed to Mrs. Deaton. She accepts it with tears in her eyes. "God bless you, every one of you. Jackie would be so proud of you." She hands the money to the Chaplin.

"Don't you dare let this set you back, girls." Mrs. Deaton

dabs at her eyes. "Instructor Shaver would have drilled you *twice* as hard, wouldn't he?" She nods brusquely at the group. "He would tell you himself, "Don't look back, don't focus on this. Keep your mind on the future, your future. And keep marching towards it."

Mrs. Deaton and the Army Chaplin then make the rounds of the cadets, offering words of condolence and sympathy. When they leave, the room becomes a sad, bedraggled place where dreams have been cut loose.

After they've gone, Coralee steps forward to see if everyone has signed off on the cards. Dodie is the last cadet to sign. She turns as Coralee approaches and sighs with resignation. "I think I'm last. They're done."

Coralee slips her arm around Dodie. "You okay?"

Dodie sighs again. "I just can't believe two more deaths so soon."

Lila comes up beside her and wraps her arm around her too. "Mrs. Deaton had it right, I think. Don't focus on the loss. Own it, incorporate it, but don't let it stop you from moving ahead. Mr. Shaver gave his all to us, didn't he? Now we should return the favor and do everything we can to graduate and earn our wings."

"Absolutely," Jinx says with determination. She and Miriam join them. Jinx puts her arm around Coralee's waist and Miriam's arm circles Jinx's waist. Patty slips into the fold to complete the circle.

Jinx looks around at the women in the circle. "None of us should give up, let down our guard or stop believing in ourselves." She looks pointedly at Coralee. "None of us."

FORMATION FLYING

SIXTEEN

The sound of a police whistle shatters the quiet morning. Lauren is stationed at the head of the hallway, just beginning her march down the center aisle of the barracks, clipboard in hand. She's doing a head count, shouting out trainee names as she passes each cubicle. Very officious—very offensive—and of course completely oblivious. "Andrews, Arthurs, Barber and Baines."

Another blast pierces the morning. "Speak UP, ladies. I can't hear you."

Slightly louder responses trickle in from the cubicles as Lauren strides past them, continuing roll call. By now almost everyone in the barracks is up and moving around: getting dressed, washing up—all except Jinx, who's still lying buried beneath a mountain of bedclothes in a lower bunk against the wall.

Jinx moans, "Would someone please rip that whistle from Lauren's mouth and shove it?" Patty interjects before Jinx can get herself into real trouble. "There ain't no such place and besides, young ladies don't talk like that."

Patty slams her locker door, jambs a ball cap on her head and crosses over to drop onto the end of Jinx's bunk. A bare foot is exposed; Patty reaches down and tickles it. Jinx jerks it away beneath the covers.

Patty grins. "Better?"

"Patty, you know I'm not good in the morning."

Patty pokes about, searching for Jinx's ribs beneath all the blankets. She's in mid-dig when one of Jinx's hands snakes out from beneath the rumple and grabs Patty's wrist in a vice-like grip. Jinx growls, "Patty, if you keep that up, I'm going to have to break your skinny little fifth-generation arm."

Another blast from the whistle, this time at the very opening of their cubicle. In the wink of an eye, Jinx rips the bedclothes off herself, turns, and is about to launch herself from the bottom bunk at the hapless Lauren. Patty is keeping Jinx pinned to keep her out of serious trouble.

Lauren, of course, is clueless. She stands in the hallway bellowing out the trainee names at the bottom of her list: "Babisch, Lee, Zimmerman, Stewart."

Jinx yells in the general direction of the cubicle opening. "Lauren Powell, if you blow that damn thing one more time...."

"Two demerits for swearing, Jinx." Lauren pokes her head in the cubicle and smiles at Jinx.

"Patty, for the love of God let me out of here so I can rip that whistle from her mouth."

Patty is still sitting on the edge of the bed, grinning like a mad woman. "Hey Lauren, I think Baines is calling you."

Lauren half turns towards the front of the barracks, listening intently. Patty adds encouragingly, "Better go see what's up."

"Thanks, Patty, you're a doll." Lauren turns to leave.

Jinx has gotten free of the blankets and lunges after Lauren, but Patty grabs her around the waist and hangs on. She wraps her arms tightly around Jinx's waist, pinning her arms down too. Jinx squirms to free herself, but she can't. Patty is laughing so hard that she's gasping for air. "Someday, you'll thank me for this, Jinx."

Jinx suddenly stops struggling; she just goes limp. As Patty loosens her grip somewhat, Jinx turns and wraps her hands around Patty's throat. The action is light, but definitely threatening.

Jinx whispers hoarsely, her voice seemingly coming from every corner of the room. "No, Patty, you're wrong. Someday—it sounds as if it's coming from an empty locker—someday I'll get you back." Jinx drops her hands from around Patty's neck. "Someday when you least expect it," says a voice from under the bed.

Patty tosses Jinx back onto the bunk and leaps up and away. Her grin has lost all its mischief. "Okay, that was downright spooky, Jinx. Don't do that, please! It totally creeps me out."

Jinx lies on the bunk and grins *maniacally,* rubbing her hands together enthusiastically. She growls, "You'll never know when I may strike."

Lila appears in the entryway and interrupts. "Can you two children make up long enough to come down to Tex's cubicle? She's packing to leave."

Both Jinx and Patty shout, "What?" They are on their feet in a moment, following Lila down the hall. As the three cadets enter Tex's cubicle, they can see the suitcase open on the lower bunk. Tex is busy emptying her locker, placing things in her bag. She's dressed in civilian clothes and her zoot suit lies folded neatly at the foot of the neatly made bed.

Lila puts out a hand to stop Tex from packing. "Tex, are you sure you want to do this?" A protracted silence follows. Tex wipes her eyes with the back of one hand, but she returns to packing. "As sure as I can be, I guess."

Jinx and Patty slink into the cubicle and come to a halt at the foot of the bed.

Jinx's hands immediately cover her cheeks in dismay at what Tex is contemplating. "But why?"

Lila asks softly, "Is it the accident? Maybe you just need some time to think."

Tex turns to face them. "That's all I've been doing. Thinking. All night long—for the last few months."

A few more trainees appear silently in the entryway.

Tex continues, "It's not just the accident; *it's everything.* You guys just don't get it. No one wants us here. Not the Army—not our parents or our beaus. They don't actually want us to fly, ever."

She wipes away another tear. Some other trainees are nodding their heads at this. "My brother says that lots of duty stations won't even let us touch a plane when we get there. Or they give us all the shit jobs that no one else wants to do."

More of the company has gathered in the doorway, quietly listening to Tex. She continues, "And if we happen to be killed doing one of those shit jobs, they don't even have the decency to pay to have our bodies shipped home."

Other cadets murmur assent. "Yeah. You know Tex is right."

Tex has finished her packing. She closes the lid on her suitcase and fastens the latches. "It's not fair!"

Finally, Jinx can't stand it any longer. "NOT FAIR? That's your big revelation, Tex?" Jinx shakes her head in exasperation. "It's not fair that I'm only five foot two. God knows I should be at least six feet. It's not fair that Patty was born dirt poor and had to work her ass off all her whole life. It's not fair that Miriam…was born Canadian."

Jinx is practically shouting. "For Pete's sake, Tex, you can't quit because life's not fair. If you quit now, *it will just stay unfair for everyone forever!* You have to stay and fight— and then fight some more."

Jinx throws her hands up in the air in exasperation. "Lila, talk some sense into her." Jinx tries to walk away from the cubicle. Lila grabs her and pulls her back inside. "What Jinx is trying to say, Tex, is that we need you! Even if the Army doesn't think they do. Can you stay, give it some time—a week at least?"

Tex picks up her suitcase from the bed. She is actively crying now. "I can't, Lila, Jinx. I know there are other things I can do for the war effort." She starts lugging her suitcase towards the barracks door. "But I can't do this. Not anymore. It's just too hard."

As Tex exits the front door and out of her friends' lives forever, she calls, "Goodbye ya'll. I'll be lookin for you overhead in the skies. Every single goddamn day!"

· · ·

Lauren spends the remainder of the morning blowing her whistle at the cadets. They've barely eaten their morning pancakes when the whistle sounds to hurry them to take their plates and cups to the bins.

They've all brought their parachutes with them to the mess hall. Now that they've eaten, they don their parachutes before they march to class. It's the final day of a whole week of wearing them everywhere they go, even to the bathroom—which is hell.

The instructors want them to notice the weight change when their 'chutes are missing. This means wearing the 'chutes until the women need to stop and *feel* if they are still strapped on. It hasn't happened yet to anyone. Shaver had assured them it would, but then Shaver said a lot of things that turned out not to be true—like training in the Link Trainer would keep them safe.

Lauren marches the cadets twice their usual distance. She blows her whistle to stop them multiple times to straighten their formations, tighten their turns, practice their right face, left face and about face. By the time they enter the Ground School classroom they're exhausted and sweaty and grim. Instructor Bittern appears to be as grumpy as his pupils, so he drills them relentlessly on pre-flight checks, post-flight checks and proper radio procedures for communicating with the tower.

He keeps hammering home to them, "The most dangerous maneuvers in flying are takeoff and landing. The closer you are to the ground, the less room you have for mistakes. Remember that!"

As if they'll ever forget.

Then it's time for Physical Training. It's still hot as hell. Again, that faultless blue sky arches overhead day after day, promising nothing but sun, sun, sun. The final day wearing their parachutes everywhere cannot end soon enough. It makes PT even worse than it usually is, and then they get to practice on the jump tower, too.

Every day has been a new series of events that tips them off balance emotionally, intellectually and physically. But the only way forward is forward, so they put one foot in front of the other and jump when the PT instructor says jump. No one even thinks to ask *how high*, not even Lauren.

After lunch, still wearing the damn parachutes, a cluster of trainees is gathered in front of the flight assignment board checking out their time slots for their afternoon flights. The two *Movietone News* guys, Connor and Cohen, approach them with their camera whirring. Cohen, who only carries a microphone, introduces himself to the group of trainees.

"Good afternoon, ladies. I'm Melvin Cohen from *Movietone News*—you know, the news reel company?"

Connor follows with a movie camera on his shoulder.

All eyes turn away from the flight board to face him.

"Conners and I are going to be around for the next few days shooting footage for a newsreel on you WASPs." Slowly the young women's worried, weary faces move from skepticism to genuine interest. Lauren weaves through the band of women to the front and steps forward, hand outstretched. "Really? May I see some I.D. please." Her tone will brook no refusal.

Cohen tries anyway. "Honestly, Miss...uh, Miss?" "Powell. My name is Lauren Powell and I'm the platoon leader."

"Well, I assure you, Miss Powell, we do have permission from Miss Cochran herself."

Lauren stretches out her hand. She is unwavering in her demand.

Cohen begins digging in pant pockets and shirt pockets. Conners zeros in on his discomfort and keeps the camera whirring. Cohen waves him away. Conners turns and shoots a sharp close-up of Lauren: stern demeanor, wisps of true-blonde hair blowing in the faint breeze off the runway.

"We met with General Hap Arnold himself, not even a week ago," Cohen offers.

"Then you'll understand my insistence on seeing I.D. This is a military training facility, not some kind of school playground, Mr. Cohen." The whole platoon perks up at Lauren's insistent demands. Some small chuckles are instantly smothered.

Finally, Cohen comes up with the security pass and picture I.D. He hands them to Lauren, who examines the papers minutely.

"You're lucky, everything seems in order. I was just about to call the military police to verify your presence here. And that would not have been pleasant, sir."

Lauren tosses her mane of beautiful tresses over her shoulder, sending them cascading from the ball cap perched on the back of her head. "As squad leader it's my job to ensure the safety of my trainees at all times."

Cohen pockets his I.D. and nods solemnly in response. "And you seem to be doing a wonderful job, miss. Miss *Powell*, was it?" He takes out a notebook and begins to scribble.

Lauren steps forward and loops her arm through his and leads him towards the aircraft on the flight line. "Now that *that* little bit of business is settled, let me show you around." As she leads Cohen off, she turns back and calls to the other cadets, "Don't forget to doublecheck the buckles on your parachutes, ladies. And remember we'll muster back here at fifteen hundred hours to march back to the barracks."

Conners has kept his movie camera whirring, capturing the whole scene in one take. He pivots the camera back to Cohen and Lauren as they walk away.

Cohen enthuses, "Wow. You've already mastered this military lingo."

"Well, my father, Admiral Winston Powell, always insisted on three things at home, no matter what part of the globe was considered home." Lauren waltzes into the distance with the two men in tow.

Jinx sashays across the exterior of the Flight Shack. "I always like to be certain people know that my father is poncie Admiral Winston Powell the third-and-a-half." She flounces back over to the flight board, finds her name, and shoves her ball cap hard on her head.

"C'mon, Dodie, looks like it's me, you and the BT-13." Jinx links her arm through Dodie's. "Let's try some military lingo out on it and see how it flies."

Fifteen minutes later, Jinx has flown the aircraft up and off the runway. She keys the mike to speak to Dodie in the front. From Jinx's viewpoint all that's visible is sky and the black shrouded cockpit in front of her, under which Dodie sweats in the fierce Texas heat.

"Okay, Dodie, before I turn the controls over to you, what's your altimeter say?"

"I've got 4000 feet."

"Perfect. Compass heading?"

"North by northeast, twenty-three degrees. And speed is one hundred forty-five miles per hour."

"Roger that, Jackson. I'll tip her over and then she's all yours." Jinx immediately rams the stick forward and puts her arms behind her head and relaxes. The aircraft drops into a steep dive.

In the forward cockpit, Dodie is already sweating beneath the completely enclosed hood. She's completely caught off guard by the dive. "Damn it, Jinx. That's not funny."

Dodie struggles to right the airplane, eyes fixed on the dials. Slowly the altimeter levels off and the horizon line comes into balance. Sweat pours off Dodie's forehead.

Jinx's voice cackles over the receiver in the darkened

cockpit. "Bring it back up to 4000 feet or the tower will have our asses."

Dodie gingerly pulls back on the stick, raising the nose of the plane. All she can see is the altimeter climbing and the horizon gauge lifting.

"Sometime this year, Dodie. There could be a dozen other aircraft out there at this altitude."

"Just shut up, Jinx. I'm concentrating."

In the rear cockpit, Jinx smiles.

• • •

Meanwhile on the ground, Miriam is sitting on one chair, with her feet up on another, scribbling on a notepad. Patty has been sacked out on a bench nearby. She awakens and lifts the brim of the ball cap that's been covering her eyes. "Is it our turn yet?"

Absorbed, Miriam barely looks up. "Nuh-uh. They've still got twenty minutes to go."

"What'cha doing? Writing home?" Patty sits up, then stands and wanders over to look over Miriam's shoulder.

"Nope."

Patty peers more closely at the page. "Essay contest?"

Exasperated, Miriam finally switches her attention from her writing to Patty. "If you ever actually listened to anyone."

Patty puts on a pouty face. "I listen!"

"Uh-huh. Like my father listens to my *mother*." Miriam pauses and looks up at Patty. "I'm writing my column for the base newspaper. "Now repeat back to me what I just said, Patty."

There's a stack of black-and-white photos on the chair next to Miriam. Patty bends down and picks them up, starts sorting through them. "Writing for the base newspaper." Patty barely glances at each photo. "And some of these photos are supposed to go with it?"

"If you get even a smidgen of engine grease on those, Patty Yin Lee…." Miriam looks up anxiously as Patty continues to sort through the pictures.

Patty is chuffing and snorting at the various trainee poses Miriam has captured.

"These are great, Mimi." Patty stops a moment. "Oooh, you took these the night of the outdoor sleep-out, right?" She comes across a picture that makes her whoop with glee. "You've been holding out on me, Mimi. I love this photo—I *want* this photo!"

Miriam stands up to see which picture Patty is shouting about. "Oh, that! Actually, it's kind of hard to even tell it's Lauren." She sits back down and resumes writing. "It would pretty much have to have her name on it before people would recognize her. Bernie looks pretty good though."

Patty hands back all the other photos, holding up her hands afterwards to show Miriam there's no grease whatsoever.

"Hmm, you're right, it's not definitive that it's Lauren. Oh well, I will still put it in my scrapbook. Good times here at Avenger Field." Patty uses the photo to salute Miriam. Feigning nonchalance, she begins to sidle away. "When did you say your article is due?"

Totally engrossed in her writing once again, Miriam

doesn't look up. "I hope to turn it in tonight, if anyone would actually let me concentrate."

Patty scampers back to her bench and her parachute tote bag. She finds a notebook and rips out a piece of paper and begins scribbling. A devilish grin is plastered to her face.

Moments later, Dodie and a woozy-looking Jinx appear in the doorway. Dodie's hair is plastered to her neck and temples, soaked in sweat. But she's grinning. "Batter up, Mimi and PY. Your turn to prove you can fly looking only at the dials."

Patty clips Dodie on the shoulder grinning. "How'd ya do?"

Dodie shrugs, her grin even wider. "Made 'er puke."

Jinx trots rapidly past Dodie, heading for the door in a hurry. She does manage to punch Dodie solidly in the upper arm in payment for her glee. Dodie doesn't even feel it—she's all grin.

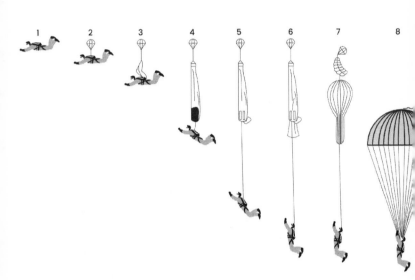

ARC OF PARACHUTE DROP

SEVENTEEN

NEW YORK CITY

Jackie is seated at a microphone inside a radio station booth, doodling on a piece of scrap paper with a stubby pencil. The radio host sits poised, awaiting his musical cue for his commercial announcement.

In the background, four women singers are harmonizing at a standing mike about the wonderful sudsing action of *SUNSHINE CLEANER*. They're singing acapella in beautifully blended four-part harmony as the announcer blasts a final pitch over the airwaves. "Sunshine Cleaner—no *clean* like it, indoors or out." The music fades and the announcer leans into his microphone, crooning. "And speaking of sunshine, we've got our own little ray of it right here in the studio today."

Jackie smiles obligingly. The announcer takes a breath and continues. "Join me in welcoming Jackie Cochran, the head of the Women's Air Service Pilots training program in Sweetwater, Texas. Winner of so many flying awards I've lost track."

Jackie interjects, "I haven't, Hank …."

Hank laughs good-naturedly. "Once again, good morning, Jackie."

"Good morning, Hank. Thank you for having me here today."

As the announcer cozies up to his microphone, he turns concerned eyes on Jackie. "So, Jackie, you've been telling me about your program at Avenger Field. Training young women to fly so they can free up men to become fighter pilots and bomber pilots at the front. Right?"

"That's right, Hank. It's critical work, and the plane doesn't care who flies it. But if a plane is damaged or brand new someone needs to fly it to a repair depot or to a Navy base to ship overseas for the war effort."

"It sounds like a *tough job*, Jackie."

"Well, I won't lie to you, Hank. Sometimes it is! But it's work that needs doing and women can do it."

"So, Jackie, here's the thing. Tell me and the mothers of America who are listening, the truth. Does becoming a WASP mean we're going to be left with battalions of *tough* young women after the war?"

Jackie rolls her eyes in exasperation.

"More importantly, Jackie, are they—pardon my *french* now, ladies at home—but are these girls who apply to the WASPs *fast*? If you know what I mean."

Jackie's laugh is like silver. It glitters across the airwaves, so genuine and bright. While she's laughing into the microphone, she stomps on Hanks's foot beneath the table. "My WASPs are *fast* only when they're flying an airplane, Hank."

More silvery laughter. "But honestly, folks, it's a good question. And I'd like to lay your fears to rest here and now. My gals are the best America has to offer. The brightest, the finest and all we do in training is to strive to make them better."

Jackie warms to her message. "Better flyers, and better mothers, too. Because most of them probably will want to be mothers after the war. And really, what better mothers for our next generation of Americans than those who have fought side-by-side with their husbands and brothers for our freedom—their own and yours, too, Hank."

Jackie throws her pencil at Hank from across the table.

• • •

It's evening and the end of a long day. Lauren is back with the *Movietone News* fellows. She has them positioned right outside the front porch of the barracks. Conners has his camera pointed towards the front door of the building, all set to go.

Lauren stands at the bottom of the porch with them and gestures towards the open door. "You can't go inside. But I've got a real treat for you." Lauren smiles into Mr. Connors' camera like she was born to it. "We're all set to march in formation over to the mess hall—the cafeteria. And you can film it."

Lauren moves over to just in front of the barracks door, raises her whistle to her lips and blows a resounding blast.

Conners is ready, his camera is whirring in a tight close-up of Lauren in command.

"FALL IN, ladies. Double time now, MARCH."

The door to the barracks slams open and a flood of trainees begins streaming from the building, taking up precise positions right in front of their squadron leader. Conners is catching it all on film.

Inside the barracks, Jinx is seated on the edge of her bunk, unlit cigarette in hand, legs crossed with a deeply foul expression on her face. Patty, Miriam and Dodie are grouped around her; expressions of dismay cloud their faces.

Miriam leans forward and takes one of Jinx's hands. "P-l-e-a-s-e, Jinx."

"Pretty please with cream and sugar on it," Patty adds.

"I am not going." Jinx looks wildly about for a match or lighter. "I would sooner eat pickled hog's feet and become a suburban housewife before I give her that satisfaction."

Dodie joins in. "Jinx, you'll starve." She can't help the smirk that spreads across her face. "I mean, you already lost your lunch!"

Jinx only glares at Dodie. Dodie shrugs, "Sorry, I'm just trying to make the point that you *need* supper."

Jinx is softening slightly. "When is this going to end?"

"Soon," Patty insists. When she sees her friends are eyeing her, she explains. "Well, I mean *Movietone* is only here for a few more days."

Jinx frowns. "But *she'll* still be here after they leave, regaling us all with how she can't decide if her left profile is more attractive than her right."

Patty suddenly drops down on one knee in front of Jinx and offers her a hand. Miriam and Dodie immediately follow suit and drop to their knees too.

"Come. Sup with us, oh Princess." Patty elbows Dodie to say something. "Yes, you must keep up your strength."

Patty leaps to her feet and throws a fist into the air. "The infidel will be punished, this I promise on my wings—*if I ever get them.*"

Jinx slides off the bed, drags the shawl that's served as a canopy on the upper bunk and wraps it over her head and shoulders. "Okay. But I'm not running. I've never heard of a princess who runs."

. . .

Night has finally put an end to a long, hot, frustrating day. Lila is standing on the porch in the moonlight, smoking a cigarette, looking out over the vast Texas panhandle. Behind her the barracks' lights are winking off, making the glow of her cigarette all the more obvious.

The door opens and Lauren stands uncertainly on the threshold, watching the other woman a moment. Lights continue to be extinguished. Without turning around, Lila whispers to her, "You know you're driving them crazy, don't you?"

Lauren shakes her head in dismay, then joins Lila on the porch. She huffs, "They're such babies. What'd they think the Army was? Summer camp?"

"They're not in the Army. They're civilians, risking their lives for their country with very little hope of adequate compensation or recognition."

Silence. Then Lauren whispers, "I just want them to be proud of who they are, Lila. Proud of what they've doing."

"Then tell them that! Trust them, Lauren. And they'll trust you." Lila stubs out her cigarette and flicks it over the edge of the porch.

"How did you stand it, Lila. How soon can you take back this whistle?"

Lila laughs quietly. "Maybe I don't want it back. Did you ever think of that?"

Lauren is quiet a long moment. "My dad's coming."

"Shit. When?" Lila draws in a breath of surprise. "Is it official?" Lila turns to study Lauren's face. The other woman's expression is a mixture of pride, excitement and dread.

"Graduation. They're making a big deal of it. Brass from all branches of the service will descend on little ole Sweetwater."

"Ah, Admiral Powell pins wings on his only daughter." Lila huffs out a laugh. "What a photo-op. The Pentagon must be turning cartwheels." Lila smiles and puts her arm around Lauren's shoulders to guide her back inside. "I guess we better be very *good*, then. Right?"

Lila and Lauren come in through the door of the barracks and notice that the lounge light has been left on. Lila motions for Lauren to go to bed. "Go on. Get some shut-eye."

Lila continues down the hallway towards the source of the light. She pokes her head into the lounge and spots Patty just sealing a large manila envelope.

Near the doorway is a bookshelf with large *in* and *out* trays for mail delivery. Patty is standing in front of the *out* tray as Lila enters the lounge. Patty turns her body to shield what she's doing. Lila whispers, "Patty what're you up to?"

When she sees it's Lila, Patty relaxes and grins, putting the finishing touches on what she's doing. She places the envelope back in the *out* box. It's clearly marked *Miriam Zimmerman / Avenger News.*

"Just doing a little editing for Miriam," Patty explains. "She had an article for the base newspaper that she absolutely had to get out tonight."

"And has Miriam asked for this editorial consultation?"

Patty's grin widens. Lila waves her away. "Oh, never mind. I suspect I honestly don't want to know." She crosses the room to the lamp. "You're done here then?"

Patty yawns and stretches, nodding vehemently. Lila switches off the light and they wander down the hall to their beds.

EIGHTEEN

Bright and early the next morning the trainees are all gathered around the assignment board. Each of them has her parachute in place and wears a large utility belt with a canteen attached to it, along with a flare gun and a small fanny pack. The fanny pack contains rations and a tiny first aid kit.

It's clear they're all nervous because when Lauren blows her whistle to get them into formation, they all jump instead to about face. A moment later they remember the routine and line themselves up into marching order.

"Okay, ladies. Take a moment to settle yourselves." Lauren pointedly makes eye contact with each of them. "We've trained for this. We're fit and we're utterly comfortable with flying. So, take a breath and just remind yourself you can do this." She smiles at them until she notices glimmers of smiles in return.

Coralee approaches the platoon from behind Lauren. She stops and presents herself at attention. "Coralee Abrahms reporting as requested, ma'am." The minute Lauren turns,

Coralee snaps off a salute.

Lauren returns the salute. "Thank you, Miss Abrahms, for volunteering this morning. With Nadine in the dispensary, we find ourselves one cadet short." Lauren turns back to her platoon and surveys them all. "As you know, the plan is that no one jumps alone today. Everyone will be paired with a jumping partner to ensure as safe a training session as possible."

None of the cadets moves a muscle, but it's clear all eyes are actively questioning just where Coralee will fit into their line-up. Lauren consults her clipboard, then announces, "Nadine's jumping partner was Miss Jackson. But I think I would rather pair Dodie with Lila for today's exercise and assign Miss Babisch to the care of Miss Abrahms."

Lauren scribbles a note on her clipboard and looks up with a thoughtful expression on her face. "Any questions, cadets?"

Jinx is frowning slightly, scrutinizing the expression on Lauren's face, trying to decipher its meaning. Does Lauren know something about her and Coralee? Or is it honest concern for Dodie? Jinx explodes a deep huff of frustration. *Oh, who cares—I get to jump with Coralee. How cool is that?*

Lauren smiles again, broadly this time. "Alright then, Stewart and Jackson pair up. Babisch and Abrahms form up at the end of the platoon." Lauren takes her place at the head of the formation and shouts: "Com-pany, atten-TION. For-ward MARCH."

The troop promptly steps out, marching towards the flight line and a waiting C-47 cargo plane idling there with loading bay doors open. As the end of the column pulls alongside them, Jinx and Coralee fall into step with it, marching shoulder to shoulder. They both risk a quick look at the other, eyebrows raised in question. Coralee shrugs and then plasters a cautious smile on her face.

• • •

Inside the cargo hold of the aircraft, the cadets are packed in like sardines. The Army loadmaster shouts above the roar of the engines as the plane lifts off from the runway. "Alright, ladies. You are lined up according to order of deployment. This will be a static line jump from 4000 feet. When I tap you on the shoulder, you and your flight buddy will rise and snap your D-ring on the static line overhead." He pauses a moment to ensure everyone is listening to his instructions.

"Remember, our flight pattern is a closed loop today. Half of you will deploy north of the road into Avenger Field. The second half will land SOUTH of the same road. Each team will position themselves in the open doorway, bracing one hand on either side of it. When I tap your shoulder again, you will jump from the aircraft, followed three seconds later by your buddy."

The Loadmaster scrutinizes all the women's faces. "Am I clear, ladies?"

To a person, the cadets call out, "Sir, yes sir."

"I don't think I heard you," he shouts back.

This time the cadets SHOUT as loudly as they can. "Sir, yes sir."

At the very end of the cargo bay, Jinx turns questioning eyes on Coralee. "You've done this before?"

Coralee nods. "Yes, when I first arrived. Jackie said to make a list of anything I felt I needed to prep for in order to assist cadets. I told her I'd trained with parachutes but had never jumped."

Jinx grins. "So they slotted you into a spot?" Coralee shrugs her shoulders. "The day after I arrived there was a class on, so I did it then." She sighs resignedly. "Be very careful what you wish for with Miss Cochran, Jinx."

Jinx grins and huffs a retort. "I guess."

It seems like minutes later the loadmaster is tapping Jinx on the shoulder. She doesn't remember the sensation of the aircraft turning, but they must have. Without thinking, Jinx and Coralee stand and trudge towards the middle of the plane and the open cargo door. They clasp hands briefly. Then Jinx snaps her release ring onto the static line and steps up to the open doorway.

"Keep your feet together, eyes on the horizon, and enjoy the ride, cadet." The loadmaster smiles at Jinx. "And don't forget to roll as you fall. You've practiced it—now do it."

Standing at the open doorway, hands braced on either side, Jinx looks over her shoulder at Coralee and attempts a smile that conveys something other than the utter terror she's actually feeling. When she looks out and down, she can see the canopies of the other cadets' parachutes blooming and falling like petals blown in the wind far to her right. Then the heavy hand of the loadmaster is on her shoulder. Without another thought, she steps through the doorway into nothing.

Jinx refuses to close her eyes as her feet meet nothing but thin air underneath them. The shock of that *nothing* literally takes her breath away, and she screams. But then she feels the jolt in the harness of her parachute arresting the fall and tilts her head up to verify the truth of it for her own scandalized brain. Nothing has ever looked as beautiful in her entire life as that great big dome of white silk billowing over her head.

And then Jinx hears someone else above her scream. For a brief moment, Jinx is certain that something has happened to Coralee. She looks wildly about her, but no body plunges past her as she continues to drift down towards the desert. In the distance, to the west, she watches a rapidly evaporating line of parachutes disappearing as they hit the ground and collapse.

Moments later, it's her turn. Jinx sees the ground racing towards her at an unbelievable pace and then her feet are rammed into the desert floor. Only pure reflex loosens her knees and hips and allows her to roll to the ground to absorb the shock. And then she's up and hauling on her 'chute, which seems determined to continue across the desert with or without her in tow.

As Jinx quickly ensnares the mounds of nylon, she turns just in time to witness Coralee contact the ground and roll. She's instantly on her feet, a huge smile of triumph on her face. Coralee rapidly begins wrangling her own 'chute into submission. The two women are so absorbed in clawing at the cloth, clutching it to their bodies, trying to squash the air out of the fabric that they almost bump into each other. They both grin like maniacs.

"You okay then?" Coralee asks gently.

"Better than okay. I'm alive…and in love." Jinx begins twirling around with her parachute in her arms. She stops suddenly. "I mean, in love with life, ya know."

Coralee slips off her harness and bends over, grinning, and begins stuffing her parachute nylon back into the seat pack. "I know there's no way this will fit in here, but it sure beats dragging it around behind us as we walk. Right?"

Jinx laughs. "Right." She too begins to shove as much of the parachute back into the pack as she can manage. She uses the leg straps to further secure the load and then drops the pack onto the ground and sits down heavily on top of it. "Let's take a break for a minute. Want a drink?"

Coralee hauls her pack closer to Jinx and then drops onto it too. "You read my mind, Miss Babisch." Both women busy themselves with opening their canteens and slurping water. The sun is tilting towards the horizon and a gentle breeze wafts across their faces. And they've survived their parachute jump. The world could not be a better place.

"Have you applied for a duty station yet, Jinx?"

Jinx frowns at the question for a long moment. "No. Not yet." She swallows more water. "I just can't make up my mind. Do I request something on the East Coast, closer to NY… or go completely in the opposite direction and aim for the West Coast? Jinx skewers Coralee with a look. "What would you do?"

"Well, if I was you, I'd ask myself what can I learn that's new, exciting and different by staying close to home? I'd say, if the government is willing to ship me off somewhere for free, why not go as far as I can go?" She pauses, "I'm just sayin'."

Jinx looks down at her boots, considering. She lifts her eyes to meet Coralee's. "It's going to be hard to graduate and leave you behind, Coralee."

Coralee looks away and exhales slowly but says nothing.

"I may have fallen in love." Jinx shrugs, feigning nonchalance, but her eyes glitter with hope.

Coralee sighs and turns to meet Jinx's gaze. "White folks don't love Negroes that way, Jinx. You'll forget me before you're twenty miles from Avenger Field."

Jinx rockets to her feet. "Coralee Abrahms, that is so unfair, not to mention it's just not true. Maybe in *your* experience it's true that love between us is impossible. I tell you New York is a big, big city where nearly anything is possible, including people like you and me."

Coralee studies Jinx thoughtfully. "Maybe you're right, Jinx. But maybe what I'm most afraid of is not that you can't love me. What if I can't love you? The hurt between the Negros and Whites is so bitter and deep in the South... what if I can't cross that line, even if I think I want to?"

Jinx's anger evaporates and she scoots closer to Coralee. She reaches down and takes Coralee's hands and pulls her up from the seat on the parachute. "Here we stand, two women who just jumped out of an airplane and survived. Are you seriously telling me that you're afraid to jump into love, Coralee Abrahms?"

Coralee can't help but grin at Jinx. "That sounds a little too much like one of the dares you fling so casually at Patty Yin Lee."

Jinx bends down and lifts Coralee's pack and helps her

slip it onto her shoulders. She then grabs her own pack and struggles into the harness. "I dare you then, Cora. I dare you to come with me to the West Coast, if that's where I'm bound. I dare you to throw yourself into this adventure and see what happens."

"Are you completely forgetting about Jackie Cochran? She stuck her neck out to put me here, Jinx."

Jinx motions Coralee forward. "Jackie put you here hoping you would find opportunities that she couldn't offer you outright because of the narrow-mindedness of a slew of certain southern Congressmen."

Coralee quirks a smile at Jinx as they walk. "So, you're saying you're that golden opportunity?"

Jinx smiles back at her. "I'm saying, I certainly want to be, Coralee. Come with me when I graduate." Jinx stops and turns to look at her. "Please. Let's give it a try."

NINETEEN

The next morning all the cadets are gathered around the flight assignment board on the lee side of the Flight Shack. They're anxiously checking out their scheduled flights for the day. The *Movietone News* guys are hanging out, shooting footage and generally getting in the way. Everyone's tired of them by now.

Over Dodie's shoulder, it's possible to view her name in big letters at the top of the list. As soon as she sees it, she turns away, a greasy expression on her face. She makes her way back through the crowd of women. For Dodie, *first up* is not a good start to the day.

As she clears the fringe of the group, Dodie and Lila notice at exactly the same moment a very crisp Army officer striding down the flight line towards the board—parachute over one shoulder and clipboard in hand.

Lila drawls, "Looks like flight checks this morning, ladies."

That does it. Dodie's expression turns sallow. She covers her mouth with her hand and scuttles away. The *Movietone* guys go to follow with their camera, but Lila doesn't give them time. The officer is only yards away.

Lila shouts, "Officer on deck. Ten-HUT, ladies."

All the women and the film crew now turn concerned eyes over their shoulders. A path magically appears for the officer to march right up to the assignment board. He checks the notations on the chalkboard, then turns—scowling, of course—to the women surrounding him. When he sees the camera, suddenly he's all smiles. He even softens his tone. "Jackson, front and center."

There's a moment of minor chaos while the trainees sort out that Dodie isn't there. It's clear from Lila's face that she's not about to volunteer any information. Finally the officer interrupts the babble. "I haven't got all day, ladies." He turns back to the board. "Next will be Lee. Patty Lee." He smiles into the camera. "Please."

Patty has her parachute on and is heading towards the flight line. Jinx spots her and points her out to the officer. "That'd be your gal, Sir."

Discomfited at being left behind, the officer pivots and strides rapidly down the flight line, attempting to catch up with Patty and still maintain his dignity. It's a hard act. The *Movietone* guys follow, camera whirring.

Back at the board, everyone is still atwitter at the surprise appearance of the officer. Jinx mutters, "Man, I'll never get used to flight checks." She looks towards the latrines where Dodie has fled. "Should one of us go check on Dodie?"

"Leave her. She didn't eat that much for breakfast. It shouldn't take her long."

Miriam shrugs. "Just think, gals, this flight check and our long-distance solo flight are all that stand between us *and our wings.*" Several young women turn and chorus, "Yeah. That's all; just a stupid little solo flight." In unison they all pelt Miriam with their caps.

• • •

The gals have requested brown-bag lunches from the mess hall, which saves them marching in the heat. It means they can eat and lounge while others are performing their flight checks. Dodie, Miriam, Patty, Lila and some others are ranged around the outside of the Flight Shack, crammed into pockets of shade where they can find it. Remnants of sandwiches and soda pop bottles and other detritus litter the ground around them. A couple of gals are already looking at their watches, nervously tracking the time for their upcoming flight check.

Jinx pokes Dodie with her toe. "Dodes, you hardly ate anything." She shoves half a sandwich at Dodie. Dodie shakes her head *no* and stretches away as Jinx tries to force it in her mouth.

Lauren immediately interjects, "Jo-ANNE, that is so uncouth. Leave Dodie alone." Jinx's temper just snaps. She turns and tosses a bit of sandwich that splats all over the front of Lauren's flight suit. Lauren screams, of course, hands flailing in disgust at the egg salad mess. She begins to lunge at Jinx, intending her serious harm. Patty slips an arm around Lauren's middle and forces the furious trainee to stop.

Patty delicately picks the egg salad off Lauren's suit. "Please, allow me!" She pops the mashed egg salad into her mouth. Everyone is stunned into silence—and then a collective *uggh* arises.

Patty turns surprised eyes on them all. "What? It was still good; it hadn't touched the ground." She licks mayonnaise from her fingers. "My pa always said, never waste good food. There are people starving in China." A long silence ensues.

Jinx looks dumbfounded. "No kidding. Did your dad really say that?"

Patty frowns. "Yeah, what about it?"

"MY mom says that every time I refuse to eat something that's good for me," Jinx laughs.

Miriam chirps in, "Mine too."

Lila and Lauren nod in agreement, along with half the girls in the circle. Patty feigns astonishment. "Go on—*they never.* Wow. What a small world." She pauses a moment and then laughs. "Hey, did they ever say *Gung hay, fat choy* at New Years?"

It takes a moment, but all the girls scowl and then chorus, *Nooo.* Patty grins and wipes her forehead in mock relief. "Whew, good. You had me worried there. For a minute I wondered if maybe we all had *one* set of parents that rotated from house to house when we weren't looking."

Everyone looks at Patty as if she's daft...and then they all burst out laughing, realizing they've been had.

. . .

Dodie is just visible climbing into the front seat of the trainer.

The Army officer settles in the rear seat, then reaches over to help batten down the thick black hood. Moments later the propellers begin to turn—slowly, then faster and faster. The officer adjusts headphones over his ears and then speaks into the microphone.

On his command, Dodie taxies down the runway until she's lined up perfectly to start her run. She points the nose of the plane towards the very center of the runway and begins to push the throttle forward, letting the aircraft gather speed. At the perfect moment, using only her instrument dials, she adjusts the ailerons to lift the nose of the plane towards the sky.

Back at the Flight Shack, all Dodie's classmates are gathered around the flight board, watching the aircraft as it hurtles down the runway. Forty pairs of eyes strain to see its every move but are hindered by the dust and the low angle of the sun. They take turns calling out what they can make out of the airplane's progress at the far end of the runway.

Jinx shouts, "Okay. She's got the nose off the ground and looking good."

Miriam moans, "I don't think I can watch."

Lauren shouts over the rising din. "And yet we have to—this is Dodie's moment."

All conversation stops as the roar of the engine passing by them obliterates any hope of commentary. The aircraft's path brings it directly opposite the Flight Shack where all the cadets are assembled. As it draws even with them, the darkened forward cockpit is clearly visible. They stare as the plane lifts clear of the ground.

Lila swears, "Jesus, it would be nice to see a bit more daylight under her wheels."

All the cadets strain to keep the craft in sight, holding their breath as the two forward wheels finally fold into the underbelly. Now a whole lot of horizon appears beneath the aircraft. Dodie is truly up and away. A loud cheer erupts from the assembled cadets.

Lila makes a point to check her watch. "Okay, she's got roughly twenty minutes to fly the pants off that airplane."

Jinx wipes her brow. "I don't think I can stay for the landing. The takeoff has nearly killed me." The whole group turns to stare at her poor choice of words. Jinx scowls back. "It's a common figure of speech. Jeez-Louise, lighten up."

The group breaks up a bit, some wandering over to sit on benches that line the exterior of the shack. Others head back to the barracks. Still others simply drop where they are, break out a book or writing pad and are immediately absorbed. Jinx, Lila and Patty choose one of the benches. They don't talk; they simply watch the sky above them.

· · ·

Inside the cloaked cockpit, the horizon gauge on the instrument panel glows like a carnival at night. The hands on the dials are turning like a ferris wheel as Dodie completes a series of rolls as part of the final portion of her flight check.

Just one final portion remains. The miniature set of aircraft wings on the dial swings to upright and level once again. Dodie lets a huge sigh escape as she sets her shoulders for the final challenge: landing, with no other information than her flight instruments.

Sweat pours off her face. The glow of the instruments lends her face an unnatural pallor. She quickly checks the altimeter: 4000 feet. A voice crackles through her headset. "Nicely done, Miss Jackson. Shall we head for home?"

Dodie's face becomes even more grim. This is the ultimate test. Instrument landing. "Roger that, Captain." Dodie keys the microphone again and calls,

"Avenger Field Tower this is Tango, Lima, Lima requesting permission to land."

The Air Traffic Controller in the tower returns her call right away. "Tango, Lima, Lima we hear you loud and clear. The runway is open and clear for landing. Wind is currently from the southwest at 5 knots and gusting." He adds, "We suggest you approach 30 degrees west by northwest at 1000 feet. Do you copy?"

Dodie wipes her forehead with the back of one hand then clicks the *send* button on her hand mike. "Copy that, Avenger. Tango, Lima, Lima. Out."

Dodie puts the microphone back in its holder. The inside of the cockpit is pitch black. She nervously taps the altimeter with the back of one finger. It doesn't budge. She squares her shoulders, lets out a deep breath, and pushes the stick forward.

As the altimeter dial begins to drop, Dodie pushes the left wing down. The aircraft begins a slow bank to bring her around to her setting. Her eyes race back and forth between the compass and its heading and the altimeter.

The compass slowly swings from south/southwest past straight west and slowly through to northwest. Dodie gently eases out of the turn and watches as the silhouette on her horizon gauge evens out.

The banking turn has dropped the aircraft's height to 800 feet. Dodie corrects it, pulling the stick slightly back towards her stomach. The plane responds and levels out at a perfect 1000 feet.

. . .

On the ground, the sound of an approaching aircraft is unmistakable. Patty, on the bench with the others, is the first to notice. She leaps up and begins searching the sky overhead, shielding her eyes with her raised hand. "I hear her. She's setting up her flight pattern for landing. Look over there on the northwest runway." The others immediately join her. They press together in knots of concerned friends.

Jinx mutters, "I can't look, I can't look, I can't look."

Miriam elbows her in the ribs. "Shut up, Jinx. You stand here and witness our Dodie's moment of triumph. 'Cause that woman was made to fly." Miriam slips an arm around Jinx's waist and whispers, "Unlike you, sweetheart, who only plays at it."

Jinx turns to Miriam in mock astonishment. "Mimi!"

Miriam merely smiles at her and turns her head towards the runway, where the aircraft is coming in low at the far end.

Lauren shouts, "There she is—coming off the northwest at two o'clock. Straight as a die."

Patty shouts, "That's our girl. C'mon Dodie!"

Silence falls as all the young women watch, helpless to change the outcome now. Helpless to aide their friend and fellow pilot.

Lila mutters, "She's looking good. Good speed, good height."

. . .

In the shrouded cockpit, Dodie is trying very hard to only see the dials in front of her. She intentionally tips her head from one side to the other to see around the sweat sluicing off her brow. She watches the figures and plugs the information into memory maps of the airfield she knows by heart.

Her radio cackles to life. "You're looking good, Tango, Lima, Lima. We have you at 15 miles and closing."

Without taking her eyes off the instrument panel, Dodie picks up the mike and keys in a response."Roger that, Avenger."

She eases the stick forward once again and the corresponding drop on the horizon gauge is definitive. She eases up just a little and checks her mileage. The prairie miles are clicking by. Altimeter 600 feet, 500, 400.

Dodie's eyes dart up to the black curtains that shroud the cockpit. Nothing seeps through. She could be landing in Timbuktu. There is nothing for her to go by except the gauges on her instrument panel and her feel for the aircraft.

One mile from the airstrip she lets out another 200 feet in altitude. She adjusts flaps and finesses the throttle and eases the stick forward. The aircraft clears the runway fence and does a slow, gradual descent to the ground. The landing gear is clearly functioning; the aircraft simply slides through its landing as if skating on ice.

On impact the roar of the engines immediately falls to a throb as Dodie cuts back the throttle and steers the aircraft towards the flight line.

All of Dodie's friends leap in the air, cheering. Through the open door of the Flight Shack the voices of the Controller, the spotter and a couple of instructors can be heard cheering as well. The Controller's voice spills out from the Flight Shack. "Tango, Lima, Lima, welcome back. That was a picture-perfect three-point landing."

More cheering erupts from the massed trainees.

TWENTY

A party is in full swing in the lounge. The phonograph is on full blast. Everyone is dressed to the nines, hair styled to a T, and they're jitterbugging as if none of them had worked at all that day. All the gals are lounging, yakking, laughing and celebrating Dodie's success—*and their own,* too. They're all on the final approach to graduation. Nothing can stop them now.

Everyone has brought some food—crackers, cheese, rumball cookies from home. There's a large punch bowl with a concoction no one's naming; everyone keeps adding to it as they enter the room. Most likely it's lethal.

Patty is on the dance floor jitterbugging with Bernice. Jinx is tagging along, dancing up a storm with Miriam. Dodie is sequestered on one of the lumpy sofas, a goofy expression on her face and a completely empty cup in her hand. Is she drunk? Or just drunk on success?

Lauren sits demurely, just slightly removed from the others, but she looks both happy and tired—like all the others. She and Lila are deep in conversation.

Jinx hauls herself over to the nearest sofa and leans on the armrest. "Wow." She stops for a breath. "I should have worked harder in PT. This is killing me."

Lauren can't help but overhear and flashes Jinx a knowing look. Jinx merely shrugs because it's true. Besides, hey, it's a party. Patty snuggles Bernice cheek-to-cheek and cruises by Jinx and Miriam.

Jinx throws her voice, coming from Bernice. "Back off, sister; I'm not that kind of girl."

Patty eyes Jinx, grinning. "Bernice, you're not any kind of girl at all."

Patty tosses Bernice's carefully coiffed wig over her shoulder and into the crowd. Of course it hits another woman—and of course she screams! The victim reacts instantly, taking the wig and launching it onto another cadet clear across the room.

Soon they're all SCREAMING. For the sheer joy of life. Jinx takes this opportunity to sit down. She motions to Miriam to join her, but Miriam suddenly remembers something mid-stride. "Hold my seat, Jinx. I'll be right back." She rushes from the room.

Miriam trots along the brightly lit hallway towards her locker. In every cubicle clothes are strewn about, makeup is spilled on dresser tops and flight suits are abandoned on the floors. When the next song on the phonograph reaches her, Miriam can imagine all the gals jumping and jiving to 'Boogie Woogie Bugle Boy'. She smiles to herself.

Miriam finds her locker, opens it and extracts a large manila envelope from the top shelf. Then she heads back towards the lounge. The music grows consistently louder as she approaches.

In the lounge, Jinx is mellowing out on a sofa with Dodie on one side and Bernice on the other. Her head begins to rock to the melody. She loops an arm through Dodie's and gets her bouncing along. Soon everyone seated on the sofas and lounge chairs is keeping time to the music.

Jinx grins. "I'm too pooped to pop." She turns concerned eyes on Dodie, who hasn't spoken all night. "Hey, you're alright, right?"

Dodie just smiles and hums along with the melody. "A little plastered…but that's the point, ain't it?"

Miriam appears in the doorway and quickly crosses to where her gang is seated. She clutches the manila envelope close to her chest. Unerringly, Jinx spots it. What'cha got, Mimi?"

Suddenly self-conscious, Miriam has a goofy grin on her face. "Don't laugh, okay." She hands the folder to Jinx. "You hand 'em out. I can't do it."

Jinx throws Miriam a questioning look as she accepts the envelope. "It's my first article in the base newspaper." Miriam is clearly torn between pride and apprehension about sharing her writing. "It's advance copies—no one else gets theirs till tomorrow."

Jinx takes the envelope and jumps to her feet, holding the folder over her head in triumph. She strides to the middle of the room and lifts the needle on the phonograph. The sudden silence stops everyone in their tracks. Instinctively they turn towards her.

Jinx grins, holding the envelope over her head. "I hold in my hand a new cause for a toast. C'mon everyone, get a drink."

Obligingly they retrieve their punch glasses. Those who still have punch pour some into others' empty glasses so everyone is ready. Jinx hastily takes a glass handed to her and raises it overhead. "First of all, to our prize soloist, Dorothy *Cornfields* Jackson."

Everyone turns to honor the cadet of the hour, who has fallen over on the sofa still clutching her punch glass. Dodie is sound asleep. Unfazed, Jinx shouts, "Hip hip hooray!" All the cadets join in.

Veteran performer that she is, Jinx can't let them go just yet. "And making her publishing debut…." Jinx waves a hand in a grand gesture towards Miriam. "Our very own Canadian scribe, Miriam *what-a-zinger* Zimmerman." Everyone shouts and raises their glasses one more time. Jinx quickly sets down her glass and begins passing out the copies of the base newspaper.

Miriam is glowing as every trainee begins scouring the paper. She bites her thumbnail in agony. *Will they like it?*

Jinx is nearly finished her task when an array of soft giggles erupts in her wake. As more copies are distributed, the laughter increases.

Jinx hands her final two copies to Lauren and Lila. Lauren has a truly beautiful smile on her face for the first time all night. Maybe, for once, she feels part of it all. Maybe, for once, she feels it might work with these gals. They both open their copies of the newspaper eager to be in on the joke.

Meanwhile, Miriam is still at center stage, watching her moment of triumph slide into a moment of...*what*? She knows what she wrote was not *that* amusing.

After Jinx studies the article, she turns to her best friend and her face warns Miriam they're headed for disaster.

"Jinx, what's going on?"

"I don't know, but I'm gonna damn well find out." Jinx shares her copy of the paper with Miriam.

Morbid curiosity pushes Miriam to find her article as quickly as possible. "Ohhhhh golly, that's my article." Miriam's eyes search out Lauren's across the room. "But that's *not* the photo I submitted."

Miriam and Jinx lift their eyes from the page at the same moment as everyone else does too—everyone except Lauren. Lauren is still absorbed in reading the whole newspaper, not having arrived at the joke. Then she turns to center page: a photo of her in bed with a *man*! The caption reads, *Lauren Powell looks as if WASP camp is way more fun than anyone expected.* Miriam's name is in the byline.

Lauren looks up from the newspaper. All eyes in the room are on her. Her expression is that of a child who has been unjustly slapped.

The piece of newspaper slips from a horrified Miriam's hands. Bedlam erupts as everyone begins to talk at once. Patty silently sneaks past the back of the sofa and out of the room.

• • •

Lila is perched on the porch railing, cigarette in hand. Patty is pacing in and out of the fan of light that bisects the porch from an open window. Jinx is seated on an overturned box with Bernice on the floor between her feet. Jinx is trying to attach the errant wig permanently to Bernice's wooden head. She winds the strands of hair through her fingers in anxiety.

Lila crosses her arms over her chest. "What the Sam Hill were you thinking, Patty?"

Continuing to pace back and forth, back and forth, Patty strides too close to Jinx, who uses Bernice's wooden hand to smack Patty's leg hard. Jinx growls. "Aaargh. She wasn't thinking. She was just being deeply, deeply stupid. I can't believe you're my friend, Patty. I don't have stupid friends."

Lila says soothingly, "Jinx, I know you're mad. But this is not about you."

Patty stops and faces Lila. "It wasn't 'sposed to be like this. I didn't know this stupid paper would go out to the whole base. She's near tears. "It was supposed to be funny, an in-joke for us." She wipes her eyes hastily. "And it was gonna let Lauren know we're all sick of her riding us *constantly*, day in and day out."

Lila looks puzzled. "Why didn't you just tell her that, Patty?"

Jinx picks up both of Bernice's hands, holding them in prayer mode. "Oh right, we're all supposed to crawl to Lauren, begging. *Oh, pardon me, madam, but the yoke around our necks is a trifle toooo tight.* Jinx makes the mistake of meeting Lila's eyes, and immediately shuts up. Silence reigns on the porch for a long, long moment.

Patty finally speaks up. "It's just that she makes me feel

so uncouth, Lila. With her sideways looks, her insistence on perfection."

"I'm couth," she retorts to Jinx's snort of derision. "Yes, there is such a word in the dictionary, oh worldly one."

Patty sits on the railing and deliberately makes eye contact with both women. "You have no idea how hard it is to straddle two such different cultures. At home, family is everything. I live with my parents, my grandparents and all my siblings. It's raucous." She grins. "A lot like living with all of you. It is never quiet at our house unless everyone is sleeping." She sighs. "But unlike all of you, everyone knows and respects the competence of everyone else in the family. My mother harangues my father for sloppiness, tardiness and slurping his soup—but she never questions his ability as a grocer or money manager." Patty shrugs.

"We all know we can rely on him to buy the produce, sell the produce and make enough money to pay the rent. And he does it week after week, month after month, year after year. What is not to respect?"

Patty levers herself up off the railing and stands a moment looking down at her feet. "I don't doubt my ability as a flyer or mechanic for a single moment in any given day. And you won't ever have to, either. Think about the importance of that for a moment, compared to whether I can color-coordinate an outfit for a date. Or know which spoon to use to eat a *soufflé*. I'd be curious to hear your thoughts." Patty jambs her fists in her pants pockets.

"Wow." Jinx looks over at Patty, frowning. "You're 'sposed to use a spoon to eat a *soufflé*?"

Lila chuckles, "What the hell is a *soufflé*?"

After a long moment of silence, Patty moans. "What're we going to do, Lila? I never meant to ruin Lauren's career in any way. It was just 'sposed to be fun."

Lila thinks long and hard, tapping her chin in concentration. Finally, she sighs. "Okay. First, the two of you are going to immediately go inside and apologize to Lauren." As Patty frowns in disbelief, Lila adds, "Just tell her exactly what you just told me, PY."

Jinx looks as if she might choke. "The TWO of us? Are you kidding? This wasn't my little caper, Lila. This was all Patty."

Lila levels a look at Jinx that would fry a lesser woman. "Belay that order. *First,* you're going to hide that damn dummy in a trunk on top of the outhouse where no one will find it if they come looking. And believe me—they will come looking if we don't fix this!"

Lila holds up two fingers on one hand. "Second, you will apologize immediately to both Lauren and Miriam. And said apology will be meaningful and heartfelt. Am I clear?"

The only response is a chorus of big sighs from Patty and Jinx.

"And third, you've got to break into the admin building to reprint that damn newspaper." This gets the attention of both girls immediately. Their faces express shock and bewilderment.

"Whaaat? Are you crazy? Crapinski, Lila, that'll get us washed out of the program for sure."

Lila flicks her cigarette away and shrugs. "Only if you

get caught." She levers herself off the porch railing and eyes the two of them. "Graduation is in three days. The place is going to be crawling with brass, *Movietone News*, Jackie, even Lauren's dad.

Jinx pales. "Holy shit. The Admiral?"

Lila turns and heads for the barracks doorway, but turns back to say, "If I hear even a whisper of this little caper via the grapevine, you can be damn certain I'll wash you out myself. You have until tomorrow at 06:00 hours to make this right, ladies."

After Lila has gone, Patty looks at Jinx and mumbles, "Look, I'm sorry you got roped into this, Jinx."

Jinx tries to stay mad, but Patty looks so genuinely pathetic, she caves. "It's okay. We can fix this, PY—but first we have to go eat crow. I hate crow no matter how you cook it!"

Moments later Patty and Jinx are standing sheepishly before Lauren and Miriam, who are perched on Miriam's bunk. It's clear PY and Jinx are doing a major *mea culpa*. At the end of Patty's spiel, they both fall on their knees and raise entreating hands towards Miriam and Lauren.

Patty notices that Miriam's been crying, which makes her feel like a toad. Miriam won't even look at Jinx. Lauren is super stoic throughout the whole debacle. A moment of silence stretches to infinity while Lauren decides whether to trash them or not.

Lauren eases herself off the bunkbed and stretches out a hand, offering to help them to their feet and shake on their apology. Jinx and Patty gratefully rise from their knees and shake hands with Lauren. All eyes now turn to Miriam. Her face says *how could you?* She rises and slides an arm around Lauren's waist and only then does she extend her hand to the traitors.

Jinx can't take the punishment from those eyes any longer. She shakes hands with Miriam but begins to cry. She feels more sheepish than she has ever felt in her entire life. Jinx lifts her eyes to Miriam's face. "Mimi, I don't know how we'll do it, but we will fix this thing. You just get some sleep, okay?"

Although they are utterly exhausted, Jinx and Patty thoroughly search the entire barracks until they have collected every single copy of the ill-fated newspaper. Their final act is to retrieve the manila envelope. They tiptoe into their cubicle and discover Miriam already sound asleep. The manila folder lies abandoned atop her dresser. Jinx silently grabs the folder and is about to tiptoe back out when she notices Miriam's hair has fallen over her face. Jinx stops a moment, bends over, and pushes the stray lock of hair off her friend's face. She kisses the tips of her fingers and places them in the middle of Miriam's forehead.

· · ·

Several hours later, long after lights out has been sounded over Avenger Field, Patty and Jinx climb out one of the barracks windows that leads to the darkest portion of the porch. They skulk the long way around the building, keeping to the shadows so they won't be seen. Each is dressed in black: watch cap, long-sleeved jacket and pants.

There's a half moon overhead, so very little auxiliary light reaches Avenger Field. They sneak to the admin building and futilely rattle the door handles. It's locked, of course. Patty steps back and looks around. Over the door is a transom, a small swinging window set over doorways to aid air circulation. Patty sees that the window has been left ajar in the futile hope that the room might cool somewhat overnight.

"There's our entrance, madam. Up you go."

Jinx looks up and then at Patty. "Me? Why me?"

"Well, if you can lift me over your head to reach it, let's go.

"I hate this stuff. I'm no good at climbing trees or illegal breaking and entering."

"Ah, just as well it's me with you tonight, then. Besides, we won't be breaking anything."

Jinx slugs Patty's arm. "If it wasn't for your harebrained practical jokes…."

"C'mon, you were in vaudeville. Alley-oop!" Patty motions for Jinx to hurry. Jinx puts her foot gingerly in Patty's hands, and before she can think about it, Patty has hoisted her aloft. Jinx pushes open the transom window and sticks her head through. Lying on her stomach, half in and half out of the room, her voice is muffled. "Okay, Einstein, now what?"

"Swing your legs through it and jump down."

Moments later Patty hears a solid thump and in seconds a rather disheveled Jinx opens the door. Patty slips quickly inside, closing the door behind her. Jinx jumps into action. "C'mon. We should check the mail slots to make sure no one else has picked up their newspapers."

Patty chuckles. "You're a natural, Jinx."

The mail station pigeonholes are just inside the door. Both girls start pulling out manila envelopes, cradling them in their arms. "Now we need to count how many copies are in each envelope," Jinx admonishes.

Patty leads the way to a small room just off the admin area. She pushes Jinx inside, then follows and shuts the door and switches on a nearby desk light. After the total darkness, the light seems blinding. Jinx raises the envelopes to shield her eyes from the glare.

The room is little bigger than a linen closet. There's a filing cabinet in one corner and a center worktable, in the middle of which sits a hand-cranked Gestetner photocopy machine. Patty tosses all the envelopes onto the tabletop and they both begin carefully opening them. Patty takes a moment to check the Gestetner machine, which is loaded with paper and ready to go. "Woo-hoo, we're in luck. It looks like Miriam never took her newspaper template off the machine. Probably in a hurry to join the party."

Patty turns to Jinx in triumph. "All we have to do now is insert the correct photo and reprint, stuff these envelopes and return them to their slots. Then we get to go to bed."

Jinx looks at the stacks of manila envelopes. "Level with me, Patty. How much sleep do you think we'll actually get?"

Patty laughs. "I dunno, a full hour...maybe two, if we're lucky."

. . .

Before dawn, Patty and Jinx sneak back into the barracks, tiptoeing down the hallway to their cubicle. Jinx stops dead in her tracks the minute her bunk comes into view. Sprawled across the top bunk, one hand splayed down, seemingly pointing at the bed below, is Bernie.

Jinx moans. "Aw shit, I've got to find a place to stash Bernie in case this still blows up in our faces. They'll confiscate him and I'll never get him back."

Patty winches, "Right. Ah, Lila said stick him on top of the outhouse. No one would ever look there."

Jinx turns and whispers angrily. "I will not stash Bernie in the outhouse."

"I'll do it, since this is all my fault anyway."

Jinx softens a bit. "You return Miriam's news article to her locker. I'm going to take Bernie to a place where he'll be respected and safe."

Patty frowns in thought. "Where?"

Jinx crosses to her bunk and hauls Bernie off the top bunk. She quickly wraps him in a sheet and tosses it over her should like a hobo. "Never you mind. I think the less you know about this the better."

Patty chuckles. "Oh, you mean Miss Abrahms' house. No one would ever think to look there."

Jinx throws Patty a scathing look and exits the cubicle. She hauls Bernie swiftly down the hallway towards the front door. Patty watches her depart and then creeps across the hall to Mimi's locker. Once the envelope is safely back on its shelf, she heaves a sigh of relief and returns to her own bed. "Gads, a life of crime is exhausting—definitely not my career of choice."

Minutes later, Jinx emerges from the copse of cottonwood

trees and approaches the small farmhouse from behind. She sees the light is on in the kitchen, and smiles. The smell of morning coffee wafts from an open window; Jinx's smile widens. But what's truly heart-stopping is the singing she hears as she rounds the side of the house. Coralee's voice is soft, yet powerful. She is singing a simple, sweet children's song with great fluidity. Jinx stops in her tracks to give it her full attention.

When the singing stops for a moment, Jinx rounds the corner to the front porch. She spots Coralee, seated in one of the rocking chairs with a cup of coffee to her lips. After swallowing, she begins to sing again in time to her rocking.

Jinx stops and simply listens, raptly watching every expression that flits across Coralee's face as she watches the dawn coloring the horizon. Without thinking, Jinx pitches her voice to harmonize with Coralee's. Startled, Coralee hesitates, but Jinx keeps singing as she steps forward into plain sight. She nods to Coralee, hoping that she'll rejoin the song.

After a moment's hesitation, Coralee raises her voice again, fixing her eyes on Jinx. The rising sun has been forgotten. They both bring the simple song to a close. After a moment's pause, Jinx bows to Coralee, grinning.

"You have a gift of a voice, Coralee. I'm so glad I got up early."

Coralee eyes her speculatively. "Umm, that in itself is suspicious, Jinx. The fact that you brought back your brother—or is it sister now—only adds to the mystery."

Coralee rises. "Would you like a cup of coffee?"

Jinx takes a step towards the porch. "I would simply love

a cup of coffee. Bernie says *no thanks.* It rots his inner core."

Coralee huffs out a laugh. "Take a seat, both of you." She returns in minutes and hands a cup to Jinx, who is sitting in the other rocker.

"So, cough up. What are you doing out and about so early? It can't be anything good."

Jinx takes a solemn sip of the coffee and sighs deeply. "Oh my God, that is good." She skewers Coralee with a look. "And so is your singing, Cora. You have a…." Jinx stops to gather her thoughts. "A luminous voice, Coralee. I'd love to hear you sing more—with an orchestra behind you."

Coralee shakes her head. "You cannot defer answering my question with compliments, Jinx Babisch."

Jinx peers over her up at Coralee. "I honestly meant what I said, Cora." She sees Coralee winding up for a rebuttal and holds up her hand. "But you're right. And you truly do deserve a complete answer to your question." She takes another sip of coffee. "Especially if you will be harboring a fugitive." Jinx pats Bernice's head fondly.

Coralee shakes her head slowly. "Oh, do tell me, what have you done now, Jinx?" Jinx shrugs apologetically and blurts, "It really wasn't me this time, Coralee. Patty implicated me vicariously when she shot a photo of Bernie and Lauren asleep together."

Coralee huffs out a laugh. "Oh, better and better. Start talking, madam."

It takes Jinx a fair bit of time to relay the parameters of her dilemma. When she has finished, she holds up her hands in supplication. "I throw myself and Bernie on your mercy. I just can't toss him on top of the outhouse as Lila suggested. This is not his fault."

"My god, life with you would be one series of comically catastrophic events after another."

Jinx smiles coyly. "But fun, Coralee. Life with me would be fun." She adroitly drops a kiss on Coralee's nose. "I promise."

Coralee takes a sip of coffee, her eyes meeting Jinx's. "Yes, Bernie can stay with me so that you don't lose him completely if this blows up in your face. I agree that would not be fair." She stands up and motions for Jinx to join her. "Fortunately, I have a small guest room. He should be quite comfortable there."

As Coralee moves towards the door, Jinx reaches out and grasps her hand. "And the question of life with me?"

Coralee purses her lips, stopping herself from responding too quickly. "One thing at a time, Miss Babisch. Let's see if you actually manage to graduate." She opens the door and motions Jinx through it. "After all, there are still three whole days to mess it up." Coralee closes the screen door firmly behind Jinx.

Jinx turns back, scoffing derisively. "I will lead the life of a saint, a monk, a holy woman from now until then to make sure I graduate, Miss Abrahms."

"Take photos for me; I'd love to witness that," Coralee calls out, laughing. "Oops, that's how we ended up in this mess to begin with."

REELING IN A 'CHUTE

TWENTY-ONE

On the day before the graduation ceremony is scheduled, before the sun is even a suspicion on the horizon, Lila is up and dressed and shaking awake a select group of twenty cadets. Consulting a list she carries with her, she moves from cubicle to cubicle as quietly as possible. She shakes a cadet and then swiftly puts her finger to her lips as each one of them bolts awake. She motions for them to hurry and dress. Holding up both hands, fingers spread, she mouths, "Ten minutes." Lila points to the rear door of the barracks and salutes to let them know she'll meet them there.

Minutes later, Lila and Lauren greet twenty cadets on the porch. Lauren nods to Lila and whispers, "Meet you at the mess hall when you're done."

All the cadets are mystified by Lauren's comment. It's clear to them that Lila and Lauren are far too serious for this to be a graduation joke in progress. Lila waves them down off the porch and whispers harshly, "Form up, ladies."

The cadets scramble into a marching formation two abreast, with Lila at the front. She snapes off a smart salute to Lauren and whispers again, "FOR-ward, MARCH."

Soon the cadets find themselves exiting Avenger Field by the front gate, held open by Coralee. As the troop passes through, she salutes Lila and then closes the gate behind the last cadet.

Although deeply curious and juggling a thousand unspoken questions, each woman marches steadily beside the others in military formation, which has now become second nature. A few minutes later, the troop can see an Army jeep in the distance, parked off the side of the road in front of a steep bluff.

Lila leads them unerringly towards the jeep with its two uniformed officers. When they are abreast of the jeep, Lila calls out softly, "COM-pany, HALT."

The Army officer on the passenger side of the jeep jumps out and approaches Lila. "Go ahead, dismiss your gals and have them fan out behind the jeep. We can explain our mission and hand out the necessary equipment at the same time."

Lila salutes and turns to face the cadets, her face impassive. "You have your orders. Dismissed." She turns back and takes up a position near the rear of the jeep's tailgate. The cadets fan out around her. The officer stands on the opposite side of the tailgate. The second officer has now climbed onto the jeep's rear and is shoving a heavy metal trunk towards the tailgate. He waves a hand towards the trunk. "It's no secret that you are very close to your graduation day. But

I caution you, what we are doing here today is an absolute secret and must remain so. Am I clear?"

The cadets turn questioning eyes towards Lila. She nods assent and says clearly, "Sir, yes sir." The cadets take their cue from her respond just as softly, "Sir, yes sir."

"Good." The officer offers a small smile. "It shouldn't surprise you that the American government is feverishly engaged in developing faster and more powerful aircraft to help it attain its military goals in this war."

He notes the surprise and puzzlement on some faces. "Some of you may be selected for duty at those bases that are developing and testing these new aircraft." He instantly sees the shift in expressions from curiosity to avid eagerness. "The work you may do, the craft you may fly, sometimes even the *location* of the base will likely be top secret." As the women's faces sober, he continues. "The government will want assurances that you will guard these secrets with your life, if necessary."

The officer turns and opens the lid of the metal locker. He pulls out a handgun, opens the barrel, and holds the gun upright for all the cadets to see. If there were ammunition inside, it would fall to the ground. "Today you will take the first step in being able to fulfill that promise. Please do not be so naïve as to think our enemies do not have spies and agents roaming throughout our country. If we are trusting you to protect our military secrets, we must equip you to do so."

He hands the empty gun to Lila, who then passes it on to the woman next to her. That cadet passes it along until it reaches the end of the crescent of cadets. Meanwhile, the officer is pulling other handguns from the locker and passing them along as well. He clearly shows that none of the weapons contains any ammunition.

"My mission here this morning is twofold: To turn your minds to work that may potentially lie ahead of you, and to teach you the most basic lessons in firearm training. This will be added to your training record so that no base commander or rifle-range manager can deny you access to hone your skills with a weapon."

All the women lock eyes with each other at this last statement.

"In order to access a military shooting range, you need to have written certification that you have received basic military arms training. This is yours. It will be documented in your records, I guarantee that. And if you find yourself in a position of being stonewalled by anyone at your future facility, you will request they call me immediately to verify your training."

Each woman now holds a handgun. The officer nods and smiles; this is supposed to be reassuring. "Let's begin. Now that we've demonstrated there is no ammunition in the chamber or in the barrel, start by closing the barrel of your pistol."

He watches as they follow his orders. He smiles again. "Okay. Now holding the pistol in your dominant hand, I want you to find the safety toggle on the handle beneath your palm." He shows them his own gun for reference.

"It's designed to slide easily on and off as you palm

the gun. These are non-regulation Smith & Wessons. We've given you guns with physical safety catches because you will not be using a holster. In most cases the guns will be carried on your person in a flight jacket pocket or a cargo pocket in your flight suit. This is partly due to space considerations in the cockpit—a holster might catch on other equipment or inhibit your egress in an emergency.

He nods as he watches the women carefully find the toggle and begin to click it up and down. "And frankly, we don't want to advertise that you're armed."

"The very first safety rule I want to burn into your memory is to always hold the gun barrel facing down, unless you intend to shoot it." Everyone immediately lowers the muzzle of the pistol so that it points at their feet.

"Good. Second rule. Always keep the safety on. Again, unless you intend to fire the weapon." He notes with satisfaction the immediate snap of safety toggles being reset.

"Very good." He genuinely smiles now at the women arrayed before him. "Now we'll practice the basics: stance, loading, and firing the weapon. All with plenty of time to get you back to the mess hall for breakfast." He pauses. "Hold your current formation. COM-pany, about FACE."

The cadets execute the command perfectly. Now the women are all facing the imposing mountain of rock and dirt that had seemed innocuous when they first marched up to the jeep. The Army officer is safely behind them when he begins to hand out small allotments of live ammunition.

"The hillside in front of you is our firing range. I want you to pick out a bush, a cactus, or a dead tree as your target.

I am going to teach you how to neutralize that target, so that if called upon, you can safeguard the military aircraft that may be placed in your care."

· · ·

WASHINGTON, D.C.

On the day before graduation, a very tired, very distracted Jackie is sitting at a table, microphone before her, listening to questions from a panel of Congressmen seated in front of her. The men do not look happy or kind. They pepper her with questions and accusations, barely giving her time to speak.

Congressman Ramspeck's voice is accusatory. "And did you then, Miss Cochran, unilaterally proceed to telegram women flyers throughout the United States and Britain offering them the chance to fly the *ARMY way*; holding out the hope of eventually becoming full-time military soldiers?"

Jackie quickly consults some notes on a paper before her. "I worked closely with General Hap Arnold to implement a women's auxiliary flying corps loosely based on a successful template used by the British."

Congressman Ramspeck hammers at Jackie. "That's not the question at hand, Miss Cochran. What this committee is trying to ascertain is whether you lied to your trainees and the U.S. military regarding the mobilization of these women flyers."

Out of patience, Jackie interrupts him. "I never lied, Congressman Ramspeck. I didn't have to. I just stated the obvious. The United States needs qualified ferry pilots to free up men for combat at the front." She takes a sip of water from her glass. "Britain had proved unequivocally that women can fill that void. And America had thousands of qualified female pilots who are eager to assist the war effort."

Another Congressman leaps into the fray. "But why as pilots? Why not as welders, or shipfitters?"

Exasperated, Jackie leans forward and growls, "It's what they do best. There are women welders, pipe fitters and bomb technicians already, Sir. No one is screaming about them taking men's jobs. My gals fly, gentlemen. And trained flyers are what we need right now to move aircraft from production facilities to the front lines. We need them to test-fly aircraft with mechanical problems, and to flight test the new and exciting aircraft innovations happening every day across America."

• • •

By 10:00 hours it is a blistering day in Texas. The sky is a cloudless blue, the sun scorching hot. The fifty-five cadets who have passed all their flying tests at Avenger Field are just finishing their preparation for the graduation ceremony.

They are dressed to the nines, no matter the heat. Eyebrows have been tweezed, facials given, permanent waves applied to tresses and lipsticks to lips. The new uniforms Jackie Cochran had designed and tailored for her gals arrived in plenty of time to be unpacked, ironed, and examined extensively in front of the five full-length mirrors newly installed in the women's barracks.

The audience is milling around temporary bleachers set up on the drill field behind the administration building. There's red, white and blue bunting draped everywhere. A happy air of anticipation glides on the hot breeze coming off the Texas plains.

Down on the drill field, a raised dais has been erected, with a microphone and many rows of chairs. Dignitaries, mostly military but some not, have begun to find their seats. A woman bugler steps up to the microphone and prepares to blow the call to order. With a nod to the leader of the small military band seated below the dais, she begins.

At the end of her brief solo, the whole band breaks into the Star-Spangled Banner, and the audience rises to their feet. The American flag billows in the slight breeze as the WASP trainees appear. Marching *en masse,* in formation. Brass buttons on their beautiful new uniforms glint in the sun. They are all smiling, perfectly in step, utter pride and joy beaming on their faces. The *Movietone News* guys are turning themselves inside out trying to capture every glorious moment.

Behind the graduating class, the younger battalions are arrayed, marching behind. Together they create an awe-inspiring sight. Nearly 500 young women in training—willing to risk their lives for their country in its time of greatest need.

As they wheel onto the drill field, the graduating class comes to a halt right in front of the dais where all the dignitaries stand. The women stand at attention, perfectly motionless, eyes straight ahead. In the front row on the dais is Admiral Powell. He is beaming down at his daughter, Lauren, who is clearly visible in the front ranks of the class.

The military band finishes its musical intro to the event. There is a moment of silence as the final note of a bugle hangs on the air. Then a rustling as everyone seats themselves for the ceremony.

After a moment, Admiral Powell rises and strides to the microphone. He looks at the crowd out on the base and finally lets his eyes fall on his daughter. "Parade Rest, ladies."

As one, the phalanx of young women widens their stance. They snap their arms behind them, folding their hands the small of their backs. Their eyes stare straight ahead, refusing to give in to curiosity and look around.

Admiral Powell gathers himself for his speech. "Ladies, gentlemen and graduating class of Avenger Field." He clears his throat. "First, I want to say I have NEVER been so proud. Not as a father, or as an officer or an American."

The Admiral continues. "I think it's important to tell you all something confidential. Something I haven't even told my daughter, Lauren." He looks about, seemingly nervous. "In the beginning, I had my doubts about this program. I confess, I thought *women flyers*—who needs them? But as the dispatches from the war in Europe have flooded into the Pentagon, we are now acutely aware that pilot mortality rates from that front have decimated our resources.

"I realized—all of America's military suddenly realized—we need women flyers.

With the war in the Pacific escalating, we will need even more young women in cockpits here at home! So before we finish today, a round of applause, please, for Miss Jackie Cochran and her incredible foresight in helping us assure victory for the U.S.A."

Loud applause erupts, and the Admiral joins in from the podium. He lets it continue for some time and then leans forward into the microphone again.

"And finally, speaking as a father, I admit I initially had very strong misgivings about *my* daughter becoming one of those women flyers." He smiles self-consciously at Lauren. "As I sent her off to training camp here at Avenger Field, I worried that this experience would change her. I feared that it might harden her to the point where I would no longer recognize her."

The Admiral wipes a tear off his cheek as he looks down at his daughter.

"Well, there she is, front row and center. And you know what, ladies and gentlemen, I do *hardly* recognize her."

The *Movietone News* guys move in for a close-up. "In these short months my girl has become so grown up and so beautiful. She's become everything I thought I feared— and more. Through her letters home from training camp, I have gained a colleague and friend. Her letters made me realize all over again how much I love flying myself. And how happy I am that she's discovered it too.

"Her absence helped me realize how much I love my daughter, and how proud I am of her and of all these fine young women here today."

Admiral Powell steps away from the podium and gallantly sweeps out his arm.

"Ladies and gentlemen, I proudly present to you...the graduating class of Avenger Field."

A storm of applause erupts in the audience, as the platoon is brough to attention and marches smartly in front of the crowd to begin to receive their diplomas. And their Wings.

As one, the crowd stands, applauding the graduating class arrayed before them on the field. After each woman receives her diploma and her wings from Jackie Cochran, they are released into the arms of their families. Small tables and booths have been set up beneath huge open-sided tents to shield the revelers from the sun. The celebration is now in full swing. Civilians and military are milling, laughing and genially comparing notes.

Patty, Dodie, Lila, Jinx and Miriam are seated in one of the huge white tents. Several tables have been pulled together and nearly the whole class is squeezed in. Lauren is conspicuous in her absence.

Dodie consults her neatly folded orders one more time. "I'm still in shock, you guys. How did the five of us manage to be sent to the same duty station?"

Jinx takes a big drink from her lemonade. "Moss Beach, California. I'm going to get a tan, and a convertible ...."

Patty laughs, "The only convertible any of us will be able to afford is an open cockpit on an airplane."

Miriam looks around, searching the crowd. "Hey, has anyone heard what duty station Lauren was assigned to?" Jinx and Patty immediately slink down in their chairs.

"Oh my god, what've you two done now?"

Jinx and Patty chorus shrilly, "Nothing, honest."

Lila smirks. "I think they still carry a steamer trunk full of guilt. That's what you're witnessing, Mimi."

Miriam turns to Lila, a smile creasing her face. "You called me Mimi, Lila! You never use nicknames."

Lila raises her glass. "To nicknames, to our gang, and to Moss Beach, California." All the girls raise their glasses in toast and shout together, "To Moss Beach."

On the far side of the pavilion, Coralee is escorting a gaggle of utterly awed new trainees. She lets them stand a moment, watching the graduates' every move. Their faces are canvases of hope, fear and trepidation.

Dodie can't help but notice their stares. She raises her glass in the new kids' direction and smiles. "To Avenger Field and the WASPs, past, present and especially *the future*. Right?"

Lila, Patty, Miriam, and Jinx fall raise their glasses, looking straight across the field at the new kids. "To the future."

Jinx gently shoves back her chair. "Back in a minute." She lifts a full glass of lemonade off the table and strides towards the new cadets. She catches Coralee's eye and smiles, offering the cold drink to Coralee. "We were just toasting our future. We've all been posted to Moss Beach, California. On the West Coast. A great place to really begin to live our lives as women flyers. I offer you the same toast: To the future!

Coralee doesn't hesitate. She reaches for the glass, shaking her head in amusement. "To the future, Miss Babisch. I have every reason to believe with you it will be fun."

Back at her group's table, Lauren arrives with her father in tow. Both are beaming. Lauren stops and smiles. "I could drink to that if anyone would hand me a drink."

The Admiral chips in, "Amen to that, Lauren. Graduating is thirsty work."

Lila leans over and passes a drink into each of their hands. From afar, Jinx and Coralee eavesdrop on the conversation at the table. Lila asks, "Have you made up your mind about duty stations yet, Lauren?"

Admiral Powell laughs and puts his arm around his daughter. "For some inexplicable reason Lauren appears to be assigned to San Diego." He shakes his head as if confused. "With me." He sighs heavily. "I guess I'm stuck with her a few more years."

All her friends laugh politely at the Admiral's comment. Lauren sighs. "I love San Diego...and it does feel a lot like home." She looks from Lila to Miriam and Patty and over at Jinx and Coralee. "At least it's only a couple of hours from Moss Beach. I could drive up and visit with you all as often as you want."

Patty blurts, "Ya, that'd be swell, Lauren."

The look Lauren gives Patty across the table is unreadable. "Honest?"

The table falls silent for a moment. As Lila takes a sip of her drink, she laughs. "Of course, we wouldn't want to break up the gang."

Now Lauren smiles. "What's even better, Daddy said that he would request another passenger car be added to the troop train that's taking him back to the coast. All of us will have a few more days together—and a safe journey to our new duty stations in our very own railway car." Lauren smiles up at her father, who grins.

Patty laughs out loud in delight. "Lauren, if you can pull this off, I'll shine your shoes for a month."

Lauren grins back at Patty. "Gee, we get to share his dining car too. What do I get for that?"

By this time Jinx has returned to the table. She pipes up, "I think undying gratitude is the going rate for dining car privileges this month."

Lila makes a *pfft* sound. "No, you're confused, Jinx—dining car privileges is naming your first-born after Lauren."

Dodie interjects. "You're both wrong. The going rate for dining car privileges is Lauren's name on an Iowa cornfield."

All the gals shout SOLD in unison and raise their glasses once again. "To Lauren and cornfields in Iowa."

FLIGHT PATTERNS
*launches my series '**Courage with a Q**'—*
LGBTQ+ historical fiction.

*Be sure to look for **FLIGHT LINES**,*
as the adventures continue.

ABOUT THE AUTHOR

I discovered the story of the WASPs just after I left my job as a photographer with the Navy Air Corps, many years ago.

I chanced upon it in a library and immediately began reading everything I could find about ALL the women flyers of the WWII era. It was the first time I'd found a book about women like me.

It took a while to get here, but I was just as excited the day I started writing this story as I had been years before when I discovered that first book detailing the lives of early women flyers.

I hope I have succeeded in invoking their passion, their daring and the *camaraderie* that developed as they pursued their dreams together.

They never let their fears stop them from doing what they loved. They never let anyone persuade them that flying wasn't for women. They stayed the course.

This is a lesson I think we all need help remembering. There have always been women who DARE to define themselves, despite cultural norms that might inhibit their dreams. These women in all their guises are worth celebrating.

RESEARCH & RESOURCES

Those Wonderful Women & Their Flying Machines—Sally Van Wagenen Kiel

WASP—Women Air Service Pilots—Vera S. Williams

Amelia Earhart's Daughters—Leslie Haynsworth

A Wasp Among Eagles—Ann Carl

Night Witches—Bruce Myles

Daring Lady Flyers—Joyce Spring

Fly Girls—P. O'Connell Pearson

Ocean Bridge—Carl Christie

Promised the Moon—Stephanie Nolan

The Originals—Sarah Byrn Rickman

Bette Gilles WAFS Pilot—Sarah Byrn Rickman

Teresa James WAFS Pilot—Sarah Byrn Rickman

Spitfire Women—Giles Whittell

Made in the USA
Monee, IL
25 August 2022